Blunt Force Trauma

Jeff Kerr

Copyright © 2023 by Jeff Kerr

All rights reserved.

No part of this publication may be reproduced, distributed, or transmitted in any form or by any means, including photocopying, recording, or other electronic or mechanical methods, without the prior written permission of the author, except as permitted by U.S. copyright law. For permission requests, contact the author at jeffkerr@jeffreykerrauthor.com.

The story, all names, characters, and incidents portrayed in this production are fictitious. No identification with actual persons (living or deceased), places, buildings, and products is intended or should be inferred.

Book Cover by Dave Provolo

ISBN: 978-0-9761152-5-0

1

Amy Morrison wiped the sweat from her palms before picking up the phone to make a call on Santa Rosa's hospital line. No sense to risk being caught by using her cell. Really, though, how big a deal would it be if she were? She wasn't dealing in national secrets. Just passing along information about the hospital's inventory. That wasn't a crime, was it?

The man picked up after the first ring. "What do you have for me?"

"The next shipment arrives tomorrow morning."

"What time?"

"They usually get here by nine."

"Which wholesaler?"

"Texan Pharmaceutical Supply."

The line went dead. He was very abrupt as usual. Amy placed the receiver back in its cradle. As she glanced around the pharmacy, she saw no unusual reactions. Just the pharmacist filling a prescription and Freddie, the other tech entering data on his computer. This was a piece of cake. And the money? She had just earned more with a ten-second phone call than the hospital paid her in a week. From now on, no more sack lunches or crappy hospital food. She'd eat out every day, maybe even hit the yogurt shop for dessert.

"What are you smiling about?" Freddie asked.

"Nothing," she said, startled that she had given herself away. "Just thinking about lunch."

2

"Hand me the wire stretcher," the older man said.

Adam Cash fished the long ratcheted tool out from the weeds and handed it to his boss. The two of them had been toiling under a blazing Texas sun since dawn, erecting a barbed-wire fence for yet another city slicker trying to get an agricultural exemption for his weekend getaway in the Hill Country. Fence a field, stick a few cows or goats on it, and property taxes plummeted. Once they stretched this last length of wire tight, they'd be done. Let the city slicker deal with the taxman.

Despite the heat, Cash wore jeans and a long-sleeved work shirt for protection against the barbs. His wide-brimmed Justin hat provided shade but did nothing about the rivulets of sweat running down his face and neck. He removed the hat and wiped his brow with his soggy kerchief. "Must be triple digits today."

The older man, a leathery wisp named Emil Bergheim, had lived in Noble County, Texas since his birth seventy-three summers ago. He grunted, "I wouldn't know. Been this way all my life."

Cash licked his cracked lips. "You got any more of that water?"

Emil's eyes narrowed. "Water's in the truck. Let's get this done first so we can call it a day."

The old man slipped his hands into sweat-stained leather gloves. He braced one end of the stretcher against the cedar fence post and clamped the other end onto the slack barbed wire. The stretcher's paint had worn off long ago, but not a speck of rust marred its surface. Emil used his tools a lot but took good care of them.

Emil roughly nudged Cash aside. He gripped the tool with one hand and worked the handle back and forth with the other. Each stroke advanced the mechanism another cog, tightening the wire.

"Go easy," Cash said. "You don't want it to break."

Emil strained to pull the handle back one last time. A loud thwack sounded, and the fifty-foot strand of wire whistled toward them from the far post. The old man stood frozen in place. Cash wrapped him in a bear hug and spun sideways, putting himself between his boss and the far end of the fence. The wire's tip grazed his cheek and snapped against his hat, sending it flying into the grass. Cash heard himself emit a loud yelp of pain.

"You can let go of me now," said Emil.

Cash released his hold. He slipped off a glove and pressed two fingers to his cheek. They came away sticky with blood. "Damn."

"It's nothing but a scratch."

Easy for him to say. And what about thank you? Cash picked up the hat and slipped his pinkie through the new hole in the felt. "This is my good hat."

The older man marched toward the dusty pickup truck parked nearby. "Hats come and go." He snatched a wire spool from the truck bed and returned to the fence. "I'll go tie this on," he said. "You tighten this time."

***

The sore muscles in his shoulders made it difficult for Cash to keep his hands on the steering wheel. The acetaminophen tablets had helped him get a decent night's sleep, but the aching hadn't gone away. It had only bided its time until morning. Cash didn't see how Emil could work so hard day after day. The man was a machine.

The ten-year-old Ford Fiesta sputtered as it crested a ridge. Cash eased off the accelerator as the view of Pinyon opened below. Not a big town, but his town. The place he'd grown up in. The home he'd come back to.

"Why Pinyon?" his mother had asked when he told her his plans.

"I grew up there."

"It's a dead end. That's why we left."

Cash didn't see it that way. To him, Pinyon represented the future, a place to make a name for himself, a chance to serve people he had known and respected all his life. People like Harold Mercer, the old man who patrolled the town square in overalls and a cowboy hat. Or Nancy Schaeffer, owner of Winkler Dance Hall, who taught Cash's brother Reid how to play guitar and once toured with Willie Nelson. Or Edie James. Yes, definitely Edie.

The road into town took Cash past the prison-like brick building that was his old high school. A decade ago he had starred as a wide receiver for the Pinyon Javelinas. Cash had time to kill, so he pulled into the parking lot of the stadium. Despite the early hour, it was already eighty-six degrees, and the short walk to the field raised beads of sweat on his brow. Sunlight glistened off the aluminum bleachers, the cropped grass blazed a brilliant green, and the purple and gold javelina on the press box looked like it had been painted yesterday. No matter how rundown the rest of a small Texas town might look, the football stadium would shine like a jewel.

Cash's eyes wandered to the spot in the end zone where his miraculous catch years ago meant that Pinyon beat its archrival, the Sonora Broncos, in the final minute. His overjoyed teammates presented him with the game ball in the locker room. He wondered if the souvenir had made the move to Austin with his parents or if they had given it away.

Cash strolled beneath the bleachers and peered up between the seats at a clear blue sky. He counted the rows and positioned himself beneath the third from the top. It was here that he had first kissed Edie. They were sixteen.

He had just walked out of the locker room after a tough loss. He had spent hours staring at Edie from across the room in algebra class, but he had never spoken to her. His heart fluttered as she sauntered up to him and greeted him by name. They chatted, and then she said, "I want to show you something" and tugged him beneath the bleachers. That's where she kissed him.

"I hope that was okay," she said. Cash laughed and told her it was just fine. He invited her for pizza at Mr. Gatti's, where he was planning to meet some friends. She said she had to check with her parents. At the house, she went inside briefly before returning, flustered, to say she'd have to take a rain check because a family friend was visiting. Cash found out months later that the family friend was an ex-boyfriend. But she went out with him a week later and every week after that. Until he joined the army.

Cash left the stadium and drove to the Noble County Sheriff's Department. The building had opened just six months ago. It was named for the recently deceased Carter Turner, the county's longtime sheriff. The complex boasted a dozen jail cells and enough office space to accommodate twice the current number of employees. Its limestone façade gleamed in the afternoon sun as Cash approached.

Brightly lit and outfitted with new furniture, the place represented a vast improvement over the cramped quarters in the old courthouse building. If Cash could get past today's interview, it would be a great place to work.

Cash froze as a uniformed deputy strode toward him from a back hallway. Holy cow, it was Gabe Santos. Dark brown skin, black hair, and a winning smile that had been the envy of every soldier in Cash's army unit for its ability to attract women.

"Gabe?" Cash said.

Santos's eyes widened as recognition set in. "Cash!" He shook Cash's hand. "I can't believe it. What are you doing here?"

"I've got a job interview with the sheriff."

"Oh, wow, that's great. You should be a shoo-in." He pulled a card from his shirt pocket. "Here. I can't stay but call me later and I'll buy you a beer."

"Deal."

Five years ago, Cash had saved Santos from certain death in Afghanistan. They were on different teams that day within a squad participating in a mission to clear a bombed-out enemy village. Covered by an overwatch team from the ridge above them, Cash, Santos, and the rest of the squad were following their sergeant to the first set of stone houses when a burst of automatic weapons fire dropped a man. Cash dove through an open doorway. Santos dragged the wounded man toward a house across the street. Before he could reach it, another burst of fire drove him to the ground.

Without thinking, Cash darted into the street, grabbed Santos, and hauled him into the house. A buddy named Sanders dashed after him to bring in the other man, sustaining a leg wound along the way. Cash saw that the man Santos had attempted to save was dead. Santos had been shot in the abdomen. Sanders was in pain, but stable.

Cash stuffed sterile gauze into Santos's wound and wrapped it with a pressure bandage. He left his injured friend with Sanders and, in a risky move, worked his way around the back of the village to reach the house from which the fire had come. His successful neutralization of the house enabled the rest of the platoon to drive the remaining Taliban fighters away. He returned to Santos in time to see him loaded onto a medevac helicopter.

Cash turned his attention to the teenager behind the reception desk. He remembered her name from when he had dropped off his job application a week ago. "Hi, Vicky," he said. She reminded Cash of the character Phoebe from the TV show *Friends*. Blonde, well-meaning but flighty, she wore a button-up blouse with one too many of the top buttons undone. Gaudy pendant earrings brushed her shoulders. A Pinyon High School senior ring graced a finger on her left hand.

The young woman's face brightened. "Hi, Cash. Are you here for your interview?"

"Yes. Is he in his office?"

"Unfortunately, he is."

"Unfortunately?"

She leaned toward him. Speaking in a conspiratorial whisper, she said, "He's not very nice to me."

No surprise there. As far as Cash could tell, Sheriff Griff Turner wasn't very nice to anyone. In high school, his bullying personality alienated Cash from the moment they first met. Now, in a strange twist of fate, Turner might be his boss. "Give it time, Vicky. Once you're used to the job, I'm sure it will be okay."

Her fingers brushed his arm. "I broke up with my boyfriend."

"I'm sorry to hear that."

"So, I'm unattached now. I can go out with anyone I want."

Catching her drift, Cash said, "Well, I'm sure you'll get lots of invitations." Her face fell, but what did she expect? She was only three weeks out of high school. "Okay if I go back there?"

With obvious disappointment, she swiveled her chair to face her computer screen. "Sure."

***

Cash shifted in the padded office chair and waited for the man behind the desk to speak. Sheriff Griff Turner, once the loudest mouth on the high school football team, leaned back and cupped his hands behind his head. A burly man, Turner possessed arms like tree trunks and a face cut from iron. The belt holding up his uniform's khaki pants bit into an ample belly that had seen more than its share of fast food and beer. He possessed the penetrating eyes of a wolf and carried himself with the swagger befitting a man who never doubted his own superiority.

"What happened to your face?" His voice boomed in the small office.

Cash didn't blink. "Cut myself shaving."

A smirk spread across the sheriff's face. "Oh, so you're shaving now? Next thing you know your voice will be changing."

Ignoring the barb, Cash flicked his eyes at the manila folder on Turner's desk. "Did you get a chance to look over my résumé?"

Turner made a show of leaning forward to open the folder. "I hardly need to, do I?" He flipped through the papers, giving each sheet only a passing glance. "Adam Cash. Twenty-eight years old, four years in the army followed by a bachelor's degree from Sam Houston State.

Police training at the CAPCOG academy in Austin." He dropped the folder. "You play any ball at Sam Houston?"

"A little."

"Football or baseball?"

"Both." When Turner didn't react, he added, "Four years of football. Baseball my freshman year."

"Why only a year of baseball?"

"I learned pretty quick that one college sport kept me busy enough."

Turner gazed at the ceiling, his mind seemingly elsewhere. "I would have played, except for tearing up my knee in that game against Junction."

"Where?"

"What do you mean, where? Hell, you were there."

"I mean, where would you have played in college?"

"Oh. Texas A&M."

Cash stifled the urge to scoff at the notion of Turner playing for a top-tier Division 1 school. Only in his dreams.

Turner's eyes refocused on Cash. "Well, I wish I could help you, but you just don't have the experience needed for the job."

Cash felt his pulse quickening. "This is an entry-level position. That's how I'd *get* experience."

"The other thing is, there's no money in the budget for another deputy."

"There's a job posting on your website."

"Must be a mistake. You can blame that airhead Vicky."

Cash didn't want to blame anyone. Especially a sweet kid like Vicky. He wanted a job in Noble County law enforcement. "Do you know when you might be hiring?"

Turner leaned forward and rested his arms on the desk. "The thing is, I don't think you'll ever make it to the top of the pile."

"I served two tours in Afghanistan," Cash said, fighting to keep his voice calm. "That should count for something."

"If we need help with Al-Qaeda, I'll give you a call."

Cash resisted the urge to punch the bastard in the face. "Is this about high school?"

"It has nothing to do with high school. It's about you not being what we need," Turner said, standing up. "Now, if you'll excuse me, I've got other things to do."

"Come on, Griff. Don't be such an asshole."

"What did you say?"

"You heard me. You know damn well that job posting was no mistake. This is just your childish idea of revenge for stuff that happened ten years ago."

The corners of Turner's mouth curled up into a wicked grin. "Sucks for you, doesn't it?"

Cash swung an arm and sent a loaded pencil holder flying from Turner's desk. Pens and pencils clattered on the floor. "This is bullshit."

Turner grabbed Cash's collar and slammed him against the wall. Seeing the fire in Cash's eyes, he said, "Go on. Take a poke at a county sheriff. See where that gets you."

Cash gritted his teeth and grabbed Turner's wrist to push it away. Turner let go and jerked his arm free. "Get the hell out of my office."

As Cash stormed back through the lobby, Vicky stopped him and said, "How'd it go?"

"Not so good."

"Oh. I'm sorry." She flashed her sexiest smile. "There's a dance over in Sonora this weekend. Dale Watson is playing."

"Dale Watson, eh? Wish I could go."

"Oh." She pursed her lips. "Have a nice day."

3

Art Santiago's stomach growled as he drove his Texan Pharmaceutical eighteen-wheeler past one of San Antonio's countless Whataburgers. This was the third burger joint he had passed in as many blocks and he was starving. But a semi doesn't fit in the drive-thru lane of a fast-food restaurant, so he sighed and kept going. Besides, his tyrant of a boss wouldn't like seeing an unnecessary stop on the truck's electronic timekeeper.

Art drove another three blocks and braked at a red light. A metallic tap on the passenger window drew his attention. A man in a ski mask was pointing a gun at him.

"Unlock the door," the man said through the glass.

Eyes glued on the gun, Art hurried to comply. The masked man opened the door and slid into the passenger seat. "Drive."

The light turned green and, heart racing, Art eased the truck into motion. "Where are we going?"

"Just do as I tell you."

A tense minute later, the man said, "Turn right up there."

Art rounded the corner and braked to a stop. "It's a dead end."

"Is the back locked?"

"Yes."

"Give me the keys."

Art fished them out of his pocket and handed them over. The gunman rolled his window down and tossed them to someone Art couldn't see. He turned back to Art. "Let me see your wallet."

"I don't carry much money," Art said, handing it over.

"I don't want your money." The gunman opened the wallet and found Art's driver's license. He studied it for a few moments and said, "Art Santiago. Morey Peak Drive. Is that a nice neighborhood?"

"It's all right."

The gunman gave the wallet back. "Here."

They sat in silence for several minutes. Art heard the truck's rear doors open. Footsteps sounded from inside the trailer. Boxes were being moved. The door slammed shut.

A hand holding the keys reached through the open passenger window. The gunman took the keys and gave them back to Art. He opened the door and tapped a finger to his head. "I've got a good memory, Art. You tell the police anything and I'll pay Morey Drive a visit. Understand?"

Art nodded. He understood.

"Good. Wait five minutes and then you can finish your route."

When the gunman left, Art waited for the required time and then shifted the truck into reverse. Back on the main street, he spotted a Burger King. This time he wasn't tempted by the thought of a meal. His appetite had disappeared.

4

Cash steered the Fiesta onto the highway and swore. That son of a bitch! Was it his fault he had been a better football player than Griff Turner? Maybe if the big slob had kept in better shape, run the laps, lifted the weights like the coaches said, maybe he would have played more.

The engine emitted several loud knocks. Cash pounded the steering wheel and swore again. He needed a better car. One without a mismatched salvage yard passenger door. One he could rely on to start every time he cranked the ignition. For that, he needed a better job, one that paid more than helping Emil Bergheim build fences. A sheriff's deputy didn't earn top dollar, but a lot more than he currently brought in. And as a deputy, he'd be doing something more useful than dodging flying strands of barbed wire.

What would he tell his parents? That he'd failed to find a job in Pinyon, Texas? A job he had been talking about since he was in elementary school? A town he had returned to against his parents' advice? He liked Pinyon. He liked being recognized by the checker at the grocery store. He liked the town square with its historic buildings that housed businesses serving the locals instead of catering to tourists. He liked the chicken fried steak at the Firewheel Café.

His parents had planned to sell off the last sliver of the ranch owned by his ancestors. Cash talked them out of it. He wanted to restore the land. He'd plant cypress trees along the seasonal creek. He'd sow native grass seed: switchgrass, Indiangrass, and little bluestem. He'd root out the invasive Johnson grass. He'd install water stations for wildlife, build check dams in the creek to reduce erosion, and rid the fields of fire ants to encourage the return of quail. He'd scatter bluebonnet seed, as much as he could afford. But without a better-paying job, that wouldn't be much.

His father would remind him he was always welcome to join his HVAC company in Austin. Learn the ropes, work his way up the ladder, and maybe even take over someday, wink, wink.

His mother would tell him to go to law school. Being a lawyer *is* working in law enforcement, she'd say. In her patronizing tone of voice she'd tell him he'd be hanging around judges and cops and people in jail and, good grief, what more did he want? And, she'd add, lowering her voice as if spilling a juicy secret, lawyers make *real* money. Way more than those bozos in the Noble County sheriff's office.

But Cash didn't want to install HVAC systems. He had no intention of spending Texas summers crawling around dusty attics in skin-blistering heat. Nor did he want to go to law school. That would only lead to being stuck in an office slaving over legal documents with language that would baffle a Nobel Prize winner, much less someone who had struggled to make Bs in college. No, he wanted a job with action, one that would take him outdoors. Something away from a city, away from Austin or San Antonio. He wanted to be a cop in a small Texas town. A town like Pinyon, seat of Noble County.

The rhythmic buzzing of cicadas reached Cash's ears as he turned onto the central square and stopped at one of Pinyon's two stoplights. He turned left and cruised past the courthouse before parking in front of Packsaddle Brewing, a brewpub housed in a one-story limestone building occupying a corner lot. His was one of only a handful of cars on the square. He exited the Fiesta, glanced at his phone—almost five o'clock—and started toward the entrance.

A sleek black Lexus backed into the space next to Cash's Fiesta. Cash turned to see Noble County district attorney Lars Newsome climb out of the vehicle. A recent transplant from Houston, Newsome was viewed by most of the locals with suspicion. To fit in, he had traded his jacket and tie for pressed jeans and an open collar. Cash appreciated the effort, but knew it took more than the right clothes to impress the people of Pinyon.

Newsome gave Cash a friendly wave. "Hey, Cash."

"Hey, Lars." Cash pointed at a bumper sticker on Newsome's car that read "Re-elect Sheriff Turner." "I didn't know you'd made an endorsement."

"He's running unopposed. It wouldn't pay to rile him."

"Guess not."

Inside the brewpub, Cash paused to adjust to the light before taking a seat at the polished mahogany bar. His gaze wandered the room in admiration and, if he was honest with himself, a tinge of jealousy. His best pal Steve Jenkins was doing all right. Steve had used the years Cash was away to fill a niche no one else had recognized. From what Cash could tell, the business was thriving. Neon letters spelling the brewpub's name glowed fluorescent blue behind the bar. Boisterous diners occupied each of the six tables. Several people shared the bar with Cash. The lone server had to hustle between her tables and the bar to keep them happy.

A lanky man with a friendly face appeared from a back room and slid behind the bar. It was Steve. He wore faded jeans and a red Packsaddle Brewing T-shirt bearing its logo, "Come and Drink It," below an image of the famed cannon that sparked the Texas Revolution.

Steve flashed a grin. "You're a day early. The beer's free tomorrow."

"Are you ever going to stop telling that stupid joke?"

"Why mess with the classics?"

Despite the lame attempt at humor, Cash appreciated Steve's sense of fun. His friend brightened any room he entered. His major fault was one that Cash had pointed out many times; he sometimes took a joke too far. Like the time in seventh grade when he removed the cartridge from his ballpoint pen and used the pen to shoot spitballs at Cash. When he tired of that, he turned his aim on their Spanish teacher, Señora Fernandez, bouncing several shots off her ample bosom until dropping one down the front of her dress. Señora Fernandez glanced up and saw Cash trying to suppress a laugh. She sent him to the principal's office. Steve found this hilarious.

When they were both fifteen, an incident that started as a lark ended with them spending the night in a Del Rio jail. After a fight with his parents, Steve took his father's truck, picked Cash up, and announced they were going to Mexico. They made it to the border town of Del Rio, where Cash paid for lunch in a diner across the street from the Val Verde County courthouse. A Val Verde deputy overheard them discussing their plans to drive across the border and picked them up. Their parents decided a night in a county jail might do the boys good. Cash was mortified at being detained, but Steve seemed to view the experience as a rollicking good time. He wheedled a deck of cards from the deputy, after which he and Cash spent the evening playing gin. As they were being released, Steve thanked the deputy and said he'd be back for another visit someday.

Now Cash's partner in crime was a successful business owner. Steve grabbed an empty glass from beneath the bar and, with a wink said,

"You *are* here at the right time, my friend. We just tapped a keg of the new stuff."

"What is it?"

Steve filled the glass with amber liquid topped by an inch of foam and set it on the bar. "Guess."

Cash lifted the glass to his lips. An odd odor drifted into his nostrils. Not altogether unpleasant, but unfamiliar. He sipped.

"Well?" said Steve, raising one eyebrow.

Cash made a face. "How the hell are you still in business?" He set the glass aside. "Give me a real beer."

"It's avocado. Goes great with chips and queso." Using a different tap, Steve filled another glass and gave it to Cash.

A man stepped up to the bar next to Cash. He plunked a sixty-four-ounce growler down and said, "Fill me up with the Packsaddle Pale Ale."

Steve began filling the growler. "I haven't seen you in a while. I thought maybe you'd given up beer."

The man laughed. "Not a chance. I live over in Junction and only come here once in a while."

Steve capped the growler and slid it across the bar. The man paid with a credit card, thanked Steve, and left.

"Regular customer?" Cash said.

"Yeah. His name is Carl Trotter. As often as he comes in, I figured he lived here in Pinyon."

"Packsaddle Pale Ale. He has good taste."

"All my customers have good taste. Hey, you haven't told me yet how it went with Sheriff Asshole."

"About as you'd expect."

"He needs to get over it. You were just the better athlete."

"Tell that to him."

"So, back to building fences?"

"No." Cash drained half his beer in one gulp. "I have an idea."

5

Enrique Javier tossed his empty soda bottle and studied the people getting off the Laredo–San Antonio bus for telltale signs. Tentative steps, wide eyes, a bewildered look, maybe a backpack, but no luggage in the hold. They'd descend the steps to the pavement, move out of the way of the other passengers, and turn a slow circle as if seeing the world for the first time. Sometimes they headed for the terminal, other times they just started walking. Not across the street to the parking lot behind the terminal, because no ride awaited the women Enrique was hunting. Instead, they'd shoulder their packs and head toward one of the side streets, either East Martin or East Pecan, and shuffle off in search of a better future. Which Enrique intended to give them. Sort of.

A pair of young women—girls, really—emerged from the bus, ticking off all the boxes on Enrique's mental checklist. He approached and addressed them in Spanish. "Excuse me, ladies, I wonder if I might be of assistance."

The women eyed him with suspicion. One of them said, "That's okay, we're fine."

Enrique pulled a card from his pocket, the one that identified him as an employee of a nonexistent Catholic church. Handing it over, he said, "I understand your reluctance. Here's my card. Call if you need anything."

He turned and walked away. About half the time, he never saw the women again. This time, though, one said, "Wait. Maybe you can help us."

He turned around and flashed a smile. "Of course."

He took them where he always took them, to the Oasis Café, only a short walk from the station. There he ordered *huevos rancheros*—the best in San Antonio—and invited them to have anything on the menu. Famished from their arduous journey, the women always ordered large meals, and these two were no exception. One had the chicken enchilada plate and a large guacamole appetizer. The other asked for a beef fajita dinner. They washed it all down with Dr Pepper.

Enrique feigned concern as they told him their stories. He had heard it all before. Grew up poor in a small village or big-city slum, no jobs, murderous drug gangs, corrupt police, heartless soldiers, abusive family members. Enrique listened and cooed sympathetic words, expressing surprise at each new revelation, shaking his head in disbelief at the mention of such terrors, professing admiration for anyone with the courage and tenacity to escape.

Now it was time for Enrique to play his hand. He insisted on dessert and smiled as the girls dug into their flan, oblivious of his true intent. "My car is nearby," he said. "I could take you to the church. Get you some fresh clothes, a place to sleep. After that, we find you something more permanent, maybe even a job. What do you say?"

They said yes. They always did. Enrique paid the bill and escorted the girls to a road-weary Dodge minivan with the name of his fictional church printed on a magnetic sign stuck to the door. Once they piled in, Enrique said, "Is everybody comfortable?"

"Yes," the women said in unison.

"Good. Here we go."

And he drove. But not to a church. To a warehouse. Where Kessler was waiting.

6

Cash caught a reflection of himself in a window as he approached the modest frame house. He attempted to smooth his wavy brown hair, but it sprang back into a disorganized mop. At least he'd had time to change clothes after working with Emil all day. Sporting mirrored sunglasses, new cargo shorts, Teva sandals, and a burnt orange polo shirt just shy of being too tight for his six-foot-two frame. Heck, he had even showered.

Cash had driven past the house many times since his return to Pinyon a year ago, but had never screwed up the courage to stop and ring the bell. Maybe that imposing concrete javelina left on the porch by the previous owner had kept him away. Or perhaps he was reluctant to tread on the beautifully manicured lawn. Or maybe, just maybe, he was reluctant to face the woman residing behind the fresh gray siding and cherry red door.

A shadow darkened the window, then disappeared. The door opened and a beautiful woman stepped outside. Edie James. Slender curves, athletic build, and flowing black hair that curled at the shoulders. A face shaped by angels, although the innocent eyes of her high school years had given way to a watchfulness gained through hard experience. She rested a hand on her hip and said, "Look at you, Mr. Frat Boy."

Cash's face flushed hot. He slipped off the sunglasses and stowed them in his shirt pocket.

"I saw you from the window. Good gracious, you were preening like a schoolboy coming to pick me up for prom."

"I was not."

"I half-expected you to hand me a corsage when I opened the door."

"Seems like yesterday I did just that."

She dismissed the attempt. "That was a thousand years ago."

"Can I come in?"

She hesitated, but then spun around and, with a glance over her shoulder, said, "Sure."

Cash followed her into a cramped den. He pushed the door closed with a loud click.

"Quiet. Luke's taking a nap."

"Sorry."

She pointed at a brown Naugahyde sofa. "Have a seat. You want something to drink? Water? Juice box? I've got mango."

"Got any chocolate milk?"

"No, but I'm glad to see you haven't changed." She dropped into a well-worn lounge chair and frowned. "Why has it taken so long for you to come see me? You've been back, what, a year?"

Cash tugged at his collar. He had known he'd have to answer that question but didn't think she'd ask it right away. "No reason. I'm here now, aren't I?"

"That you are. The question is, why?"

"Well." He cleared his throat. "I'm planning on running for sheriff."

Her expression didn't change. "Is that so?"

"Yes, and I need someone to run my campaign." He spit out the words so fast they almost ran together.

She laughed. "Your campaign? Aren't you the big-time politician! How come I haven't seen any signs around town?"

"I'm picking them up from the printer later this week. I just filed yesterday."

A toddler ambled into the room. His golden hair reminded Cash of the boy's father, the man who had swooped in to marry Edie while Cash was dodging IEDs in Afghanistan. The boy rubbed his eyes and said, "Mommy, I'm hungry."

Edie rose and scooped him up. "Let's get you something to eat." She looked at Cash. "This is Luke."

"Hello, Luke."

"I'll be right back."

Cash settled back into the sofa and took in his surroundings. Other than the sofa and chair, the only other furniture in the room was a flimsy coffee table bearing countless water stains and a wall-mounted TV with a diagonal of no more than forty inches. Hanging next to the TV was a framed studio portrait of mother and son. Cash stood up to get a closer look.

"That was taken right after the divorce," Edie said as she swept back into the room. "That's why I'm smiling."

They both sat. "Where's Randy now?"

"As long as he's not in Pinyon, I really don't care. Now tell me, why on earth would you want me to be your campaign manager?"

Cash was ready for that question. "Because you're smart. And you're capable. You're a real go-getter."

She emitted that quick crystal laugh that Cash remembered from high school. For a moment he was back in tenth-grade algebra, gazing across the room at her.

"Yeah, I'm a real go-getter. That's why I wait tables at the Firewheel."

"You're just as pretty as ever." He squeezed a fist in frustration. He hadn't meant to say that.

Her eyes narrowed to slits. "That ship sailed when you joined the army."

"I'm sorry." He was always sorry with Edie. Sorry that he'd joined the army instead of marrying her, sorry that four years later he had headed off to Sam Houston State without seeing her, sorry that she'd married Randy Webster without giving him another chance. "Maybe I should go."

"Don't be so sensitive. I haven't said no yet. It's just ... damn it, I would have married you."

"Like you said, that was a thousand years ago. And you didn't want to be an army wife."

"I didn't want to be an army *girlfriend*." Her voice had an edge to it. "I *would* have been an army wife. It was you that didn't want to be an army husband. Then when you got discharged, you went straight to college. Why didn't you look me up?"

Cash said nothing. Why the hell hadn't he done that?

"That's when I married Randy."

"That didn't turn out so well." He instantly regretted saying it.

"Thanks for reminding me. Now I'm a single mom with no college degree waiting tables to pay the bills."

"I'm sorry."

"You said that already." She waved a hand to sweep the past aside. "How much money have you raised?"

"What?"

"For your campaign."

"Oh. Steve gave me five hundred dollars."

She fluttered her lips. "That's it?"

"Uh, and I've got a couple thousand in the bank."

She laughed again, and Cash felt his heart melt. "I guess that's a start," she said.

"So, what do you think?"

"What do I think? I think you haven't got a chance in hell. But, sure, I'll help you throw your money down the drain."

"Thank you. That's great." Before he could stop himself, he added, "Maybe we could discuss strategy over dinner some night?"

She rose, crossed the room, and flung the door open. "Don't press your luck."

7

Nate Kessler reached out his hand for a quick shake with the nervous man across the table. "Remember, this is not something you talk about. Ever."

"Of course," the other man said. "You have my word."

Kessler suppressed the urge to laugh. There was nothing to be gained by insulting his new customer, but how many times had he heard that statement before? The most recent man who had uttered it now lay in an unmarked grave on a desolate ranch twenty miles southwest of San Antonio. He had failed to keep his mouth shut. Kessler gave this man no better than a fifty percent chance of avoiding the same fate.

The nervous man nodded at the tequila bottle on the table. "Mind if I have another shot?"

"Be my guest."

"This is good stuff," the man said as he filled his glass. He downed it in one quick gulp.

"Herradura Silver. Fifty dollars a bottle."

"Holy shit."

"I'll give you a bottle when you leave. Call it a party favor."

"Wow. Thanks."

Kessler chuckled to himself. Some people were so easy to impress. "Now to business. Before we can go any further, I need to see the money."

They sat at a table in an otherwise barren warehouse in a rundown section of San Antonio. Enrique stood nearby, ready to jump at an order from Kessler. Another man patrolled the building's entrance.

The nervous man hoisted a briefcase onto the table. He popped it open and swiveled it to face Kessler. "It's all there. You can count it if you want."

"There's no need for that," Kessler said, smiling.

The man moved to shut the case.

Kessler held up a hand. "Don't be an idiot. Of course I want to count it." One by one, he removed the bundles of bills and rifled through them. Satisfied, he returned them to the briefcase and whistled to the guard by the door. "Go get those women."

"Which ones?"

"The two that got here last week."

The guard strode to the rear of the warehouse and pulled a set of keys from his pocket. He unlocked a door and disappeared. Moments later, he reappeared with Enrique's latest prey in tow. As he relocked the door, he ignored the muffled shouts coming from the other side.

The guard prodded the two women toward Kessler. They made eye contact with Enrique, but in their drugged state, didn't recognize him. Kessler watched them approach and nodded in appreciation. Enrique certainly knew how to pick them. Young, nubile, and docile. Now and then he returned with a wildcat, one that was more trouble than she was worth. That was why Kessler had the ranch. It gave him a place to dispose of the feisty ones.

"Hurry up, ladies, we haven't got all day," Kessler said. He grinned at his customer. "Don't know why I bother. They don't speak English."

"What language do they speak?"

"Spanish, I guess. Who gives a shit?"

"I was just wondering."

"It really doesn't matter, does it? Pull your van inside."

Both men stood. "And remember," Kessler said. "You gave me your word."

8

"Anybody want to split that last one?" Steve said, eyeing the slice of Canadian bacon-mushroom pizza left on the tray.

Cash patted his belly. "It's all yours."

Steve raised an eyebrow at Edie, who flicked a hand to invite him to it.

"Great." He snatched the slice and dropped it onto his plate.

They sat around a table in Bill and Ted's Excellent Pizza Parlor, one of two pizza restaurants in Pinyon, the other being a national chain. While Cash liked to eat and shop at locally owned establishments, he couldn't deny the place was a dump. Faded green wallpaper and a pressed tin ceiling that sagged in multiple places begged for attention. A concrete floor with cracks large enough to swallow a small dog threatened to trip unwary customers. Diners sat at primitive tables made by screwing a plywood circle to a plastic base. Because the owners, Bill Carpenter and Ted Hubbard, hadn't bothered to sand the plywood, patrons sitting at these tables ran a constant risk of splinters.

The bar along one wall also appeared homemade, although at least its pine surface had been smoothed and painted a dirty gray. What passed for decor included a dozen mounted deer heads interspersed with random Texas sports team pennants. A lone javelina head snarled at patrons from behind the bar.

Edie tapped a finger on the spreadsheet displayed on her laptop screen. "How many yard signs are up?"

"Enough," said Cash.

"How many?"

"Uh, five."

"And three of those are in our yards." She threw him an accusing glance. "How many houses did you visit?"

"Enough."

"You said that already."

"I don't like knocking on strangers' doors."

"This is a small town. There are no strangers."

Cash said nothing. That was precisely the reason he hated knocking on doors.

"Steve, did you hit up the businesses on the square?"

"I did," Steve said, stuffing the last bite of pizza into his mouth. "Nobody wants to take sides."

"Which means they've already taken sides. Nobody's giving us a chance."

Cash sighed. He had known he faced an uphill battle but he had expected their initial efforts to at least budge the needle toward success.

"Guys, we have to do better than this," said Edie.

Cash said, "I guess I have to get used to asking people to vote for me."

Edie patted his arm, her touch distracting him from any thoughts about door-to-door campaigning. He tried to recall the last time he and Edie had kissed. Graduation night?

"You can't do it all by yourself," Edie said. "When I said we're a team, I meant it."

Rusty hinges groaned as the restaurant's door opened. A uniformed figure filled the doorway. The man removed his hat and strode over to their table. "Well, if it ain't the Noble County political whiz kids."

Cash nodded a greeting. "Hello, Clovis."

Clovis Ward was the county's chief deputy, second in command to Griff Turner. He was the longest-tenured of the department's employees, with seventeen years on the force. Built like a linebacker, with thick muscles and a flat stomach, Ward carried himself with the same swagger as his boss. Unlike Turner, he spoke little, and when he did he used a quiet, but stern voice of command.

Ward had run for sheriff two years ago when the previous sheriff, Carter Turner, suffered a fatal heart attack in his sleep. He lost to the dead man's son Griff in the special election. Despite the humiliation of losing to someone with so little experience, Ward had swallowed his pride and agreed to stay on as chief deputy.

Cash had known Ward since he was a gangly preteen and Ward was the new deputy in town. Theirs had been an uneasy relationship. Cash had long suspected that Ward didn't like him, but he didn't know why. He did know that Ward despised his father, Del, a feeling that was mutual, from what Cash could tell. Del Cash referred to Ward only as "that son of a bitch deputy." Cash had asked his father about it once and was told to mind his own business.

Ward dropped a meaty paw onto Cash's shoulder, causing him to flinch. "You guys figuring out a way to pull off an upset?"

Cash emitted a noncommittal grunt. He had no desire to endure sarcasm from Clovis Ward.

"Listen, if it's any consolation, I wouldn't mind seeing that happen," Ward said, leaning in close. "Between you and me, maybe it's time for a change. Know what I'm saying?"

"No, Clovis, what are you saying?"

"I'm saying that Griff Turner is a real son of a bitch."

Cash saw every head in the restaurant swivel toward them. Oblivious, Ward slapped Cash's back. "You think so too, don't you? I mean, he gave you a giant middle finger, didn't he?" He shifted into a perfect impression of Turner's voice. "Sorry, Cash, I know you're qualified and all, but I'm not gonna hire you because of a bunch of shit from high school."

Cash stared at the big man. What on earth was he doing?

Ward caught the eye of a man at the bar. Using his own voice, he said, "You heard about that, didn't you? If anybody has cause to hate Sheriff Turner's guts, it's Adam Cash."

No one ate, no one drank. All eyes in the restaurant were glued on Clovis Ward. Cash couldn't think of anything to say to make the big man go away. As if sensing he had overplayed his hand, Ward released his grip on Cash's shoulder and said, "Good luck in the election, Cash. I'll be seeing you."

When Clovis left, Steve said, "What the hell was that all about?"

"He's just screwing with us," said Cash. "There's no way in hell he's voting for me."

"Well, I say screw him."

Edie sighed and turned her attention back to her laptop screen. "Come on, guys. We've got a lot of work to do."

"In that case," said Steve, rising, "I'm gonna order another pizza."

***

Thirty minutes and one sausage pizza later, Edie snapped her laptop shut and extricated herself from the booth. "I'll see you boys later."

"Sure thing," said Steve.

Cash watched Edie until she was out the door, mesmerized by the rhythmic swaying of her hips.

"Man, you have got to get over her," Steve said.

"What are you talking about?"

"The way you look at her. She's not coming back."

Cash stared into his iced tea. "Who says I want her back?"

Steve laughed. "You're so full of shit. It's obvious."

"Maybe if you'd ever get a girlfriend, you'd understand."

"Maybe you should go fuck yourself. I've been with plenty of women."

Now it was Cash's turn to laugh. "Hookers don't count."

"I've told you before," Steve said, his voice turning cold. "I didn't know she was a hooker."

"Sorry."

They glared at each other. Cash tried unsuccessfully to suppress a muffled laugh. "You should have seen the look on your face when she asked you for a hundred bucks."

"That's the last time I go to New Orleans without enough cash."

"Good times," Cash said with a sigh. He raised his tea glass. "To good friends."

Steve returned the salute. "No, to best friends. Which is why you've got to listen to me. Forget about Edie."

Cash tossed back the rest of his tea. "Who's Edie?"

9

"My God, she's beautiful," Cash said as he stroked the infant girl's silky hair. He marveled at her tiny fingers as they wrapped around his thumb.

"Momma says she takes after me," said the child's mother, twenty-two-year-old Bernadette Fenster, who was perched on the edge of a flimsy rocking chair in a double-wide trailer. "I know half comes from you. I think Momma's just going off the red hair."

Bernadette was a full-bodied woman with curly red hair, a prominent chin, a pointed nose, and oversized ears. She wore faded blue sweatpants and a T-shirt that said, "Hands off this sexy bod." Her face was pleasant but not beautiful. Not like Edie's. Nevertheless, Cash said, "I can see that. She's pretty like her mother."

Bernadette snorted. "You're laying it on thick, aren't you? Is there something you want?"

Cash handed the six-month-old back to her mother. "No, I just wanted to see my daughter."

"Well, now you've seen her, so I guess you can go."

He wasn't ready to leave. He had something to say. "I like the name you picked. Emma."

"It was my great-grandma's name," she said, pleased. "I always said if I had me a girl, I'd name her Emma."

Cash cleared his throat. "I did want to talk to you about what I suggested on the phone."

"You mean spending the night here with me?" She scoffed. "I don't think so. One night of drunk sex was enough."

"We wouldn't have sex. We'd sleep in different beds. Different rooms, for that matter. And it wouldn't be every night, just now and then. You could have a night out when I'm here. Go on dates, whatever you want."

"Dates. Right. If there's a man in Pinyon worth dating, I ain't met him yet."

"That's just an example. Don't you want a little freedom?" He cringed at the pleading tone in his voice.

"Don't need that," Bernadette said with a firm shake of her head. "I got Momma to help me."

Cash drew a deep breath and released it. He looked around the room at the shabby furniture and stained carpet, trying to think of something to say that would change her mind. Despite knowing it wouldn't sway Bernadette, he stated the obvious. "She's my daughter too, you know."

She stared past him and rocked. The rickety chair emitted a loud squeak each time it came forward. "Don't make me hire a lawyer, Cash. I can't afford it." When he didn't respond, she added, "I don't think you can either, judging by how much you send me."

Cash knew she was right. The campaign for sheriff had strained his bank account, leaving him with little left for child support. Still, he had sacrificed to send as much as he could. "All I'm saying is, I want to be a good father. I want to be responsible."

"Hell, you *are* responsible. At least your dick is." She closed her eyes. "Damn it, I'm sorry. It's not as if I pushed you away. I sure was drunk that night."

"You know I didn't take advantage of that. I was drunk too."

Opening her eyes, Bernadette gave him a look soft enough to almost be sympathetic. "I know you didn't. If I'd have said no, you would have stopped. Heck, you even asked if it was okay before you slid it in. If there's one thing I can say about you, Cash, it's that you're a gentleman."

Cash's jaw slackened. This was the first time she had ever said anything remotely nice to him. He'd never forget the fury on her face when she informed him of the pregnancy. He saw no trace of that now. "If you ever need anything, just ask," he said.

"I never know where you are."

"You've got my number."

"What if you're out of range building fences or something?"

"If you can't find me, check with Steve at the Packsaddle. He'll put you in touch."

Bernadette rewarded the offer with a smile. "I appreciate you wanting to be her daddy." Her eyes narrowed. She was done playing nice. "But don't ask me about sleeping here again."

10

Cash gripped the sides of the lectern and took a deep breath. He hated situations like this, standing in front of a crowd of people asking them for something they probably didn't want to give. He knew most of the people present, or at least knew their names and faces, but why would they want to help *him?* Edie had suggested it—no, ordered him to do it—so here he was. If the suggestion had come from Steve, he would have ignored it. But Edie could tell him to stick his finger into a light socket and he'd do it, fantasizing it would somehow earn him another chance with her.

The room was familiar enough. When he was a boy, his father had brought him along to the occasional Rotary Club meeting in the private dining room of the Firewheel Café, hoping to instill a sense of service in his son. Not much about the room had changed over the years. Attendees sat on the same plastic chairs at the same laminate tables. They pledged allegiance to the same dusty American and Texan flags hanging from the same upright poles behind the lectern. If they were bored, their eyes wandered to the Little League team photographs lining the walls or the faded map of the Republic of Texas. Or the framed print of the painting *Dawn at the Alamo*, depicting Davey Crockett swinging his musket like a club and Colonel Travis stepping on one Mexican soldier while shooting another. The only change Cash noticed was an influx of more Little League pictures.

Cash glanced at his notes and forced himself to concentrate. "In conclusion, I pledge that as sheriff I will always act in the best interest of the people of Noble County. I hope I can count on your vote. Thank you."

A polite ripple of applause broke out. Cash hadn't expected a standing ovation, but clearly, he hadn't set the room on fire. His mouth watered as he glanced down at the juicy slab of cherry pie a server had placed before him as he rose to speak. Would it look rude if he took a bite? Probably. He reached for the glass of water beside it and sucked down a large gulp.

Virgil Hall, president of the Pinyon Rotary Club, swallowed a last bite of his own cherry pie and said, "If anyone has questions for young Cash, I'm sure he'd be glad to entertain them."

Several hands rose. Cash pointed at an elderly man in a blue denim shirt and bolo tie with a scorpion embedded in the slide. He forced himself not to stare at the scorpion and said, "Yes, sir."

The man rearranged the cowboy hat in his lap and leaned forward. "My neighbor let them wind farm people put up some of those giant windmills on his property. I hear they got cameras on those things. If you was to be elected, what would you do about that?"

Cash felt sweat soaking the back of his shirt. Damn that Jackson Metzger. Hauled himself away from his forty-two game on the café porch so he could torment Cash with stupid questions. "Are you sure there are cameras?" Cash asked.

The old man scoffed. "Hell, yes, I'm sure. I see those red lights blinking all night long. Them people are spying on me."

Virgil spoke up. "Jackson, those red lights are to keep airplanes from crashing into them. They're not spying on you."

"Airplanes?" Metzger looked at Cash. "Is that right?"

Cash nodded. "I believe it is."

"So, they ain't spying on me? I can see them damn things through my bathroom window."

"Nobody wants to watch a crusty old man take a dump," said Virgil, eliciting a round of laughter.

The room fell silent. Cash squirmed as all eyes turned back to him. "Are there any more questions?" he asked.

A heavily made-up woman in business attire raised her hand. Cash didn't know her name but recognized her as the manager of the local credit union. "Yes, uh ..."

"Jeanine," the woman said. "I can't help but notice that you've never worked in law enforcement. That doesn't exactly inspire confidence in a voter."

Cash was ready for that one. He had rehearsed his answer with Edie. "I may not have experience as a police officer, but I've had the training. I graduated from Sam Houston State with a bachelor's degree in criminology and completed police training at the CAPCOG academy in Austin. Before that, I served two tours in Afghanistan, where I faced many challenging—no, dangerous—situations. I don't anticipate running into anything in Noble County that I haven't come across before."

Cash spotted several people nodding in approval. Jeanine, though, appeared unconvinced. Before she could ask a follow-up question, the man next to her stood up. Cash had never seen him before. He wore a checkered flannel shirt, faded jeans, and well-worn cowboy boots. A salt-and-pepper beard obscured the lower half of his ruddy face. He looked like a farmer who had just stepped off his tractor. The man stuck his thumbs in his belt and said, "Mr. Cash, I'm sure you're aware that Texas has the right to secede from the Union if it wants to. I was wondering if you think that would be a good idea."

Cash's jaw dropped. Where had that question come from? How would his answer bear any relation to the job description of a county sheriff? Looking to buy time, he said, "I actually wasn't aware of that."

The man smirked. "Now that you are, what do you think? Should Texas be its own country? It's a simple question."

Cash noticed several people leaning forward to listen to his answer. He sucked down some water and racked his brain. "It would seem to me that the Civil War settled that issue a long time ago." He glimpsed Edie off to the side, shaking her head. Ignoring her, he said, "Here's the bottom line. I'm an American. I fought for this country. Some of my comrades died for it. I would never do anything to harm it. Just like I would never do anything to harm the good people of Noble County."

The man's eyes narrowed. "You may be an American, but with an answer like that, you sure as hell ain't no Texan."

Cash felt something in his brain snap. "I was born and raised right here in Pinyon. What about you?"

"Takes more than a birth certificate to make a man a Texan."

"So, you're *not* a Texan."

"I didn't say that, you jackass."

Cash stepped around the lectern and faced the man. "If anyone's a jackass, it's the man who wants to refight the Civil War."

"Good answer," shouted a woman from the back.

"No, it ain't," said the bearded man. "A real Texan would support independence."

The woman stood up. "Are you saying I'm not a real Texan?"

"That's exactly what I'm saying. Hell, you were born in New Jersey."

Other people stood. Everyone began talking over one another.

"It's right there in the Treaty of 1845."

"You done drank the Kool-Aid, Frank."

"My daddy didn't fight in Vietnam for this."

"I tell you, the government is spying on me from them windmills."

Virgil rose and raised his arms. "People, people. Let's come to our senses." The room quieted. "That's better. Now, Frank's not completely off his rocker. If you look—"

A general uproar drowned Virgil out as a dozen fierce debates broke out around the room. Cash sighed and sat down. Spotting his dessert, he pulled it toward him and picked up a fork. There was no sense in wasting a free piece of cherry pie.

***

"I don't think that got me many votes," Cash said.

Edie dunked a napkin in a glass of water and dabbed a red spot on his shirt. "I see you enjoyed the cherry pie."

"Leave it," he said, nudging her hand away. "Don't you have to get back to work?"

She pointed at Jerry, the cook, perched on a nearby stool working a crossword puzzle. "Does it look like it's busy out there?"

"Guess not. You know, I expected more pertinent questions."

"Don't you get it? It doesn't matter what people ask. For that matter, it doesn't matter a whole lot what you say. The important thing is for you to come across as a good old Texas boy." She sighed. "I'm not sure citing the outcome of the Civil War accomplished that."

"Come on, Edie, that question was insane."

"Maybe, but a crazy person's vote counts just as much as a sane one's."

"There were thirty people in that room today. I doubt if I changed the mind of a single one of them."

"That's where you're wrong. Jeanine told me she's voting for you."

"Jeanine? Miss You-never-worked-in-law-enforcement Jeanine?"

"One and the same. I'm telling you, Cash, this race is closer than you think."

"Yeah, right."

"Don't be like that. I want you cheerful at your luncheon tomorrow."

"Luncheon?" He didn't like the sound of that.

She studied a slip of paper from her pocket. "The Silver Cowgirls. Twelve o'clock at the community center."

"The Silver Cowgirls. Is that the group of old ladies you see wearing pink hats around town?"

"Yep."

"If there's a Silver Cowgirl younger than eighty, I'll eat that napkin."

"Bessie Eagleton is seventy-eight. She was in here celebrating a birthday last week," she said, handing him the soggy napkin.

He tossed it into a nearby trash can. "I'll be there."

"Just remember one thing," Edie said, pointing a finger.

"What's that?"

"Texas lost the Civil War." She rose and strutted toward the exit.

"That was the whole point!"

Cash followed Edie out into the dining room, where he bumped into Gabe Santos. The deputy's eyes lit up with recognition. "Hey, Cash."

"Santos. Hey."

"Can I buy you lunch?"

"I just ate."

"Oh. Another time then."

"I'd take a chocolate shake."

***

Santos ordered the daily special, chicken fried steak, mashed potatoes with cream gravy, and green beans. Cash nodded in approval. He thought it was the best chicken fried steak in Texas. Although he was still full from the Rotary Club lunch, he asked for "the biggest chocolate shake you make, hold the whipped cream. And can you ask Jerry to put an extra scoop of chocolate in it?"

"Sure," the server said and left.

Santos grinned. "Adam Cash. I still can't get over running into you."

"I never told you I was from Pinyon?"

"You probably did. There's a lot from back then I've forgotten."

"A lot of it deserves to be forgotten."

Santos raised a finger for emphasis. "I'll tell you what I haven't forgotten. The way you saved my butt."

"I was just doing my job."

"Thank God for that. I was a dead man. Shot all to hell and barely able to hold my weapon. Then you showed up."

"You'd have done the same for me."

"I'd like to think that's true."

Cash ignored the attempt at modesty. Instead, he voiced a question he'd had for a long time. "You know, I always wondered what happened to you after that day."

"It's all a blur," Santos said, shaking his head. "They operated on me at the base, took out a piece of my gut. From there they sent me back to the States. While I was in the rehab center, my enlistment ran out. I wasn't in much of a mood to reenlist."

"I don't blame you."

"So, you're running for sheriff?"

"You didn't know?"

"No."

Cash pressed his lips together. "There's the problem. Nobody does. I'm going to get creamed."

"Never say never. I'll vote for you."

"You'd vote against your boss?"

Santos stirred slightly. Not obeying a superior officer went against the grain. But he said, "Between you and me, Turner's sloppy. Kind of a loose cannon. He wouldn't have lasted five minutes in Afghanistan. No way he'd be sheriff if it wasn't for his daddy."

"You better keep that to yourself."

"I plan to." He signaled to the server. "Can you bring me one of those shakes?"

"Sure."

Turning back to Cash, he said, "So, what will you do if you lose?"

"I don't know. Keep building fences, I guess."

"Too bad. We could use a good man like you."

Cash sat back in his chair and sighed. "If only Griff Turner agreed with you."

11

When Santos returned to the department after lunch, Vicky jerked a thumb toward the hall and said, "The sheriff wants you back there."

"What for?"

"Do you think he tells me?"

Santos strode down the hall to the department's meeting room. He entered to find Sheriff Turner seated at the head of the rectangular conference table. To his right sat Clovis Ward, to his left, deputies Judd Noteboom and Deke Conrad. Turner glanced up and said, "Gabe's here. Everybody switch to Spanish."

Everyone laughed, Turner the loudest. Santos forced a weak smile and took the last seat at the table. Why did Turner keep making jokes about his ability to speak Spanish? The online notice advertising his position had stated, "Fluency in Spanish a plus." Yet Turner made wisecracks about it every chance he got.

As the laughter died down, Noteboom said, *"Sí, Jefe,"* eliciting more laughter. This didn't surprise Santos. Noteboom was an ass, always sucking up to the boss. Like Turner, Noteboom had a gut that hung over his belt like a balloon begging to be popped. His thick neck connected a massive head to his barrel chest. He kept his lips pushed up in a constant scowl. Although barely into his thirties, his scalp was visible through an unkempt mop of stringy brown hair.

Deke Conrad was the opposite. With his departmental uniform of khaki pants and short-sleeve button-down shirt, Conrad could have been plucked from a catalog of Texas law officers. His shaved head, square jaw, and thick shoulders gave him the look of a man not to be trifled with. Unfortunately, in Santos's opinion, physical prowess did not come packaged with much in the way of brain power. He was a good man to work with as long as he left the decisions to others.

Turner folded his hands and leaned on his elbows. "All right, down to business. I picked up a shitload of campaign signs this morning that I need you guys to put out. Ward and Noteboom, you take the square. Deke, Gabe, you guys hit as many businesses as you can get to. And don't take no for an answer."

"You got it," said Noteboom.

Santos held up a hand. "Excuse me, Sheriff. I'm not sure regulations allow us to work on a private political campaign."

Turner scowled. "This isn't a private campaign. Hell, I'm the sheriff. I work for the county."

"Maybe we should run this past Lars," Santos said, referring to the district attorney.

"Or maybe you should just do as you're told."

Ward said, "Santos has a point, Griff. It is indeed against regulations. We could be fined. Fired even. You know how picky some of the county commissioners are."

Turner's jaw muscles tightened. "Never mind, then. I'll get me a couple of high school kids."

"You don't think you could lose, do you?" Noteboom asked.

Turner laughed. "To Adam Cash? Not hardly."

"Okay. It's just, I know he's been out campaigning. He spoke at the Rotary Club the other day."

"He can talk to those old farts all he wants. He's a piece of shit and everybody knows it." He looked at Ward. "Am I right?"

Ward nodded. "He doesn't have a chance. He's weak. People aren't stupid."

Turner looked at the other deputies. No one spoke. "All right," he said, pushing himself to a standing position. "Carry on."

They stood.

"And Santos."

"Yes?"

Turner's face tightened into a scowl. "*Gracias* for the legal lesson."

12

Barry Novak rolled over to look at the woman lying next to him on the two-person cot. He thought her name was Rosa, although it could have been Felicia. She was asleep, her soft breaths drifting from her mouth in rhythm with the rising and falling of her chest. A puddle of drool stained the pillow beneath her chin.

Taking care not to wake her, Novak stroked the woman's jet-black hair. When she arrived yesterday, it had been greasy to the touch. He made her and the other woman shower to cleanse themselves of the grime they'd accumulated during their long trip from God knows where. Colombia? El Salvador? Brazil? He didn't know and didn't care. All he knew was they would each fetch a handsome price. He already had buyers lined up.

The woman beside him was the prettier of the two. The other one had rotten teeth and a chin that jutted out. Her figure was nice enough, but Novak's decision on which one to bed had been easy enough. He had given the big-chinned woman a dose of oxycodone and banished her to the other cot in the room while he had fun with Rosa. Then, as promised, he gave his bed partner her own dose of the synthetic opioid. The women had arrived hooked on the stuff, a brilliant management tool initiated by Kessler, the San Antonio supplier. After purchasing the two women, Novak and his partners had to find their own supply of drugs. Thanks to their connection at Santa Rosa Hospital, that had been easy.

Novak got out of bed and slipped on his boxer shorts. A big man, he had big appetites, and frequent sex was one of them. He smiled at the thought he could now have it anytime he wanted. Sure, he would still wine and dine a woman if she was hot enough, but he could walk away if his date didn't put out and still get laid. Why hadn't he thought of this arrangement years ago?

Glancing at the drool-soaked pillow, he decided to make the women change the sheets when they woke up. Maybe sweep the room and clean the commode too. Why not make use of them while they were here? He would just be preparing them for their new lives of service, whether providing sexual favors or vacuuming the den. Probably a combination of the two.

An open pill bottle on the floor caught Novak's eye. He picked it up and screwed on the cap, reminding himself not to be careless with the drug that kept the captive women so docile. Until last night he had been skeptical of oxycodone's ability to live up to its promise, but the woman on the cot had proven its value. He would send her and her partner on their way with two pills each. Their purchasers would have to feed their habit after that.

The woman with the big chin stirred and sat up.

"*¿Señor?*"

"What is it, Rosa?"

"Felicia."

"Whatever."

She stared at him with uncomprehending eyes.

"What do you want? *¿Que quieres?*"

"*Quiero salir.*" Her words came out slurred.

Novak searched his rudimentary Spanish vocabulary for the word *salir*. "Leave? You want to leave?"

"*Sí*," said Felicia, nodding, eyes half closed. "*¿Cuándo podemos irnos?*"

"*No puedes*," Novak said. You can't.

Felicia's face fell as comprehension set in. She glanced at Rosa, still asleep. Looking back at Novak, she said, "*Señor, por favor.*"

Novak stood and put on his pants. "You're not leaving. Understand? *No salir.*"

She broke into sobs. Novak slapped her, and she cried louder. He pushed her backward onto the cot. The noise woke Rosa.

Novak left the room, closing and locking the door behind him. He had built this room himself, framing it, putting up the drywall, and stuffing the walls and ceiling with extra insulation for soundproofing. He sealed the only exit with a heavy metal door and attached padding on the side that faced the room to muffle the sound of anyone pounding on it. The room had a sink, a commode, a shower, a wall-mounted television, and two cots. He had more cots available in case they were ever needed. He hoped they would be.

The room was located in the basement of a former Fort Worth gelato shop he'd purchased a year ago. He had intended to keep the shop open, figuring he could use it to launder the money he expected to make from selling the women, but on the advice of a friend, he bought another shop in a pissant town called Pinyon. The Fort Worth location became superfluous, so he shuttered it. With the building's main floor empty and the basement room soundproofed, the women could scream all they wanted and no one would hear them.

Novak sauntered over to a fold-up card table that held a laptop, a glass, and a bottle of bourbon. He poured himself two fingers of the amber liquid and dropped into a metal folding chair. A few taps on the keyboard brought up a live video feed showing the women. They were seated next to each other on a cot, sobbing. Novak felt no sympathy for them. There were sheep and there were wolves. The sheep always cried when caught. As far as Novak was concerned, if you didn't want to get eaten, then don't be a sheep.

Novak sipped the bourbon and held the glass up to the light to peer through the translucent liquid. He smiled at the irony of his disdain for drug addicts while he downed a half-pint of Michter's a day. But bourbon provided a civilized means of self-medication, while drugs like oxycodone dragged their users into savagery. The income flowing from his pipeline of human cargo would buy his ticket to rub elbows with Fort Worth's elite, maybe even the fat cats at the Petroleum Club. After that, he would never drink a mid-level bourbon like Michter's again. He'd have nothing but the best: Blanton's, Parker's Heritage, maybe even Old Rip Van Winkle 25-Year-Old Kentucky Straight Bourbon at $50,000 a bottle.

Reviewing the plan cooked up by him and his partners once again, Novak found no weak spots, at least none with unacceptable levels of risk. Except for one. And he intended to eliminate that weak link with the phone call he was about to make.

He fished a cheap Nokia burner phone from his pants pocket and pulled up the three contacts in its directory. The screen displayed no names, just numbers as untraceable as the one for the phone in his hand. He placed a call to the first number on the list and waited. A man answered. "What's up?"

Novak swallowed and relished the warm feel of the bourbon trickling down his throat. "I've been thinking about what you told me. There's only one way to handle this."

"Are you sure? That's a big step."

"I know it's a big step. But you don't get anywhere by taking small ones."

"That's easy for you to say way up there in Fort Worth."

"Listen, Goddammit. I'm in this as deep as you. I've got a business right there on the town square. In fucking Pinyon, for God's sake. Which I bought on your advice."

A loud sigh came through the phone's speaker. "You're right. I'll take care of it."

"When?"

"Soon enough."

"Keep me posted."

Novak ended the call. He refilled his glass, leaned back in the chair, and stared at the ceiling. This was indeed a big step. But it was worth it. After all, you don't get to drink Old Rip Van Winkle by taking small ones.

13

Cash woke up on election day in a foul mood, knowing he was going to get creamed. He had made telephone calls, knocked on doors, spoken to several service clubs, kissed up to the Silver Cowgirls, and stood outside the feed store to hand out flyers in a drizzling rain. He had courted judges, attorneys, ranchers, prominent business owners, and the principal of each school in town, begging for endorsements. None came. Everyone said the same thing. "I didn't know there was anyone running against the sheriff." He even asked Emil Bergheim for his vote, but Emil told him he needed Cash for building fences, not handing out speeding tickets.

Cash broke two eggs into a bowl while trying to think of what else he might have done to improve his odds. Radio interviews? The only station in the county preferred agricultural extension agents as guests over wannabe sheriffs. A rally? The last thing he needed was to show up at an auditorium that was empty save for Pam Beasley, the nosy reporter from the *Pinyon Herald*. An election day barbecue? How would he have paid for that?

Stirring the eggs with a fork, Cash dropped in some leftover grilled onions, cumin, and a dash of garlic powder. As the eggs cooked, he added crumbled tortilla chips and grated cheddar cheese and then scraped everything onto a plate.

Cash loved migas. He had them for breakfast at least once a week. This morning, though, the first bite tasted like soggy cardboard, as did the second. He couldn't stop thinking about the election. There was no denying it. He was going to lose and lose big. A swig of orange juice went down like battery acid, and he poured the rest of the glass into the sink. After dumping the eggs into the compost bucket, he leaned on the counter and shook his head. It would be an epic loss. He was certain of only three votes: his, Steve's, and Edie's. And could he really count on Edie?

He showed up to work still sunk in his pity party. Emil got on him several times for sloppy mistakes, the worst of which necessitated the resetting of four fence posts when he added too much water to the concrete mixture. At noon, he told Emil he was leaving to vote and wouldn't be back until tomorrow. "Tomorrow, eh?" Emil said, not bothering to hide his irritation. "I won't finish this by myself today and it's supposed to rain tomorrow."

Cash waved a hand and plodded toward his car. "It never rains around here when it's supposed to rain."

At the elementary school, Cash got in line to vote. He watched Harold Mercer struggle with the electronic voting machine before banging a fist on the screen in frustration. The old man left. On the way out, he caught Cash watching him and winked.

Cash stepped forward when it was his turn and slapped his driver's license on the table. The volunteer, an elderly woman with crooked glasses, studied it and said, "Hey, didn't I see your name on the ballot?"

"Yes, ma'am. I'm running for sheriff."

"Oh." The woman handed the license back. "That's too bad."

After leaving the school, Cash drove past the historic courthouse dominating the town square and parked in front of the Firewheel. As he stepped up onto the restaurant's concrete porch, he spotted

Jackson Metzger studying his dominoes at one of the tables. With him were three other retirees, one of whom, Sid Brower, had taught Cash's high school algebra class.

Cash threw a friendly wave. "Hey, Mr. Brower. Who's winning?"

Brower rolled his eyes. "These guys are killing us."

Metzger said, "Sid, are you gonna flap your gums or play dominoes?"

"Relax, Jackson, it's just a game."

"See, that's why you're getting your ass kicked."

Cash left the men to their game and pushed through the restaurant door. He had been eating at the Firewheel since he was old enough to walk. He loved that so little had changed over the years. The cracked concrete floor, pressed tin ceiling, bare plaster walls, and cast-iron support columns looked exactly as they did in the century-old photographs hanging along one wall. A neat row of white plywood signs displaying rainfall totals going back to 1893 hung on another wall. The annual totals ranged from 14 inches in 1923 to a high of 54 inches in 1957. Any monthly total of zero was in red. There was a lot of red.

Cash heard a familiar booming voice calling his name above the background din and cringed. Griff Turner. The sheriff sat at one of two rectangular tables pushed together to make room for himself and a dozen others. Cash noticed the tables were situated in the center of the room where everyone in the restaurant could see them. He doubted this was a coincidence. Along with Turner, Cash recognized district attorney Lars Newsome, Frida Simmons, Cash's former babysitter, now the county medical examiner, and Barbara Mixon, a local judge. The others were strangers to him. Judging by the lively conversation and smiling faces, everyone was having a good time. It stung to see Frida enjoying herself in Turner's company.

"Cash, come on over here," Turner hollered, holding up a hand. When Cash was slow to respond, the sheriff stood and waved him over. As he drew near, Turner reached out to shake his hand. "Good luck in the election, but I think we know how it will turn out. No hard feelings either way, right?"

"Right."

"Hey, we can pull up another chair. Why don't you join us?"

"No, thanks."

Turner kept his grin plastered in place. He knew he was putting on a show. "Come on, now, don't be like that. We're all friends here, right?"

Conversation at the table ceased as everyone waited for Cash to reply. Cash drew a deep breath. Should he go along with the charade or speak his mind? He knew what Edie would say but decided to go with the truth. "Griff, you know as well as I do that we've never been friends. So why don't you just cut the bullshit?"

Someone, maybe Lars Newsome, said, "Ouch."

Griff's smile disappeared. "You don't think you're going to win today, do you? Because from where I'm sitting, it looks like you're going to get your ass kicked." He flashed a leering grin. "But don't feel bad. You can come to the victory party at my house tonight. I invited Edie."

Picturing Edie partying with that fat slob of a sheriff boiled Cash's blood. He walked around the table to stand directly in front of the big jerk. "Here's the thing, Griff. If I lose today, I'll be just fine. If you win, you'll still be an arrogant asshole."

Several people laughed. Turner's face reddened as the insult sank in. He shoved Cash hard enough that he had to catch himself on a chair to keep from falling. "Bite me, Cash. You were a loser back in high school and you're an even bigger loser now."

Cash righted himself and thrust out his chest. "Do you know what eats at you, Griff? I was the better athlete in high school and I'm the better man today. And no election result will change that."

Griff shoved him again. "You're just pissed because I wouldn't give you a job." He looked at his dining companions. "Y'all know that? Cash applied for a job with the sheriff's department, but I wasn't desperate enough to hire the miserable loser." He thrust a finger into Cash's chest. "Why don't you man up and admit the truth? You're just not good enough."

Cash's temples flushed hot and, before he could stop himself, he swung a fist into Turner's jaw. Turner stared open-mouthed for a moment and then shot his own fist into the side of Cash's head. With a roar, Cash grabbed Turner's shirt with one hand and cocked his arm to strike with the other. Hands grabbed him from behind and yanked him away. Turner swung and missed, his momentum causing him to stumble against a chair and send it flying.

More chairs slid on the concrete floor as people jumped from their seats. Turner balled his fists, his jaw tight, his face fiery red. Cash tried to pull free to resume the fight, but Newsome wrapped his arms around him from behind and locked the two of them together. "Stop it, Cash," he said. "You don't want to do this."

"I ought to throw your ass in jail, you son of a bitch," Turner said through clenched teeth. "There are a dozen witnesses here that just saw you punch the Noble County sheriff."

Cash struggled against Newsome's grip but couldn't free himself. Newsome jerked him back another step. "Cash, you've got to stop."

He didn't want to stop. He wanted Newsome to let go so he could punch Griff Turner in the face. "Let go of me, Lars."

But Newsome didn't let go and Cash's fury subsided enough for him to realize the DA was right. He relaxed and Newsome released his hold.

Turner removed a pair of handcuffs from his belt. "Turn around," he said, his voice simmering.

Newsome stepped between them. "Don't, Griff."

"Get out of the way. I'm arresting him for assault."

"Don't," Newsome repeated. "You put a hand on him first."

Turner thought for a moment and reattached the cuffs to his belt. He glared at Cash. "You're lucky I'm in a good mood. Now get the hell out of here."

Humiliated, and unable to think of anything to say, Cash turned and trudged toward the door.

"Cash, come here. Let me get some ice on that."

Edie. Of course. The only thing he could think of that was worse than being punched by Griff Turner was for Edie to see him being punched by Griff Turner. "I'm all right."

She took his hand with one that was warm and soft. "Don't argue with me." Leading him into the kitchen, she lowered him onto a stool. "Wait here. I'll get some ice." While she was doing that, she said, "I saw what happened. What the hell were you thinking?"

He ignored the question.

As she applied a bag of ice to his head, she said, "Some of those folks at the table have told me they're thinking of voting for you. I can't see that happening now."

"Who said that?"

"Frida. Lars too, although I wouldn't trust that city slicker any further than I could throw him."

"Maybe they already voted."

"Nope. They were all going after lunch."

Griff's party invitation popped into his head. "You're not going to Griff's house tonight, are you?"

"I was thinking about it. You're not throwing a party, and it never hurts to be cordial."

Cash blew out a deep breath. This was too much. "Are you done talking? Because I was having a lousy enough day already without you to make it worse."

"Fine." She dropped the ice in his lap. "I've got tables to wait."

14

Cash slunk out of the Firewheel, and the first thing he saw was the historic two-story courthouse. The white limestone façade had been cleaned and the original slate roof replaced. In high school, Cash had lost a bet to Steve that he could heave a football over that roof. Losing the bet had cost him ten dollars. Not to mention a damn good football. Great, he thought, my losing streak started all the way back then.

Hal Donaldson climbed aboard a riding lawn mower parked on the lawn and started the engine. Dust swirled around him as he threw the machine into gear and took off at a plodding pace. Coughing from the hot dust, Cash waved at him.

Cash passed the bank, with its year-round Christmas lights, and the pharmacy, reputed to be the oldest in the state. An ancient sign in the window of the latter advertised hamburgers for ten cents and ice cream for a nickel. The pharmacist, Phil Jacoby, loved to tell people how he had found it behind a wall during a long-ago renovation project.

He passed Steve's brewery and the pizza restaurant and entered Erfurt Park, where he followed the crushed granite path to the Nolina River. The water level was lower than usual this year. Little rain had fallen in the past few months, and normally submerged cypress roots protruded from the muddy banks. Cash hurried past a dense thicket that stretched a hundred feet along the riverbank. With its hidden paths and secret clearings, the spot had been one of his favorite boyhood playgrounds.

From there, Cash walked the short distance to the Pinyon Public Library, a squat, one-story yellow brick building a block off the square. Incongruously, the busts of Western author Elmer Kelton and country music singer Hank Williams were stationed on either side of the doorway. Inside the library, he settled into a chair with a six-month-old copy of *Sports Illustrated* and fell asleep. When he awoke, he glanced at his phone and saw he had slept for over an hour. Stumbling out into the late afternoon sun, he squinted and shielded his eyes. His stomach growled. After skipping breakfast and lunch, he needed food.

His phone buzzed. He yanked it from his pocket and looked at the screen. "Hey, Mom."

"Hi, Adam. I was calling to see if you had any news."

"About what?"

"Don't be silly. The sheriff's election. Do you know anything yet?"

Great. Just what he needed. A conversation with his mother about his humiliating day. "The polls are still open, but I don't think I'm going to win."

"Why do you say that?"

"Just a hunch."

There was a long silence before she spoke. "You know, Adam, the offer your father and I made is still good."

"What offer was that, Mom?"

"I swear, sometimes your memory is worse than your father's. The offer to pay for half of your law school tuition. You could start in the fall."

"I'm not going to law school, Mom."

"You don't have to decide right now. Just think about it."

"Mom, I'm not—"

"Just think about it, okay?"

"Okay."

He ended the call and headed for the square, where his car was still parked in front of the Firewheel. He ducked into Bill and Ted's and found a seat in a corner booth. With his back to the wall, he could see the entire restaurant. Except for two teenagers inhaling a sixteen-inch pizza at a nearby table, he was alone.

From behind the bar, Bill Carpenter caught his eye and waved. Cash returned the greeting. Carpenter ambled over to him. "Hey, Cash, what's up?"

"Nothing much. I'm just waiting to get my ass kicked in the election."

"How do you like the Cowboys this year?"

"What do you care? You're an Eagles fan."

"Give me a break. I was born there."

"Wish I was there now."

"What can I get you?"

Cash gave him his order. After Carpenter left, Cash laid his head in his arms and closed his eyes, fatigue and self-pity threatening to overwhelm him. When a soft tap on the table startled him, he raised up to see a teenage girl setting a glass of soda before him. "Sorry. Here's your Coke," she said.

He sipped the ice-cold liquid and reflected on his misery. Crappy car, dead-end job, no prospects, humiliation at the hands of Griff Turner, and the certain embarrassment of a landslide election loss looming over him. Why the hell had he come back to Pinyon? Maybe he should listen to his mother and become a lawyer.

But he knew that was out of the question. He would hate being a lawyer. He probably wouldn't even get into law school. That would give his parents one more thing to ride him about. Besides, Pinyon was home. His life was here. Edie was here. He loved the place and its people. Most of them, anyway. Griff Turner was a jerk.

The front door banged open and a man breezed past. His heavy boots clomped against the wooden floor. Griff. Good grief. How many times did he have to see the guy in one day?

Striding with purpose, the sheriff circled behind the bar and disappeared into the kitchen. A shouting match ensued, with Griff's deep voice blasting through the walls, and Bill Carpenter's reedy twang sounding more distant. A loud crash startled one of the teenagers into dropping his slice of pizza. The kitchen door flew open, and Griff charged back into the dining room. He spotted Cash on his way out and said, "What the hell are you doing here?"

Without looking up, Cash raised a middle finger.

By the time his pizza arrived, Cash had lost his appetite. He forced himself to eat two pieces and took the rest in a to-go box. Outside, he climbed into his car and stuck the key in the ignition. It was only six-thirty. He didn't want to go home. Back to an empty house surrounded by two hundred acres of empty land.

A blue glow beckoned at the end of the block. The Dizzy Dillo. Why not? He hadn't been there since running into Bernadette Fenster that night over a year ago when he got drunk, banged her in her trailer, and got her pregnant. Something like that couldn't happen again, could it? Not in his depressed state. No woman would come near him.

Cash got out of the car. A light rain was falling, and the pavement glistened in the evening sunlight. As he pushed the Dillo's door open, a handful of drinkers occupied the bar. Both pool tables were in use, one by a young couple, the other by four men with bushy beards and bloated bellies. The occasional click of pool balls blended with the soft country ballad pouring from an overhead speaker.

Despite the sizeable crowd, Cash saw no familiar faces. Good. The last thing he wanted was for a friend or, worse yet, a casual acquaintance to console him for his upcoming electoral debacle. He shuffled to a stool at the far end of the bar and sat down.

"Give me a beer," he told the smiling young woman behind the bar. Her cute face tempted Cash to flirt, but he knew his mood would doom the effort.

"What kind?"

"Your choice."

The response appeared to stump her. Her smile faded. "Bottle or draft?"

"Surprise me."

Unused to wielding such power over her customers, the woman studied the contents of the cooler for a long time before selecting a bottle of Lone Star, popping its cap, and setting it on the bar.

"Thanks."

"No problem."

A baseball game was playing on a wall-mounted television behind the bar. Cash watched with only mild interest, neither team being one he cared about. The game reminded him of his freshman year on the team at Sam Houston State. When he quit at the end of the season, he told the coach he needed more time to study. That had been a lie. In truth, he hit .213 that year and lost his starting job at second base to a guy now playing professionally at the AAA level. Just one more failure on his résumé.

Mired in misery, Cash worked his way through three beers, sticking with Lone Star to avoid confusing the cute bartender. By now Griff Turner's victory party would be in full swing. He wondered if Edie was there. The thought tied his stomach in knots. Well, let her go. She didn't owe him anything, did she?

When Cash was halfway through his fourth beer, a man dropped onto the stool next to him. "Buy you another?"

Clovis Ward. Unbelievable. "Jesus Christ, are you guys following me?"

"What?"

"Never mind."

Ward waved the bartender over and asked for two beers. "What kind?" she said.

"Bud Lite. In a bottle." He pointed at the empty Lone Star bottles. "Way better than that shit."

Obviously relieved at the order's precision, the young woman fetched the beers and set them on the bar.

Ward wrapped his thick hand around a bottle and held it up in a toast. "To the candidates. May the best man win."

Cash clinked with him and took a long pull. "I think it's too late for that."

"I'll let you in on a secret," Ward said, leaning in and lowering his voice. "I voted for you."

Cash couldn't help but laugh. "That gets me up to four."

Ward missed the humor. "I'm serious. It's time for a fresh start. Out with the old, in with the new."

"I thought you guys were friends."

The chief deputy shrugged. "We're friendly enough. He can be a pompous ass, though."

"He invited me to his victory party."

"See what I mean?"

"Aren't you going?"

"Yeah, I have to put in an appearance."

"I've got a question." Cash was now slurring his words. "How come you didn't run?"

"No thanks. I got my ass kicked two years ago. I don't need that again."

Cash giggled and closed his eyes. When the room stopped spinning, he opened them and said, "So, you voted for me, eh? I always thought you didn't like me."

"Now, what makes you think that?"

"I don't know. I know you and my dad hate each other."

"Water under the bridge," said Ward. "If he was here right now, I'd buy him a beer."

Cash didn't know how to respond, so he flashed a stupid grin. He chugged the rest of his beer and stood on wobbly legs. "I'm gonna get going. Have a great time at the party. Tell old Griff hello and give him a big middle finger from me."

"Whoa, partner," said Ward as Cash swayed side to side. "You're not driving, are you?"

"No. I've got me a ride."

The lie seemed to satisfy Ward. "All right, then. I'll be seeing you."

Cash dropped two twenties on the bar and stumbled out of the building into a light rain. Across the street, he collapsed onto a park bench on the courthouse lawn. His eyes took in a row of signs lining the sidewalk. They were plywood cutouts of purple javelinas, each bearing the name and uniform number of a member of the school baseball team in gold lettering. The school drill team had planted them on the courthouse lawn to support the team during its recent playoff run. Cash remembered the first time he had seen his name on a similar sign. His mother had taken a picture of him in uniform standing next to it. It was probably still hanging somewhere in his parents' house.

The rain stopped, but Cash knew better than to get behind the wheel of a car. Wouldn't Griff Turner love to haul him in on a DWI? No, he'd just spend the night right here on the town square. If it started raining again, he'd sleep in his car. He closed his eyes and dozed off to the repetitive call of a nearby whippoorwill.

He found himself standing on the lawn of Edie's house. Not her current house, but the house she grew up in. Edie and a group of girls were on their knees, huddled together to work on something. One looked up, pointed, and laughed. The others joined in. He turned to leave, but Edie called his name. She held up a plywood javelina cutout with his name scrawled on it. Beneath it was the word 'loser.'"

A car engine hummed to life across the street. That brought Cash out of his dream. As the headlights flicked on, he wondered how long he had been asleep. He didn't know. A black Toyota Prius eased out of its space and started past him before it stopped. A door opened.

"Cash? Is that you?"

"Edie?"

Footsteps approached. "What are you doing out here?"

Cash spread his arms. "I'm just enjoying this beautiful evening."

"You're drunk."

"I cannot deny that."

"You shouldn't be driving."

"I cannot deny that either."

She took his arm and tugged. "Come on. I'll drive you home."

He fell asleep on the way. At the house, Edie roused him and led him inside. He stumbled toward the den sofa, but she caught him and said, "Let's get you to bed."

He laughed. "I've been waiting a long time to hear you say that."

She ignored the quip and led him into the bedroom, where she bent over to help him out of his jeans. After kicking them off, he swayed in place, waiting for her to tell him what to do next. She straightened. Acting on a drunken impulse, he grabbed her and pulled her in for a kiss.

She pulled back, but not right away. His reeling mind took solace in the brief hesitation. She said, "We're not doing that."

"Did you go to Griff's party?" He sounded more aggressive than he meant to.

She nudged him onto the bed. "No."

Cash struggled to force the fogginess from his mind. "I messed up, Edie."

"Don't worry about it. We've all had a few too many at times."

"No. I messed up with you. I should have never—"

She covered his mouth with her hand. "Not now, Cash. Save it for another time."

He didn't want her to go. "I'm sorry I dragged you into this election. What an embarrassment."

She eased him onto his back. "I'm just sorry I couldn't make it happen for you. You'd make a good sheriff."

His eyes slid shut. Already half asleep, he mumbled, "I just want a job in law enforcement."

15

County medical examiner Frida Simmons had seen dead bodies before. Old men suffering heart attacks in their sleep, depressed wives ending it all with a bottle of pills, a teenage boy who hanged himself in his family's barn. She had even seen a murder victim, a drunken husband shot to death by his long-suffering wife after he hit her one too many times. All these deaths tugged at her heartstrings. Even that of the wife beater.

Frida recorded the evidence associated with their deaths. Fingerprints on the pill bottle, strangulation bruises on the boy's neck, claw marks on the wife beater's face. She had poked and prodded and measured and taken photographs and later written her reports for Sheriff Turner. He would read them, ask a few questions, and accept her explanation of how the person died. The cause was never much of a mystery. Even the murder case was straightforward. Husband beats wife, wife shoots husband in self-defense, case closed.

This morning's find presented a unique challenge for Frida. A mysterious jigsaw puzzle she couldn't yet assemble in her mind. The dead man lay on his back, his arms at his sides and his legs akimbo. His head lolled to one side. Frida knelt beside the body to examine the linear gash on his right cheek. The right side of his jaw was broken, and one side of his skull had been crushed by a heavy object.

Even more intriguing to Frida was what she found in the victim's mouth, a wadded-up sheet of paper. She unfolded it with gloved hands before slipping it into a plastic bag. Reading through the clear plastic, she saw it was a flyer promoting the candidacy of the loser in yesterday's election for sheriff, Adam Cash.

Frida gently turned the victim's head for a closer look at the wound. She shuddered at the deep indentation in the skull. Clotted blood matted the hair into a thick tangle. Bits of brain tissue protruded through the opening. Frida knew that scalps bleed a lot when breached. This one had done so, as evidenced by the bloody, matted hair. But where was the gigantic pool of blood that should lie underneath that shattered skull? Where she should see a dark red lake, Frida saw only a small red stain.

She stood up. "He didn't die here," she said to the man beside her, chief deputy Clovis Ward. "He was killed somewhere else and moved."

Ward sucked air through his teeth. "Why would somebody go to all that trouble?"

"To hide evidence."

"Or they killed him right here and there's no more evidence to find."

Frida explained about the lack of blood in the grass.

"But there is blood, right?"

"It's not just that. Look at the postmortem staining on the front of his neck. That's from pooled blood that clotted while he was face down. That means he was lying prone for a good while before the killer brought him here."

Ward shook his head but said nothing. Frida studied his face and saw no trace of emotion. Just a man doing his job. Another stoic Texan hiding behind a mask of indifference. He reminded her of her ex-husband.

Ward's phone rang. He tapped the screen and held it to his ear. "That was Noteboom," he said after ending the call. "The car is on the square. Get over there and get me some fingerprints. After that, we'll tow it to the garage so you can examine it in more detail."

Frida couldn't take her eyes off the dead man. His death would be big news in Pinyon. "Okay."

Ward followed her gaze. He put his hands on his hips and heaved a sigh. "Now who in their right mind would kill a county sheriff?"

16

Cash sat in an army troop carrier, shoehorned into a tight space among seven other soldiers. He couldn't remember where they were going. Afghan names flowed together in his mind as random arrangements of guttural sounds. All he knew was what the sergeant said. He'd have a chance to fire his M4 when they got there.

Taut nerves roiled his gut. Sweat ran down his face and pooled in his armpits. His stench mingled with that of the other men, fouling the air in the cramped space. Seeking relief from his nausea, he craned his neck to catch a rush of hot breeze from the open window. The blast did nothing to ease the assault on his nostrils.

The earth tilted as a deafening roar reverberated inside the vehicle. Someone screamed—was it him?—and gravity pulled the men together in a writhing mass of tangled arms, legs, and equipment. His helmet slid down over his nose. Dust filled his world, choking him, blinding him, stinging his eyes. His head rattled against something hard, twisting him first one way, then another. The roar gave way to a high-pitched squeal.

He couldn't move, was afraid to move. Squirming bodies pressed down on him with the weight of an elephant, squeezing the air from his lungs. His temples throbbed. He couldn't breathe. A thousand hammers clanged inside his skull until he wished for sleep, wished for death, wished for anything that would make the pain and the noise and the terror stop.

He opened his eyes. He could see again. He could breathe and cool air filled his lungs. His helmet was gone. The men had disappeared. He was in his bed, sweating and panting, alone and unharmed.

Cash sat up. How could the dreams seem so real? The heat, the Humvee, the explosion. How many times must he relive that awful night, with all its pain and terror? How many times must those men die? Why was he still among the living?

The dream had been a mirage, but the headache was not. Cash stumbled out of bed, clutching his throbbing temples, and staggered to the bathroom. He found a pill bottle, twisted the lid, and dumped four tablets into his hand. After swallowing them in one gulp, he chased them down with a long drink of water.

His phone rang. Where was it? He wandered back into the bedroom, trying to remember what he had done with it before tumbling into bed the night before. There it was. On the nightstand next to the paperback copy of *Lonesome Dove* he had been reading for a month. He picked it up and tapped the screen. "Hello?"

"You sound like you're still asleep."

"Edie?"

"Did you think I'd forget driving your drunk ass home last night?"

"No ... uh ... what do you want?"

"I want to lie around in my pajamas with a hot cup of coffee. Instead, I've got to come get you so you can pick up your car."

Cash rubbed his eyes to clear his head. "Oh, right. Okay. Thanks."

"One thing, though."

"What?"

"You better not puke in my car."

***

Cash had driven the dirt road between his property and the highway hundreds of times, but never had it felt so jarring. Edie must be hitting the potholes on purpose, so often were the jolts coming. His stomach lurched with each dip or bump, threatening to make him break his promise not to heave. He consoled himself with the thought that, because he had skipped breakfast, nothing much would come up if he did.

Edie said, "Hey, you got thirty-one percent."

"Thirty-one percent of what?"

"The election, dumbass. For sheriff."

Fighting to contain his nausea, Cash stared out the window and watched a flock of wild turkeys scatter at the car's approach. "That means Griff got sixty-nine percent. That's a slaughter."

"Come on, that's way more than we thought you'd get."

Edie turned the car onto the paved road leading to town. The smoother ride gave Cash hope that he'd survive the trip. "You told me I might win."

"I was trying to stay upbeat. Seriously, thirty-one percent is great. That means one in three people would rather have you as sheriff than Griff Turner. I'd say you're in pretty good shape for the next election."

Cash glimpsed the Nolina River through the trees. Only a thin ribbon of water trickled through its exposed limestone bed. "If I'm still living here."

"Come on, don't give up. I'd miss you if you moved away."

"Really?"

"Really."

That sounded encouraging. Then he remembered something. Squirming, he said, "Did I kiss you last night?"

"You did." Her hands tensed on the wheel.

"I'm sorry."

"I've had worse."

Minutes later, Edie turned onto the town square and braked to a hard stop. "Isn't that your car?" she said, pointing at his Fiesta.

Cash followed her gaze to see his car surrounded by yellow police tape. A handful of onlookers milled around outside the tape, kept at bay by a deputy Cash recognized, Judd Noteboom. "What the hell?"

Edie parked the car and said, "Let's go see what's going on."

Befuddled, Cash got out. As he and Edie approached the tape, Noteboom raised a hand. "Sorry, guys. I can't let y'all go in there."

"Like hell you can't. That's my car."

"Seriously, I can't let you pass."

"Why not?"

"It's part of an ongoing investigation of a crime."

"What crime?"

Noteboom hitched up his pants. "Somebody killed Sheriff Turner last night. They found his body over in Erfurt Park."

"Griff's dead?"

"Yeah."

"Who did it?"

"We don't know yet. Ward and Frida are over at the park looking at the body. Ward sent me over here."

"And you put tape around my car? Why?"

"I have no idea. I was told to come over here and make sure nobody touches it."

"Screw that," said Cash, lifting the tape and stepping beneath it.

Noteboom moved to intercept him. "Really, I can't let you do this."

"For real?"

"For real. Now get back outside the tape."

Cash considered his options. He could force his way past Noteboom, get in the car, and attempt to drive away. That would likely lead to a confrontation with the deputy that wouldn't end well. He could stand around and wait. But for what? And for how long? Or he could go somewhere else and wait. Maybe have breakfast if his queasy stomach would allow it. He turned to Edie. "Want to get something to eat?"

"I can't. Julie's watching Gabe and she has to be at work at ten."

"Okay. Thanks for last night. And for picking me up this morning."

"Thanks for not barfing in my car."

When he opened his arms for a hug, Edie hesitated. Cash said, "Don't worry, I'm not going to kiss you."

She gave him a quick embrace. "Let me know what happens."

"Will do."

Cash left his car and walked to the only place on the square open for breakfast, Shelly's Donuts. He bought a pint of chocolate milk and an egg, potato, and cheese breakfast taco and found a seat by the window. He could watch his car from there.

Nothing seemed to be happening. Noteboom paced around the car with his thick arms folded, shooing away anyone who got too close. People stopped, tried to peer through the car's windows from behind the tape, and then moved on.

Cash had just popped the last of the taco into his mouth when a silver Ford Fusion parked on the square and Frida Simmons got out. He dropped his taco wrapper into the trash and hurried out of the shop. "What's going on, Frida?" he asked, jogging to catch up to her.

"Adam?" She seemed surprised. "What are you doing here?"

"That's my car behind the tape."

"Really?"

"Yes, really."

"Sorry. I didn't know. Clovis Ward sent me here to pull prints from a Ford Fiesta parked on the square. He didn't tell me who it belonged to."

"Why does he want prints from my car?"

"You'd have to ask him that."

Cash tried a different approach. "So, Griff Turner is dead?"

"You heard? I just came from the body."

"How did he die?"

She pursed her lips while mulling a response. "I won't know for sure until I've done an autopsy. I probably shouldn't be telling you this, but it looks like blunt-force trauma to the head."

"So, he was murdered."

"I didn't say that."

"Who did it?"

"That's for Ward to figure out. And I'm not saying he *was* murdered. By the way, I'm sorry about the election. I voted for you."

"Thanks."

She gestured at the Fiesta. "If you'll excuse me, I have to do my job."

Cash stepped aside to let her pass. He crossed the street and sat on the same park bench Edie had found him on the night before. With a quickening heart rate, he watched Frida go to work. She sprinkled powder on the driver's door handle, produced a small brush, and with short, quick strokes, removed the excess powder. Next, she affixed a length of tape, pulled it off, and stuck it to an index card she took from a small kit bag. After repeating the process on the other door handles, she signaled to Noteboom. They held a brief conversation, after which Noteboom pulled out his phone and made a call.

Minutes later, a tow truck turned onto the square and backed up to the Fiesta. Cash bolted from the bench and jogged across the street. He waved for Noteboom's attention. "Why are you towing my car?"

Noteboom spat a stream of tobacco juice. "Sheriff Ward wants it back at the station. Frida can continue her search there."

"Sheriff Ward?"

"Acting sheriff."

"What is she searching for?"

"I don't know. Evidence, I guess."

Cash wanted to wipe the smirk from Noteboom's face. "Son of a bitch. When will I get it back?"

"When they're done with it."

"Come on, Judd. Can't you tell me anything else?"

Noteboom shrugged. "I can't tell you what I don't know."

Cash spotted Frida heading for her car. He ran to intercept her. "Frida."

She turned.

"What did you find?"

"A few fingerprints. Nothing else."

"My fingerprints, I'm sure. What's going on?"

Frida dipped her head to look over her glasses. "Cash, I'm sympathetic. This must seem very confusing. But this is an active investigation. I'm not supposed to talk about it." She glanced back at Noteboom. "All I can tell you is you're a person of interest."

Cash's jaw dropped open. "I'm a person of interest? Do they think I killed Turner?"

"A lot of people, me included, saw you throw a punch at him yesterday. Now he turns up dead? It doesn't make sense to ignore you as a suspect."

"Christ, Frida. You were my babysitter. You know I didn't do it."

"I believe you. But you must admit, what happened at the Firewheel yesterday gives people a reason to think you might have."

She opened her car door. "Clovis will want to talk to you. I'm sure you can clear everything up then."

17

Still hungry, Cash returned to the donut shop. He bought another chocolate milk along with three cherry kolaches and resumed his seat at the window, running the events of the morning through his mind. So, Clovis Ward thought he killed Griff Turner. That didn't happen. Or did it? Last night he had drunk himself into a stupor at the Dizzy Dillo before wandering outside to fall asleep on the courthouse lawn. The next thing he knew, Edie was driving him home. Could he have woken up before she found him, stumbled upon Turner in the park, and killed him? The more he thought about it, the less likely it seemed. In his inebriated state, he'd have been no match for the sheriff. But what if Turner was also drunk?

No, it couldn't be. As much as he had disliked Griff Turner, he had never been tempted to resort to murder. But now they were searching his car. For what? All they'd find was a box of cold pizza.

Cash watched the tow truck pull the Fiesta from the square. He expected to see Noteboom leave, but the deputy remained rooted in place, hands in his pockets, glancing around as if waiting for someone. A Noble County sheriff's department squad car rounded a corner and stopped in front of him. Clovis Ward got out.

The two men conferred briefly before Noteboom pointed at the donut shop. Motioning for Noteboom to follow, Ward headed directly that way. Cash stopped eating and waited. Maybe now he'd get some answers.

A bell tinkled as Ward pushed the door open and scanned the room. Removing his hat, he swaggered over. "Morning, Cash."

Cash nodded. "Clovis."

"I guess you heard about Sheriff Turner."

"I did. Do you know who did it yet?"

Ward pressed his lips into a thin line. "I've got my suspicions. I wonder if you wouldn't mind coming with me to the station to clear a few things up."

Cash held up a kolache. "As a matter of fact, I would. I'm still eating breakfast."

"Bring it along. Hell, I'll even give you a cup of coffee to go with it."

"Am I a suspect?"

"No, but I do have a few questions." When Cash didn't move, Ward leaned in and lowered his voice. "I don't want to embarrass you in here, but I will if I have to."

"Hell, Clovis, I thought we were friends."

Ward tapped the handcuffs at his waist. "Don't make me use these."

Cash returned the kolache to the bag and stood up. "I take my coffee black."

***

During his time studying criminology at Sam Houston State, Cash had participated in the Citizens Academy, a nine-week program offered by the Huntsville Police Department that provided a close-up look at police procedure. Part of the program involved riding along with an officer on patrol. Cash's brief ride in a squad car with Ward and Noteboom was therefore not his first time in a police vehicle. It was, however, his first time riding in the back seat.

Cash knew the doors could not be opened from the inside. He also knew that the polycarbonate partition separating him from the front seat could withstand any amount of force he could bring against it. The effect on Cash during the ride-along in Huntsville had been reassuring. Today he felt trapped.

At the sheriff's office, Cash followed Ward into the interview room, mystified about his reason for being there. Someone killed Griff Turner last night? Fine. It wasn't him. He had spent the evening wallowing in self-pity. Making a fool of himself with Edie. Falling into bed as the world swirled around him. Having a flashback nightmare. Waking up with an incredible hangover. Which wasn't getting any better, thanks to chief deputy Clovis Ward.

Ward directed Cash to one of two chairs at a small wooden table against the wall. An electronic recording device was waiting there. The room was barely big enough to accommodate the furniture. Its dark blue walls seemed to close in on Cash, kicking his pulse rate up a few notches. A window ran along the wall opposite the table. Its blinds were closed.

Noteboom ambled in with a cup of coffee and set it before Cash. "Thanks, Judd."

"No problem."

As Noteboom left, Ward settled into the other chair and flicked a switch on the recorder. "I'm going to be taping this interview. Do you understand?"

Cash nodded.

"There's no video, so please state your answer."

"Yes, I understand we are being recorded."

"For the record, please state your full name."

"Adam Charles Cash."

Ward leaned forward. After reciting his own name and the date, he said, "Cash— Mr. Cash—I'm going to ask you some questions about the death of Sheriff Griff Turner last night. The more truthful you are, the quicker we'll be out of here."

"Okay, I get it."

"We found Sheriff Turner's body this morning in Erfurt Park. Death seems to have been caused by blunt-force trauma to the head."

"Did you find a murder weapon?"

"I'll ask the questions."

"Fine. But this is all news to me."

"Of course. I wonder, though, if you could explain something else we found."

"What's that?"

Ward pulled a flyer from his shirt pocket. "One of your campaign handouts."

"Big deal. Those are all over town."

"The one we found was wadded up and stuffed in Griff Turner's mouth."

Now Cash understood the line of questioning. "I didn't put it there if that's what you're thinking."

"Where were you last night, Cash?"

"Drinking at the Dillo. You saw me."

"How about after that?"

"Edie James took me home."

Ward bit his lip but otherwise kept his face a blank slate. "Right away? I mean, right after you left the Dillo?"

"I'm not sure. I fell asleep over on the courthouse lawn."

"You fell asleep. For how long?"

"I don't know."

"What time did you get home?"

Cash could also see where this was going. "Like I told you, I don't know. I was pretty wasted."

"You didn't like Sheriff Turner, did you?"

"We weren't the best of friends."

Ward leaned forward. "You weren't friends at all, given what happened at the Firewheel yesterday. I understand you started a fight with him."

"I'm not sure it's fair to say I started it. He called me over to his table."

"What happened then?"

"He was being an asshole. Showing off for his friends."

"And you threw a punch at him."

"Only after he pushed me. Twice. And he punched me back."

"So, it would be fair to say that you had cause to hold a grudge against the sheriff."

Cash wasn't falling for this line in the slightest. "I didn't say that."

"He beat you pretty bad in the election. That must hurt."

"I wasn't really expecting to win."

"So, you hated the man," Ward said, tenting his fingers as if he had just proved a point.

"You're putting words in my mouth. Just like you did at Bill and Ted's." They stared at each other. Neither man blinked. Cash watched Ward's expression transition from smug confidence to puzzlement as he tried to think of his next question. Cash said, "Look, are you charging me with something? Because if you're not, I'd like to get on with my day."

"All right, Cash." Ward clicked off the recording. "You can go."

Cash stood up.

Ward got up to block the door, though. "I know you did it," he said through clenched teeth. "And I'm going to prove it."

18

Frida approached the old Ford Fiesta with a pit in her stomach. The notion of Adam Cash, the polite kid she had once babysat for, as a murder suspect had turned an exciting case into a depressing chore. But she had a job to do. And the sooner she did it, the sooner Adam would be cleared.

The Fiesta had been left in the sheriff department's garage, a two-bay aluminum addition to the main building. Even with the bay doors open, the garage felt like an oven. Beads of sweat dripped down the back of Frida's neck as she popped the Fiesta's trunk and peered inside. She didn't see much. Just a well-used baseball glove, a socket wrench set, a sweat-stained pair of leather work gloves, and three reusable grocery bags. "At least he's green," she muttered.

A thorough search of the trunk revealed nothing else of interest. No hair from the victim, no bloodstains, and no other body secretions that might have come from a corpse. The components of the socket wrench set didn't seem big enough or heavy enough to have inflicted the wound found on Turner's skull. Even so, Frida used gloved hands to examine each piece. She found nothing suspicious. She had just extricated herself from the trunk and put a hand on the lid to close it when she heard Vicky's voice. "Excuse me, Dr. Simmons?"

Frida clicked the trunk shut. "Yes?"

"One of the deputies asked me to tell you to look in your car for a bag of evidence they can't find."

"Is it for this case?"

"No, for an older one."

"That's crazy. I don't carry old evidence around in my car."

"I'm just the messenger. They said it was really important."

"Okay."

This is idiotic, Frida told herself as she strode out of the garage to her car. Here she was, actively searching a vehicle suspected of being involved in the sheriff's murder, and they needed her to go look for old evidence bags? What a stupid waste of time.

Still grumbling, she checked the front and back seats, glove box, and trunk of her car but came up empty. Deciding she was on a fool's errand, she returned to the garage. Vicky was nowhere in sight. Frida cursed as she strode into the office, marched down the hall, and found the young secretary at her desk. "Tell them there's nothing in my car. And if anybody else wants something, I'll do it when I'm finished in there."

Before Vicky could respond, Frida spun around on her heel. She didn't like leaving a vehicle mid-search, even though she knew security cameras were monitoring the garage. Donning a pair of fresh gloves, she resumed her search.

Could Adam Cash really have killed Griff Turner? Frida found it hard to believe. She had known Adam since he was in grade school. Respectful and unfailingly polite as a child, he had never struck her as someone capable of killing a rabid dog, much less a county sheriff. On the other hand, he had fought in Afghanistan. She couldn't even imagine what he'd seen there. Perhaps the experience had changed him.

Frida opened a rear door and swept her gaze along the back seat, spotting only the to-go pizza box from Bill and Ted's. She lifted the lid and peered inside, seeing nothing but six slices of cold pizza. She closed the box and left it on the seat. Leaning farther in, she reached an arm under the passenger seat and felt nothing. She walked around to the other side of the car and repeated the process under the driver's seat. Her fingers brushed up against something hard. When she tapped it, she could tell it was made of glass.

She retrieved a short length of dowel from a nearby workbench and nudged the object into view. It was a glass beer bottle. There was a dark smear on the label. Blood. At least it looked like blood. She used the dowel to hold the bottle upside down as she pulled herself out of the car. Upon closer inspection, she had no doubt that she was looking at a blood smear. She would run some tests, but one big question was blooming in her mind. What was this bloody bottle doing in Adam Cash's car?

19

"Holy shit! Why does he think you did it?"

Cash adjusted himself on top of the upturned paint bucket to keep the rim from digging into his rear. "Hell if I know. But he's gunning for me, that's for sure."

They sat in Steve's basement office at Packsaddle Brewing. Steve called the room an office, but it was tiny and Wi-Fi couldn't penetrate the thick limestone walls. Steve said that for internet access, he had to take the laptop upstairs to the dining room.

"You didn't do it, did you?"

Cash fixed his friend with a withering glare. "What do you think?"

"Okay, okay. I had to ask. So, what are you going to do?"

"I don't know. I didn't kill the guy. All I can do is hope that the stupid son of a bitch Ward figures that out."

"That's not much of a plan."

"Tell me about it." Cash rose, and his head thumped into an overhead pipe. "Damn it, Steve. When are you going to get a real office?"

"What's wrong with this one?"

Cash tried to rub away the pain. "Forget it. Would you mind taking me home? I don't feel like showing my face around town today."

***

Cash usually enjoyed the drive up to his house. From the main road, a quarter-mile dirt lane led to a sharp right onto another path, this one of crushed granite. A clump of cedar obscured the house until after the turn. The fifty-year-old structure rose beyond a field of native prairie grass. Sometimes he encountered a herd of grazing white-tailed deer or a flock of turkeys clustered around a feeder in the field. The approaching car might send long-eared rabbits scurrying for cover.

Today Cash cared little about viewing the local wildlife. How could he enjoy the scenery with a possible murder charge in his future, waiting for him, ready to pounce like a pack of hungry wolves?

Steve drove up the driveway to the three-bedroom, two-bath house Cash was raised in. Aside from a few spots of peeling paint along the trim, the place was in good shape. Cash had been planning to apply a fresh coat of paint after the election. Now he wondered if he would ever get to it.

Steve switched off the engine of his Ram pickup. Cash pushed the front door of the house open, strode through the den, and headed to the kitchen for something to drink. "Want a beer?" he called out to Steve.

"Is it one of mine?"

"No. There's no vegetables in it."

"Very funny. I'll pass."

Back in the den, Cash sank onto the sofa. The only thing different about the familiar room was the leatherette lounge chair he bought on sale at a San Antonio Costco. Everything else was as he remembered from childhood, from the cedar paneling to the river rock hearth to the painting over the fireplace depicting two cows grazing in a field of bluebonnets. The room comforted him amidst his growing despair. "What the hell am I going to do, Steve?"

"I don't know, bro. It's crazy."

"Edie drove me home last night. She can vouch for me."

"Yeah, but what about after you saw Ward at the bar? Didn't you say it was another thirty minutes before Edie found you?"

"I don't really know. I fell asleep."

"He won't stop, you know. Clovis Ward is one persistent son of a bitch."

"That's what I'm afraid of. He told me he knows I did it and he aims to prove it. I don't see a way out of this mess."

Steve pointed a finger for emphasis. "There's always a way."

"Maybe in the movies."

"Look, I never thought I'd be able to open a brewery. I needed equipment. I needed space. I needed employees. For all that, I needed money. A lot of money."

"Are you going somewhere with this?"

"Hear me out. Like I said, it seemed impossible. Then Dad told me to break everything down and make a list of all the little things I could do that would add up to success. Then he said to pick just one of those things and get it done. Then pick another. And another. And keep going until I got where I wanted to be."

"And now you own a brewery."

Steve sat back, a satisfied smile on his face. "And now I own a brewery."

Cash thought about that, then bolted from the sofa.

"Where are you going?"

"I'll be right back."

He found a backpack in his bedroom closet and began stuffing it with items from his dresser. Underwear, socks, T-shirts, a pair of jeans. He grabbed toothpaste and a toothbrush from the bathroom and added them to the pack. He tossed in his phone's charging cord. From a high closet shelf, he pulled a waistband holster and a hard plastic gun case just bigger than the Ruger LCP 380 it contained. He strapped the holster to his belt and took the gun out of its case. After checking the chamber to make sure it was empty, he snapped a clip into place and slipped the pistol into the holster. He found a box of spare ammunition on the shelf and stowed it in the backpack with everything else.

Cash eyed his phone and realized the danger of using it. Ward could track the signal and find him in a heartbeat. He used his thumbnail to pry the back open and lift the battery out. This he slipped into a zippered pouch on the backpack. He stuck the phone in his pocket.

He dropped to his knees, pulled a rolled-up sleeping bag from beneath the bed, and returned to the den. Grabbing his hat from a peg on the wall, he said, "You still have those fermentation tanks in your basement at the Packsaddle?"

Steve raised an eyebrow. "Yeah."

"You don't use them anymore, do you?"

"Not since we opened the new building north of town. Why?"

"My goal is to stay out of prison, right?"

"Right."

"So, to do that, I've got to prove I didn't kill Griff Turner. For that to happen, I've got to find the person who did. That means I'll need to conduct an investigation. And to do that, I need to stay away from Clovis Ward. So, I need a place to hide."

"You're going to hide in my basement?"

"If you'll let me."

"Sure, but—"

"I'm just following your dad's advice. That's step one."

"What's step two?"

Cash slipped the backpack over his shoulder. "Solve the murder."

20

To play it safe on the drive back to town, Cash pulled his hat low over his eyes and slumped down in his seat. Steve parked in the alley behind the brewery and told Cash to stay put while he made sure no one else was around. Moments later, he opened the truck door and said, "All clear."

Cash followed Steve down a set of dank limestone stairs to a dimly lit room with a concrete floor and unpainted cinder-block walls. Four stainless steel fermenters took up most of the space. Each fermenter consisted of an inverted cone beneath a cylindrical tank supported by three steel posts. Even though the tanks hadn't been used for months, the odor of malt and yeast still permeated the room.

Cash gestured at the fermenters. "Why are these still here? Seems like you'd need them at the new place."

"They're so small compared to the new ones that it's not worth the trouble."

Cash dropped the sleeping bag and slipped off the backpack. "All right. Well, thanks."

"What are you going to do for food?"

That was step two, for sure. "I was hoping you could help me out there."

"Sure. I'll pick up a few things at the store."

"Get some chocolate milk."

Steve smiled. "Want a Silly Straw to go with it?"

"I like chocolate milk. You got a problem with that?"

"Guess not."

"Can I use that laptop in your office?"

"Yeah. Just keep it anonymous." He started up the stairs and then stopped. "What's the next step? To solve the murder, I mean."

Cash had been thinking about that. So far he had drawn a blank but he didn't want to admit that to Steve. "I have a plan."

"Let's hear it."

His mind labored to squeeze out an idea. All he could come up with was, "I need to see the murder scene. Ask around and see if you can find out the location. Any other details you can get would be helpful. Just don't be too obvious."

"Okay. Oh, I almost forgot." He pulled a key out of his pocket and tossed it to Cash. "That's for the back door."

After Steve left, Cash unrolled his sleeping bag and lay down. He was lucky to have such a loyal friend. They had met on the first day of fourth grade when Steve got on the school bus and found no empty seats. When he asked Cash to scoot over so they could share his, Cash refused. Steve shrugged and dropped onto his lap. Cash ordered him off and Steve said, "Why? I don't fart." The quip made Cash laugh so hard that he forgot about being angry. He and Steve had been fast friends ever since.

Cash surveyed the cramped basement. It occurred to him that being stuck down here was not much different than being confined to a jail cell. Other than the occasional sound of footsteps overhead, the place was deathly quiet. A weak shaft of light struggled through a filthy window just above ground level. The single overhead light bulb provided the only other illumination.

A dark cloud settled over Cash as he realized this was his home until—when? Could he prove his innocence? Without a stronger alibi, that seemed a daunting task. Would he be able to identify the actual killer? Maybe, but he lacked clues and the resources to find them. Could he elude Clovis Ward long enough to clear himself? Ward was no Sherlock Holmes, but even he should be able to find a wanted man in a town of fewer than two thousand residents.

Cash paced the floor and glanced at his watch. Three o'clock. Several hours of daylight remained. He needed to wait until dark to emerge from the safety of the basement. What could he do until then? He knew the answer, and it killed him. Nothing.

21

Barry Novak massaged his throbbing temples and swore. Did he have to spell everything out for these idiots? "You shouldn't have left a body for them to find," he said into his phone.

"If there's no body, there's no suspect," said the man on the other end of the call. "If there's no suspect, they never stop looking for one. Besides, a body always turns up eventually."

"And you think this guy Cash will get the blame?"

"I'm sure of it."

"I guess I'll have to take your word for it."

"Don't be such a baby. We can't go back and undo it."

Novak closed his eyes and took a breath. His friend was right. They had crossed a line they couldn't uncross. There was no sense in assigning blame. Not when untold riches loomed on the horizon. "When will you have another shipment for me?"

"As soon as we hear from the supplier."

"Think your guy can get more than two this time? I can fit a lot more than that in the van." And he could squeeze more cots into the basement's soundproofed room.

"The first one was just a test run. You provide enough funding, and we can get as many as we want."

Novak's eyes lit with greed. "I'll tell you what. I can come down there this week. I'll bring some cash."

"Sounds good. So, how did the sale go?"

Novak drummed his fingers on the card table. "The first one went fine. Some oil fat cat I've done some contract work for. He's already put her to work."

"And the other?"

"The other client is out of town, so I've still got her."

"Is she any good at giving blow jobs?"

"How would I know?"

Raucous laughter came through the phone. "I'll take that as a yes. She can't go anywhere, can she?"

"No, that room is secure. And the oxycodone keeps her too groggy to try anything. You've got enough of that to last a while, right?"

"Sure, no problem."

"All right. I'll see you later this week."

"One more thing. Do you have a gun?"

"Yeah, why?"

The man snorted. "Buddy boy, we're in the big leagues now."

Novak ended the call and pocketed the phone. Checking the video feed on his laptop, he saw Rosa lying on the cot watching television. He paced to the door of her temporary prison and released the deadbolt. She didn't move when he pushed the door open and stepped inside. He closed the door. After clicking off the TV, he dropped his khakis and slid onto the cot. The woman swung a drugged look his way. "Wake up, Rosa," he said. "It's party time."

22

Edie swept the coins from the table and tallied them up. Two dollars and forty-five cents. On a tab of over thirty bucks. Why were little old ladies such lousy tippers? At least these two had been polite. Complimenting her hair, asking about her family, remaining calm when the over-medium eggs came out too hard. She knew of several elderly women who would have flipped their blue-haired wigs over that.

As Edie wiped off the table, the memory of the kiss Cash had stolen the night before popped into her head. Yes, he had been drunk, but Edie thought it was more than the alcohol fueling his clumsy play. Even when he was sober, his comments these days leaned toward the flirtatious. She had to admit feeling flattered, maybe even interested. And he had always been a good kisser. Even last night.

Ten years ago, she thought she loved him. But what did an eighteen-year-old know about love? He broke her heart when he joined the army. They had talked of going off to college together. They even narrowed it down to two schools, Sam Houston State and UT Dallas. Both of them he'd chosen for their strong criminology programs, a field of study that held no interest for her. She wanted to be a nurse. Although both schools offered nursing programs, they wouldn't have been in Edie's top five if not for Cash. But she was willing to compromise because she loved him. Or thought she did. God, he was such a good kisser.

Edie still harbored dreams of becoming a nurse. Her father's sudden death from a heart attack at age forty-seven had derailed her academic plans. Her mother died in a car accident years before that. Finding herself tasked with caring for Dana, her younger sister, Edie left school and got a job. Dana graduated six years ago, after which she married and moved to Kerrville with her new husband. But Edie remained stuck waiting tables in Pinyon. A single mother working her tail off to save enough money to go back to school.

Her thoughts returned to Cash. How did she feel about him? Was she interested enough to rekindle a relationship? Should she? She knew marrying Randy had been a mistake. She had ignored his many red flags in a misguided attempt at a rebound relationship. Now, thank God, she was rid of him. And here was Cash, back in her life, unattached, ready to plant roots, and apparently interested in her.

As Edie wiped the last crumb from the table, she spotted a family—mom, dad, and three children—entering the restaurant. Another busy day at the Firewheel. She tossed the rag behind the counter and hustled across the room to greet them. Suddenly, Clovis Ward pushed in front of them. "Edie. I need to talk to you." His tone was curt, demanding.

Edie gestured at the family. "Can this wait? We're pretty busy."

"No, it's urgent."

The father noticed Ward's uniform. "It's all right, miss, we can wait."

Edie flashed an apologetic smile. "Thank you." Pointing at the table she had just cleaned, she said, "Just have a seat and I'll be right with you." She turned to Ward. "What's going on?"

Ward strode past, leaving her no choice but to follow. "Let's talk in the back."

In the kitchen, Edie said, "All right, Clovis. What is so important?" She didn't bother to hide her annoyance.

"It's about Cash."

Her heart skipped a beat. "Did something happen to him?"

"Yes, but not like what you're thinking. He tells me you drove him home last night."

"That's right."

"Why?"

"I was leaving work and saw him sitting on the bench across the street. When I stopped to talk to him, I realized he was wasted."

"So, you told him to leave his car and you'd take him."

"That's right."

"What time was that?"

"Tell me what happened to him."

"Relax, he's not hurt. Now, what time did you take him home?"

She brushed a wisp of hair from her face. "Let me think. I guess it was about eleven."

"Isn't that late for you to be going home? The restaurant closes at nine."

"Later than usual. After we cleaned up, I got to talking with Diedre."

"Who's Diedre?"

"One of the other servers. She's getting married next month. We were looking at bridesmaid dresses online."

"Did Cash say anything to you on the way home?"

"No. Like I said, he was drunk. He fell asleep in the car almost right away."

"Did you spend the night with him?"

Edie frowned. "Is that any of your business?

"It is when I'm investigating a murder."

"What?"

"Answer the question." He jabbed a finger at her. "Did you spend the night with him?"

He was such a jerk, but Edie resisted the urge to tell him off. "No. I put him to bed and went right home." She decided he didn't need to know about the kiss.

Ward wrinkled his forehead as if trying to think of what to say next.

"Come on, Clovis," Edie said. "Who's dead?"

Ward hiked up his pants and stepped past her. On his way out of the kitchen, he said, "Ask Cash."

23

Cash began the search for Griff's killer by trying to draw up a checklist of the dead sheriff's enemies. As much as he had disliked Griff, though, he couldn't think of anyone holding enough of a grudge to resort to murder. He needed to ask someone who knew Turner more intimately. Someone like his wife, Mia. Would she talk to him? Cash doubted it. Unless she harbored animosity toward her dead husband that he was unaware of. Particularly if she shared Clovis Ward's suspicions. But he had to start somewhere.

The Turners lived in a historic limestone house two blocks off the square. Built in 1902 by Pinyon's first physician, the two-story structure was once the finest residence in town. Though surpassed over the years by other homes, the place remained impressive. Expensive too, as Cash remembered his father once commenting.

Cash waited until dark before venturing outside. Since it was a weeknight, he wasn't surprised to find no pedestrians about. He hurried past the square to reach the Turner house. There he spotted three vehicles in the driveway—Griff's truck, a late-model sedan, and a Toyota Highlander. Either the sedan or the Highlander had to be Mia's, but who owned the other vehicle?

Not wanting to risk revealing himself to Mia's guest, Cash found a spot in a dry drainage ditch halfway down the block from which he could watch the house. The location afforded him a perfect view. When thirty minutes passed with nothing happening, he began to lose patience. It occurred to him that the extra car might belong to a relative spending the night, in which case he might as well try now as later. Just as he rose from the ditch, the front door opened. He dropped back to the ground. A man and a woman stepped out of the house. Cash recognized Mia from the real estate signs around town bearing her picture. The man looked familiar. Of medium height and build, he appeared older than Mia, probably in his mid-forties. A neatly trimmed beard covered the lower half of his face.

Mia escorted the stranger to the driveway. The man removed a key fob from his pocket, but before he could use it, Mia flung her arms around his neck and delivered a passionate kiss. Afterward, they clung to each other. The man said something, and Mia kissed him again. He stroked her hair. She buried her head in his chest.

The man pulled himself away and pressed his key fob to flash the taillights on the sedan. He opened the car door and the interior light illuminated his face well enough for Cash to make out his features. It was Carl Trotter, the man Cash had seen filling a growler at Steve's. Trotter fired the engine, backed out of the driveway, and drove away.

Armed with his new knowledge, Cash strode up the walk to the Turner house and knocked on the door. As the door opened, his mouth fell open. He had never seen Mia Turner up close. He had never fully appreciated her fashion model looks from the picture on the real estate signs around town. Now that beauty hit him like a blast of ice water. Straight, silky hair running halfway down her back. A perfectly formed face. Just a touch of lipstick. A blouse that squeezed her sides and pushed up on her breasts. Jeans so tight they could have been painted on.

Cash forced himself to speak. "Mrs. Turner, I'm Adam Cash."

"I know who you are." Her eyes were cold.

"I wonder if I could come in and speak to you for a moment. It's about your husband."

She slipped a hand behind the door as if to close it.

"Don't," Cash said. "I really need to talk to you." Receiving only an icy glare, he added, "I'm sorry for your loss."

"Sorry? What the hell are you sorry about? Clovis Ward told me you did it."

"He's mistaken. It wasn't me."

"Bullshit. They found the murder weapon in your car. A beer bottle with your fingerprints on it." Contempt oozed out of her. "You killed Griff with a fucking beer bottle."

"The murder weapon? In my car?" He knew how weak he sounded.

"What the fuck do you want? Did you come here to kill me, too?"

"No. I'm not going to hurt you. I just want to talk. I didn't kill Griff. I want to find the person who did."

The corners of her mouth turned down. "Right. It seems to me the guy's standing on my porch."

"Mrs. Turner, please—"

"Get the hell out of here."

"Who was that man you were kissing?" Cash said, trying a different approach.

Her eyes became slits. "I'm calling Clovis." She slammed the door.

Cash stood rooted to the spot. A beer bottle . . . ? The weight of that statement finally sank in, along with how severe his predicament was. He forced his legs into motion and sprinted back to the square. A beer bottle in his car? With his fingerprints on it? How did it get there? He was screwed. Clovis must have obtained an arrest warrant by now.

When he reached the square, Cash ducked beneath the awning of the pharmacy and slowed to a walk. What now? He thought of

Bill Carpenter. Perhaps the shouting match he'd witnessed between Carpenter and Turner the night of the murder had played a role in Turner's death. But he couldn't just waltz in and demand information. That would never work.

He reached Bill and Ted's Excellent Pizza at the end of the block. He remained unsure of how to approach the restaurant's owners, so he kept going straight to Erfurt Park. He found a spot behind a hedge separating the park from the street from which he could surveil the pizza joint. Because the building had been constructed on a slope, the basement could be accessed from the rear. A light over the basement door illuminated a beat-up Honda Accord parked nearby.

An engine roared as a Noble County sheriff's squad car blasted through the square. Clovis. On his way to see Mia. Probably hoping to arrest him. Cash held his breath until the car was out of sight.

Heart pounding, Cash returned his gaze to the restaurant. He didn't know if the Accord belonged to Bill or Ted. Before he could investigate, he heard the sound of an approaching engine. A white cargo van with a dented fender turned into the alley and braked to a stop behind the Accord. The driver, a tall man with a thin frame and stooped shoulders, got out. Ted Hubbard.

Ted disappeared through the basement door. Moments later, he reappeared with Bill. Ted opened the rear cargo door of the van, and the two of them manhandled a large, flat box out of the vehicle and dragged it into the restaurant. As they passed under the light, Cash recognized the logo of a popular electronics brand on the box. It held a flat-screen TV.

Cash checked the street in both directions and jogged to the van. He peeked into the cargo area: more boxes. Some looked like the one Bill and Ted had carried into the restaurant. Others were smaller and contained sound bars.

A shadow darkened the van's interior. Before Cash could react, a man's voice growled, "Don't move. I've got a gun."

24

The menacing voice chilled Cash's blood. "Hands where I can see them."

Cash raised his hands and turned around to see Bill Carpenter, clad in jeans and one of his restaurant's signature green T-shirts, aiming a gun at him. Bill sported the bushiest beard Cash had ever seen, although his hirsute appearance did not extend to the top of his bald head. From the way his gun hand trembled, Cash suspected he had never pointed a weapon at another person.

Bill said, "Cash? What the hell are you doing?"

"I need to talk to you."

"You sure as hell do. Why are you poking around in there?"

"I wasn't poking around. I was just curious."

He lowered the gun. "Nosy, I'd say."

Cash glanced at the open basement door. "Can we go inside and talk?"

Bill cocked his head while considering a response. "All right. Just as soon as we get this stuff unloaded." He shoved the pistol in his belt and slid a box out of the van. "Grab the other end."

Cash helped Bill unload the van and bring everything inside. After the last box was deposited in the basement, Bill said, "Come on upstairs." In the dining room, he pointed at a booth. "Take a seat." He grabbed three water bottles from a cooler and followed Cash across the room.

Ted arrived with a bowl of salad. He slid into the booth and began shoveling the greens into his mouth. Speaking through his food, he said, "Hey, Cash."

Bill handed his partner a water bottle and pushed another across the table toward Cash. "So, why were you snooping around back there?"

The act of unscrewing the bottlecap and taking a drink gave Cash time to think of an answer. "Have you guys heard about Griff Turner's murder?"

Ted nodded. "Yeah. We didn't have anything to do with it."

"I didn't say you did."

Bill said, "We've heard some rumors about you, though."

Cash's eyes darted between the two men. "That's all they are. I didn't do it."

"Okay, why are you here?"

"I'm trying to clear my name. Clovis Ward is anxious to nail me to the wall. I need to find the real killer and get Ward off my back."

"Okay," said Ted. "He's not here, though."

"What's with the TVs?"

"They're for the dining room. The ones we have aren't worth a damn."

"Who did you buy them from?"

"Some guy from Boerne. I think he's Turner's cousin. He owns an electronics shop down there."

"Is that your van out back?"

"No, it belongs to that guy. He's over at the gelato shop. He let us borrow it."

Cash wrinkled his brow. "The gelato shop is open?"

"No, but Novak is there. That's who the guy is there to see."

"What's this guy's name?"

"I don't know."

"I was here last night. I sat right over there."

"I remember," said Bill. "You wanted extra sauce."

"While I was eating, Turner came storming in. You two had a pretty good shouting match back in the kitchen."

"Okay, I get it now. You thought maybe that had something to do with his murder."

Cash shrugged.

"I'll tell you what. We didn't kill the man, but we won't cry about his death. He was a total son of a bitch."

"We can agree on that. What were you guys arguing about?"

"You don't know?" When Cash didn't answer, Bill added, "Geez, I thought that was an open secret. Turner has been squeezing money from us ever since we opened. Said he'd sic the health inspector on us if we didn't go along. Threatened our liquor license, too."

The news that Griff Turner had been dirty didn't surprise Cash. "How much were you paying?"

"Not a lot. That's how he keeps it—my mistake—kept it going for so long. Three hundred a month. He'd always say, 'That's only ten bucks a day. And I'm giving you a free day in the longer months.'"

"Yeah, he was pretty fucking generous," said Ted.

Cash said, "So, what were you guys shouting about? Did you refuse to pay him?"

Bill shook his head. "Business hasn't been so good lately. I asked him if we could drop back to two hundred a month. He said no."

"I guess that pissed you off."

"You bet."

"Enough to kill him?"

"Goddamn it, no. It wasn't us."

Cash studied Bill's face and saw nothing to indicate he was lying. "Who else was paying him?"

"The Dairy Queen, the gun range, and the Firewheel are the only ones I know for sure," said Ted, rubbing his chin. "Probably others, but I don't know."

"What about the brewery?"

"I don't know. Ask your pal Steve."

"Was Clovis Ward involved?"

"If he was, I never saw it."

Cash slipped out of the booth. "Thanks, guys. This gives me something to go on."

"No problem," said Bill.

Cash took a step toward the stairwell, then stopped. "I'd appreciate it if nobody knew I was here tonight."

Ted made a motion like he was zipping his lips together.

"Thanks again."

25

To guard against Bill or Ted discovering his hideout, Cash left the restaurant and headed back into the park. He stumbled through the dark before emerging back onto the street a block past the entrance. On his right was a church, shuttered for the night. Next to it was the Dairy Queen, also closed.

Cash strode to the end of the block and turned right to reach the alley. This allowed him to approach the brewery from the rear. He could see the white van still parked behind the pizza joint. Bill and Ted were nowhere in sight.

He arrived at the back door of the brewery and found it locked, but Steve's key opened it. He retrieved the laptop from Steve's office. Remembering his warning about spotty Wi-Fi in the basement, he took it upstairs to the dining room.

He didn't dare sit at a table. Someone might see the light from the laptop screen through the front window and recognize him. He crouched behind the bar, plugged the device in, and fired it up.

Cash performed an internet search on Carl Trotter and learned that he lived in Junction, where he worked for the Frank Soechting Insurance Group. Cash memorized the address. He fumbled along the counter behind the bar and found a landline next to the cash register. Kneeling behind the bar, he punched in Steve's cell number on the keypad. After four rings, Steve's voicemail picked up. He tried again with the same result. On the next attempt, Steve came on the line. "What's going on? Is everything okay?"

"Yes, I'm fine," Cash said, keeping his voice low. "I need to use your truck in the morning."

"What for."

He explained his need to see Trotter.

"Wow, Trotter and Mia Turner. I'll be damned."

"Can I use the truck tomorrow?"

"I don't know. That would be aiding and abetting."

"You're already doing that, dumbass. I'm calling you from behind your bar."

"Right. Okay, sure. I can drive the brewery van."

"Hold on. One more thing."

"Yeah?"

"Were you paying Griff Turner protection money?"

The ensuing silence gave Cash his answer. He heard his friend clear his throat.

"How did you know that?"

"Good grief, Steve. When were you going to tell me?"

"When I thought it might be any of your damn business."

"They think I killed the man. Doesn't that make it my business?"

"Not unless you think I did it. In that case, fuck you."

"Geez, sorry."

Cash hung up and returned to the basement. Sleep proved elusive. He lay on his back and stared at the ceiling, wondering how long it would be before Ward caught him. He imagined his parents' reaction to the news that their son had been arrested for murder. That would be humiliating. Even worse, his daughter would grow up without a father. And he'd lose Edie forever.

Giving up on sleep, Cash crawled out of his sleeping bag, went upstairs, and opened the laptop. Another internet search on Trotter revealed no arrests. His biography on the insurance agency's website mentioned a wife and two children.

Cash knew that many family men had extramarital affairs. Family women, too. But how many of them would kill because of it? And not just anyone, but a county sheriff? Any person with sense would know that the act would trigger a highly motivated hunt for the killer. Had Carl Trotter been willing to take that risk? Only if he was an idiot.

Cash went back down the stairs to the deformed-looking sleeping bag but sleep still eluded him. As he stared into the darkness, he scripted the conversation he would have with Trotter. The insurance agency opened at nine. If he left at seven, he'd make it in plenty of time to be there when Trotter arrived for work. He went upstairs and called Steve.

"Can you be here by seven?"

"Would you please stop calling? Some of us are trying to sleep."

"Last time, I promise."

"Does it have to be so early?"

"I want to get to Trotter's agency before he does."

"All right. I'll be there."

"Thanks. You can go back to bed now."

Cash returned to the basement. He saw a cockroach on his sleeping bag and raised a foot to stomp it, but something stopped him. The poor roach was just going about its business when random fate intervened to deliver it a killing blow. Much like fate had lowered the boom on him. He flicked the insect away and crawled into his sleeping bag.

26

A brilliant orange sunrise greeted Cash as he followed Interstate 10 east toward Junction. He drove through a landscape of green hills blanketed by ash juniper, mesquite, and Spanish oak. Highway cuts through the ridges had created walls of chalky limestone on either side. The linear rock layers of these walls gave the appearance of enormous ribbons glued to the cliff faces.

Cash exited the highway onto Junction's North Main Street and followed the road to the center of town. He found the Frank Soechting Insurance Group at one end of a plaster and limestone building a block and a half from the courthouse square. He eased Steve's truck into a parking space and killed the engine.

The dashboard clock read eight fifty-one. He was early. Checking the rearview mirror, he saw a municipal office building across the street. The parking lot contained several vehicles, including a squad car for the Junction Police Department. He donned his hat and lowered himself into his seat.

Cash tensed when a white Nissan Sentra pulled into the next space. A bearded man wearing khaki slacks and a button-down shirt got out. Carl Trotter.

Trotter unlocked the building and disappeared inside. Cash forced himself to wait two minutes before he got out to follow. As he circled

Trotter's Sentra, he spotted a Texas Tech University sticker in its rear window. Another sticker next to it bore a shield over a gold phoenix. He tried to place it but couldn't.

Inside the agency, an unoccupied laminate desk filled most of the tiny lobby. To the left, a hall led to several private offices. Trotter was nowhere in sight.

"Hello?" Cash called out.

An unseen desk drawer slammed and Trotter stepped into the hall. Cash couldn't help but notice his movie star looks. The insurance agent and Mia Turner matched up well.

"Can I help you?" Trotter asked.

Cash extended his hand for a quick shake. "Mr. Trotter, I'm Brad Ramsey. I wonder if I could speak with you. It's about Sheriff Griff Turner."

Trotter furrowed his brow. "Are you with the police?"

"Why do you ask?"

"It's just ... wasn't the sheriff killed the night before last?"

"How did you know that?"

"I heard it on the radio."

"To answer your question, I'm not with the police, but I knew the sheriff. I have some concerns about the quality of the current investigation into his death."

"But you're not with the police."

"No."

"Then I don't have to talk to you."

Cash hadn't expected that, and he remained in awkward silence until an answer came to him. "That's true. But I'm only asking for a minute of your time. I just have a couple of questions, and then I'll let you get on with your day."

"I could tell you to leave and get on with my day even sooner. Besides, what makes you think I even knew the man?"

Cash realized it was time to play hardball. "I saw you and the sheriff's widow at her house last night. You two were very friendly with each other."

The color drained from Trotter's face. "How long have you been spying on us?"

"Last night was the first time I've ever seen you." He saw no point in mentioning the visit to the Packsaddle. "Look, I don't give a damn about whatever you and Mia Turner are doing behind closed doors. I'm just trying to figure out who killed her husband."

Trotter said nothing.

Cash gestured at the hallway. "Can we go to your office?"

Trotter grunted and led Cash down the hall. He shut his office door and sat behind a desk identical to the one in the lobby. A Texas Tech pennant hung on the wall behind him. Beneath it was a plaque bearing the same phoenix and shield logo Cash had seen on Trotter's car. He tried to place it again as he dropped into a flimsy plastic chair opposite the desk.

Trotter fixed Cash with a defiant scowl. "I didn't kill Griff Turner."

"I'm not accusing you. But somebody did, and I need to find that person."

"Why?" said Trotter with a snort. "Does he get a reward?" When Cash didn't respond, he added, "The guy was an asshole. He hit Mia a few times."

"I didn't know that."

"I guess you're not as good a spy as you thought."

Cash uncrossed his legs and leaned in. "Did Sheriff Turner have any enemies that you know of? Anyone who disliked him enough to kill him?"

"Hell, that's half the town. It always amazed me that he was elected in the first place. I guess it was because of his dad."

"Where were you the night of his death?"

"I told you, I didn't kill him." His words crackled with anger.

Cash met Trotter's glare with a blank look and said nothing.

"All right, I was here," Trotter said. "In Junction. My son had a Little League game. After that, me and his mom took the kids out for pizza. Then we went home."

"What team does your son play for?"

"The Mets."

"Who did they play?"

"The Dodgers." Trotter leaned back in his chair and cocked his head. "You know, I just figured something out. Your name isn't Brad Ramsey. You're that guy Mia called me about. Alex Cash. You ran for sheriff."

Cash's throat went dry. His cover hadn't lasted five minutes. "It's Adam."

"They think you did it, don't they?"

"It would appear so. I didn't."

"I don't guess you'd tell me if you did."

"No, but I wouldn't come here either, would I? Think about it."

A wry smile creased Trotter's face. "I guess it won't hurt to tell you that Turner was dirty."

"I heard about the extortion."

"It's more than that. Mia told me. She said there were all kinds of late-night meetings with some real creeps."

"Who?"

"She didn't see them. Just heard rumors from people around town. They saw Griff with some real sleazebags."

"That's not much to go on."

Trotter shrugged. "I'm sorry, but that's all I—wait a second. The gun range."

"What about it?"

"She said a lot of those meetings took place at the gun range. He went there a lot. Stayed until all hours."

"Wouldn't it be plausible for a sheriff to go to a gun range? Being a good shot is kind of a job requirement."

"I'm just telling you what Mia told me. She was suspicious of something. At first, she thought he was having an affair. Not that she cared, but hey. Later, she heard he was spending a lot of time with a guy who works there. Pete something. I don't know his last name. If you're looking for Turner's killer, I'd start there."

A bell sounded out in the lobby as the front door opened and closed. Trotter rose. "Sounds like I've got a customer."

Cash stood. "I appreciate your help."

"No problem."

"You're not going to call the sheriff's department on me, are you?"

Trotter laughed. "And have you tell the world I've been sneaking around with a dead sheriff's wife? I don't think so."

27

Ward took a sip of the coffee and frowned. "Who made this shit? It's weaker than a newborn calf."

"I think Vicky did," said Conrad.

Ward set the cup down. "Somebody needs to tell her that to make coffee, you have to actually put some coffee in the damn machine."

"You could make it," Frida Simmons said. "That way you'd get it the way you like it."

Ward scowled. "Ain't my job." He glanced at the wall clock: 9:05. Where the hell was Noteboom?

Ward sat at the head of a small conference table in the department's meeting room. He leaned back in his chair and surveyed the other people present. Smirking, he noted that DA Lars Newsome must have been busy on Amazon again. The collar of his plaid snap shirt circled his neck stiffly, as if the shirt had just been removed from its package. And you could cut a ribeye with the crease in those jeans. Ward half expected to see a label still attached to the pocket. Still, the faux casual was better than those damn banker suits the guy used to wear.

Frida wore an outfit that better fit what Ward expected to see. Her untucked polo shirt hung past the waist of neat but faded jeans. A pair of worn hiking shoes added to the rustic feel. *If only she'd put on some makeup, she might be worth a second look,* Ward thought.

Conrad looked as regulation as ever, with his pressed khaki pants, button-down shirt, and gleaming badge. Next to him was Gabe Santos, the son of a bitch who was always questioning orders. Ward had told Turner not to hire the guy, but Turner did it anyway, claiming he was under pressure from the county commissioners to bring a Spanish-speaking officer onto the force. Ward thought Turner should have told the county commissioners to take a hike, but the weasel didn't have the guts. As a result, Ward was now saddled with a real pain in the ass.

Conrad stirred in his chair. "I was wondering about the arrest warrant. Do we really need it? It's a murder charge."

Ward gave him a withering look. The guy was a couple of beers short of a six-pack. "Yes, we need an arrest warrant. Especially since we'll probably be arresting him in his house. Although if Noteboom doesn't get his ass here soon, he could bolt."

"Mixon's probably busy putting on her morning makeup," said Conrad, referring to local judge Barbara Mixon.

"Keep it up," said Frida. "Hostile workplace lawsuits are a gold mine."

Ward put up a hand. "Can it, Frida. Nobody's suing anybody."

Before she could respond, Judd Noteboom burst into the room. Waving a single sheet of paper, he strode up to Ward and slapped it on the table. "Got it."

Ward glanced at the warrant while Noteboom found a seat. "All right, people, let's review," the chief deputy said. "As you all know, Sheriff Turner was found dead in Erfurt Park. In a minute, Frida will explain why it looks like murder. The evidence so far suggests the killer is Adam Cash. He had motive, opportunity, and means." Ward clicked his tongue. "Bastard crushed his skull in with a beer bottle. We're going to make sure he doesn't get away with it. Frida?"

All eyes turned toward the medical examiner. She cleared her throat. "What I've found so far indicates that the sheriff was killed at an unknown location, and his body was taken to the park. The cause of death was blunt-force trauma to the head. The murder weapon could have been a beer bottle, but a lot of other heavy objects would fit the wound pattern."

Ward made air quotes. "Lots of other heavy objects weren't found in the suspect's car."

"I'm getting to that. A campaign flyer for Adam Cash was stuffed in Turner's mouth. A search of Adam's car revealed blood on the driver's-side door handle along with his fingerprints. Inside the car, we found a bloody beer bottle with his prints on it."

Ward said, "That's about as straightforward as it gets."

"Not quite. There were no fingerprints on the flyer, but there were prints on the bottle. It doesn't seem likely that the killer would have left prints on one and not the other. Furthermore, the prints on the bottle are clustered at the base in an orientation suggesting someone holding the bottle right side up, like you would if you were drinking from it. To crush somebody's skull with a beer bottle, it'd be necessary to hold it by the neck and wield it like a club. There were no prints on the neck."

"All plausible discrepancies," said Ward with a wave of his hand. "What she's not telling you is that Cash was drunk that night—hell, I saw him at the Dillo—and he can't account for a significant stretch of time. The estimated time of death is between ten p.m. and midnight." He looked at Frida. "Right?"

She nodded.

"He left the bar around nine-thirty. Edie James drove him home around eleven. That leaves an hour and a half for him to kill Turner and move the body. Plenty of time."

"That's awfully fast for the post-mortem lividity I saw to have formed." Frida was referring to the pooling of blood in lower parts of a body after death, resulting in purple discoloration of the skin.

"Where did you see post-mortem lividity?" Santos asked.

"All over the front half of his body. That suggests he lay prone for quite a while. We found him on his back."

"Yeah, well, bodies react in different ways," said Ward. "Cash is our guy."

"Lars, what do you think?" Frida asked. "Is there enough for an indictment?"

Newsome ran a hand over his chin. "Enough for an indictment, yes. Enough for a conviction? I don't know."

"Nothing's ever certain in a courtroom," said Ward, butting in. "But this seems like plenty to me. Now, is there anything else?"

Santos raised a hand.

"What is it?"

"I'm sorry, but I'm having trouble seeing this as an open-and-shut case. Frida just pointed out at least two holes in your theory that a good lawyer could drive a truck through."

Ward squinted at his deputy. "This isn't a theory. It's supported by facts."

"Yes, but some of the facts would seem to lead in another direction. At the very least, you'd have to have a better explanation than 'bodies react in different ways.'"

"Are you making fun of me, Deputy?"

Santos blanched. "No, sir. I just thought—"

"When I want to know what you're thinking, I'll ask. Got it?"

Santos didn't answer.

"Good." Ward folded the warrant and stuffed it into his shirt pocket. "Noteboom, you're with me. Conrad, Santos, you guys stay here in case he shows his face in town." He stood up. "And remember, no matter what you may think of Adam Cash, the fact is he brutally murdered our friend and colleague. We have to assume he'll be armed. If that's the case, he'll be plenty dangerous."

"Meaning what?" said Santos, irritation creeping into his voice.

"Meaning, keep your hand near your sidearm."

***

Despite what Ward told his deputies, he expected no resistance from Cash. The man had folded in the donut shop and there was no reason to think he wouldn't do so again. What else could be expected from someone with no backbone? Thank God he lost the election. Noble County would be the laughingstock of Texas if he'd won.

Ward parked his squad car in the circular driveway in front of Cash's house. Making no effort to keep quiet, he got out and signaled Noteboom to follow. "Go watch the back," he told his deputy.

As Noteboom mutely obeyed orders, Ward reflected on how easily some people went along. He'd had his way with the deputy ever since Noteboom's first day on the force six years ago. Back then Noteboom had reminded Ward of a puppy, not too bright and eager to please. As the seasoned veteran in the relationship, Ward had quickly established his dominance. So had the previous sheriff, Carter Turner, but Ward had been able to prevent his son Griff from establishing a similar relationship. A few behind-the-back comments and well-timed innuendos from Ward had been enough to seed doubt in a simpleton like Noteboom.

Ward strode up to the door and rang the bell. "Cash, it's Clovis Ward. I need to talk to you." When there was no response, he banged on the door. "Come on, Cash. Open up." He still was left there hanging. With a curse, Ward gripped the knob and turned. The door was locked. He stepped back, raised a foot, and slammed it into the door, opening it with a splintering crash. "Cash? Are you in here? It's Clovis." Silence.

Ward pulled his sidearm and began a search of the three-bedroom house. He made his way from room to room, each time swinging his weapon around the corner before stepping into the doorway. The last room he came to was an enclosed sun porch in the back. Even as he entered it, Ward knew it was vacant. To compound his frustration, he saw Noteboom outside staring through a window, a blank expression on his face.

Noteboom rapped his knuckles against the glass. Ward opened the back door and let him in.

"No luck?" Noteboom said.

Ward re-holstered his weapon. "No. He's not here."

"What now?"

Ward headed toward the front door. "Now we go find the son of a bitch."

28

Back in Pinyon by ten o'clock, Cash parked the pickup behind the brewery and surveyed the alley. Seeing no one, he pulled down his hat, slid out of the truck, and hurried through the back entrance. He closed the door and paused to listen. The place was quiet. After a quick peek into the empty dining room, he retrieved the laptop from the basement and took up his usual position behind the bar.

Had Carl Trotter told him the truth? Cash had taken a class in criminal investigation at Sam Houston State that included lectures on suspect interviews. Physical signs such as excessive fidgeting, a change in speech pattern, and putting a hand over one's mouth while speaking suggested lying. He had seen no signs like that with Trotter. If the man had lied, he had covered it well. What about Bill Carpenter and Ted Hubbard? Nothing they had said seemed to betray untruthfulness either.

Cash powered up the laptop and found the Junction Little League website. He clicked on the schedule and scanned the list of games played on the night of the murder. There had been two, Cubs vs. Astros and Dodgers vs. Mets. No results were posted yet, but at least there had indeed been a game involving the teams cited by Trotter.

Trotter had suggested starting a search at the gun range. Cash had never gone there. He didn't even know its name. He only knew it occupied a former plant nursery a few miles south of town. A search of the terms "Pinyon" and "gun range" brought up only one result: Roadrunner Pete's Shooting Range. The home page bore a photograph of a hard-looking man with a scruffy beard and plenty of ink on his arms and neck. The caption read, "Pete Klein—owner and firearms expert."

Cash clicked the "About" button. He learned that Pete had opened the business three years before with the goal of "helping you hit what you aim at." Pete prided himself on his strong support of the Second Amendment, which he claimed gave every law-abiding citizen the right to carry any weapon anywhere at any time.

The range opened each morning at ten o'clock. That was fifteen minutes ago. Should he risk a visit? Today was Thursday. A regular workday for most people. The place shouldn't be too crowded. As far as Cash knew, none of his friends frequented the range, so his chances of being recognized seemed low.

Cash returned the laptop to Steve's office. As he checked the load in the Ruger, he was reassured by the feel of its cold steel grip. After putting on his hat, he ducked his head and bolted through the back door to the truck. Confident that no one had seen him, he cranked the engine and drove away.

Ten minutes later, Cash steered into the parking lot of the rectangular metal building housing the gun range. Years of Texas sun had bleached its paint to a dull green. A plywood sign that read "Roadrunner Pete's—Guns—Ammo—Shooting Range" hung over the front door. The only other vehicle in the lot, a brown Toyota Tacoma pickup, was plastered with NRA and gun rights stickers. Cash figured it had to belong to the owner.

During Cash's youth, the building had been home to Sunnyside Lawn and Garden. He recalled accompanying his mother there every spring when she picked out perennials. Her garden had always looked great in April, less so in May, and even less so in June. By July, the plot could only be described as a plant cemetery. The weed-choked beds lining the modern building's front fit that description as well.

Cash entered the building and found no one in the lobby. He strolled past a shelf stocked with ammunition and approached the counter. A forest of guns—rifles, pistols, shotguns, and more—filled the wall on the other side. A sign read, "Do not handle the guns without permission." He spotted a countertop bell and gave it a tap.

A scruffy man shuffled out of a back doorway and nodded a greeting. Taking in the man's unkempt beard, faded T-shirt, ink sleeves, and neck tattoos, Cash knew he was looking at Pete Klein.

"If you're here to shoot, I'm just getting things set up," said Pete. "Or you're free to browse if you're looking to buy."

"Thanks, I'm here for a little target practice."

"Okay. It's twenty bucks an hour. You pay before you shoot."

Cash fished two tens out of his wallet and laid them on the counter. "Got something I can shoot with? A handgun will do."

Pete gestured at the gun at Cash's waist. "What's wrong with that Ruger?"

"Nothing. I'm looking to branch out."

"That's another twenty." Before Cash could respond, Pete pulled several pistols from the wall and spread them out on the counter. "Take your pick."

Cash picked up a .460 Smith & Wesson revolver. "This one."

Pete smirked. "Everybody wants to be Dirty Harry."

Cash added a twenty to the bills already on the counter. When Pete asked for identification, he pulled two more twenties out of his wallet and held them out.

"What's this?"

"My identification."

Pete frowned but took the bills. After leading Cash into the back of the building, he stopped at the first of ten shooting lanes. "How far away do you want the target?"

"Let's try thirty feet."

"Okay, boss." Pete pushed a button and the target slid away with a high-pitched squeal, jerking to a stop when it reached the correct distance. "I'll leave you to it, then. Make sure that gun's unloaded when you leave your lane. Eye and ear protection are right there."

Cash donned the safety gear and loaded the pistol. As he lifted the heavy weapon, he realized that, except for his deer rifle, he hadn't used a firearm since his discharge from the army. He eyed the target, a silhouette of a man. In Afghanistan, he had fired at real flesh-and-blood targets who were shooting back at him. One that he hit still haunted him, a boy who looked no older than twelve or thirteen. When Cash reached him, the boy lay on his back, clutching his stomach with bloody hands, pleading with his eyes for a miracle. Cash grabbed the medic kit from a colleague and did his best, but the boy died. The youthful face lived on in Cash's nightmares, adding another layer of guilt to an already thick foundation. He hadn't joined the army to kill children, even the ones that were armed.

Cash stuffed the memory into a far recess of his mind and pointed the barrel at the target. When he squeezed the trigger, the blast almost knocked him off his feet. He steadied himself and fired again. When the cylinder was empty, he flicked a switch to bring the target up close. All five shots had hit the silhouette, with three arranged in a tight center cluster.

Cash set the gun down. After a glance over his shoulder to make sure he wasn't being watched, he strode to a door beyond the furthermost shooting lane. He surmised it led to the only other unknown space in the building. The knob turned.

The room proved to be a letdown. On one wall was an enormous flat-screen TV. Flanking it were three well-worn sofas. The air reeked of tobacco smoke mixed with the pungent aroma of marijuana. Empty beer cans overflowed a filthy trash can in the corner.

Cash wandered among the sofas, spotting nothing suspicious. He heard a noise and saw Pete glaring at him. "What the hell are you doing in here?" the range owner said.

Cash shrugged. "I was looking for the way out."

"This ain't it."

"Sorry."

"Come on, then."

Cash retrieved the Smith & Wesson.

"Are you done already?"

"Yeah, I just remembered I have a dentist appointment."

Pete scowled and waved a hand. "The exit is this way."

Out in the lobby, Cash handed the gun over and said, "Do you ever get law enforcement in here? Or do they have their own place to shoot?"

"I don't ask folks what they do for a living."

"Surely you know who they are, though."

Pete pointed at the exit. "Have a nice day."

29

"Here you go, fellas," Edie said, setting two cheeseburger plates on the table. "Enjoy."

"Thanks, Edie," said Deke Conrad. He wrapped his hands around the enormous sandwich and hoisted it to his mouth. Biting into it, he let out a groan of satisfaction. "Nobody does them like the Firewheel."

Conrad's dining companion, fellow deputy Gabe Santos, stared at his plate and said nothing.

"Aren't you going to eat?"

Santos picked up a fry and nibbled at it. "Do you think Adam Cash killed Sheriff Turner?"

Conrad took another huge bite of his burger. Talking through his food, he said, "I don't know. I guess. I mean, who else is there?"

"That's what bothers me. We haven't considered any other possibility. Ward saw that flyer and jumped to one conclusion."

"It's Cash's flyer."

"Yeah, but there are no prints on it. Nothing to connect him with it at all. Those flyers were all over town. Anybody could have left it with the body."

"But why would they?"

"Could be somebody that wanted to make it look like Cash was involved."

"Are you saying he was framed?"

"It does happen."

Conrad popped the last bit of the burger into his mouth and started in on his fries, downing one after another in rapid succession. "I might need to get another plate." He eyed Santos's untouched food. "You gonna eat yours?"

Santos picked up his cheeseburger. "Yeah."

"So," Conrad said with a grunt. "Who do you think did it?"

"I don't have anyone specific in mind. But that's not the point. My problem is, I don't think we have enough evidence to convict Cash."

"We don't need to convict him. That's up to Newsome."

"Come on, you heard Frida. There's plenty of room for doubt."

"Frida's a whiner. Nothing's ever good enough for her."

Santos sighed. Talking to his partner was like trying to explain the concept of eating only at mealtimes to a dog. Nothing you said would sink in. "I'm just saying we should be absolutely certain before we put somebody away for murder."

"Why do you care about this so much? Is Cash a friend of yours?"

Santos contemplated the question. He couldn't exactly call Cash a close friend. After all, he had only run into him recently after not seeing him for several years. But they shared a bond that he wouldn't be able to explain to someone like Conrad, a civilian with no military experience. You didn't have to be close friends to feel an obligation to a fellow soldier. That bond held tighter than friendship.

"He saved my life once."

"How?"

Santos told him the story.

"Okay, he saved your life. I guess you owe him."

"I do."

"You gonna eat your fries?"

Santos shoved the plate across the table. "They're all yours."

30

Cash returned to the brewery unsure of his next step. He came in through the back door, followed the stairs down to the basement—and found a bag of groceries on his sleeping bag. Bread, peanut butter, strawberry jam, a bag of apples, a half-gallon of chocolate milk, and a box of oatmeal cookies. Enough to last for several days. Except for the chocolate milk. That would be gone by nightfall.

Cash opened the cookies and popped one in his mouth. Footsteps sounded from the stairwell. He tensed but relaxed when Steve appeared in the doorway. "Damn, you scared me," he said.

"I see you found the food. I can bring you something hot from the kitchen too if you want."

"Thanks. This will do. No need to risk making the cook suspicious."

Steve found an upside-down bucket to sit on. "Got any answers yet?"

"Nothing solid. The guy at the gun range is a little shady, from what I hear."

"Who's that?"

"His name is Pete Klein. Do you know him?"

"No."

"Me either. Did you find out where the body was?"

"Sorry, no. Only a few people would know, and I can't exactly walk up to them and ask. I walked through the park, but I didn't see anything."

"Did you check with Frida?"

"Now, how am I going to do that? 'Hey, Frida, I was just wondering, where exactly was Griff Turner's body when you saw it? The guy hiding in my basement wants to know.'"

"You don't have to be a smartass about it."

"I'm just a little tense, is all. I heard there's a warrant out for your arrest, so now I'm officially harboring a fugitive."

Cash had to concede that Steve was right to be nervous. If Ward caught him here, his friend would be in real trouble. "I can leave."

"I didn't say that. Just stay put. You'll figure this thing out."

"Thanks."

"I do have one piece of good news."

"What?"

"I got a Wi-Fi extender. You should get internet service down here now."

More footsteps sounded on the stairs. Cash ducked behind one of the fermentation tanks.

"Relax," said Steve. "That will be Edie."

Sure enough, Edie appeared in the doorway. Seeing only Steve, she said, "Is he down here?"

"He's hiding."

Cash stepped out from behind the fermenter. "What the hell, Steve?"

"Don't be mad," said Edie. "We're a team, remember?"

Steve said, "I'll leave you two to hash things out." He disappeared up the stairs.

"Edie, you shouldn't be here."

"I'm glad to see you, too."

"You know what I mean."

"I just wanted to tell you: I know you didn't kill anybody."

"I appreciate that. But Clovis Ward thinks I did. And unless I can prove otherwise, I'm going to prison."

"Steve told me you've got some clues about the identity of the real killer."

"I'm at a dead end," Cash said with a sigh. "Heck, I don't even know where they found the body."

Edie strutted over to him. "That's another reason I came by. Working in a cafe lets me hear things Steve doesn't."

"What are you talking about? Steve serves booze to people. They pour their hearts out to him."

"Do you want to hear this or not?"

"Sorry. What is it?"

"I *do* know where the body was found."

"Where?"

She pulled a folded piece of paper from her jeans pocket and handed it to him. "Here, I drew you a map."

***

Cash couldn't go to the park in broad daylight. That would have to wait. He wanted to dig deeper at the gun range but couldn't go back there either until after dark. Instead, he fetched Steve's laptop and returned to the basement to learn more about what Pete Klein might be doing at his gun range.

Cash navigated to the Texas state records website and searched the arrest database for anyone by that name. He found files on ten different men. Five were at least sixty-five years old. Cash estimated Pete's age was between thirty-five and fifty, so he ruled those men out, as well as four others twenty-five or younger. That left only thirty-seven-year-old Peter Lawrence Klein, arrested six months ago for a homicide in Tarrant County. Cash doubted that someone accused of murder only six months ago would now be allowed to operate a shooting range. So, his Pete Klein had a clean record, at least in Texas.

What about Bill and Ted? Bill's record revealed only a ten-year-old misdemeanor marijuana possession charge. Ted's showed nothing. He tried Carl Trotter and once again found no record of trouble with the law.

Cash snapped the laptop closed and swore. What was he missing?

He reopened the laptop and pulled up the Junction Little League site. Someone had updated the game results. On the night in question, the Astros defeated the Cubs 5–2. What about the Mets? His heart jumped. There was no game. The Dodgers forfeited for lack of enough players, meaning Trotter had lied to him. Cash decided to go back to Junction and confront the son of a bitch. He grabbed two apples and the box of cookies and headed for the door.

An hour later, Cash steered Steve's truck into the insurance agency's parking lot in Junction. He switched off the engine. His pulse rate picked up at the thought of the upcoming confrontation with Trotter. He forced himself to take several deep breaths and wait for the pounding in his chest to stop. After climbing down from the truck cab, he took another deep breath and stepped into the office.

A young woman with a nose ring and green-streaked hair greeted him from behind the reception desk. "Can I help you?"

"I'm looking for Carl Trotter."

"You just missed him."

"Do you know where I might find him? It's important."

"I'm not sure. I think he went home."

"Oh."

"I could call him for you."

Cash shook his head. "No, I need to give him some papers. Could you tell me where he lives?"

She eyed him with suspicion.

"It's important," Cash said. "It's about a bank loan he's applying for."

"What's he need a bank loan for?"

"You'd have to ask him that. I just know that if he doesn't get these papers signed, it will be delayed until next week, and he'll be madder than hell."

Though not totally sold, the woman plucked a business card from the holder on her desk. She flipped it over and scribbled an address on the back. As she handed it over, she said, "Here. Please don't tell him you got this from me."

Cash winked at her. "Your secret is safe with me."

***

Cash neared the Trotter home still mulling over how to confront the insurance agent. Should he play it coy, hoping to catch Trotter in an obvious lie? Or should he come right out and accuse the man of murdering his girlfriend's husband?

He didn't want to spook Trotter, so he parked around the corner from his house and walked the rest of the way. It was built on a small slope, with steps that led from the sidewalk to the front door. It stood out from its neighbors because of its size—the imposing two-story structure had to have at least four bedrooms. A beautifully landscaped yard disproved his mother's contention that "nobody can garden in this kind of heat."

Cash took note of the two cars in the driveway, Trotter's Nissan Sentra next to a silver Toyota Rav 4. He stepped past two bird baths flanking the sidewalk and ascended the steps. The blue enamel coating on the door looked fresh. As he knocked, he caught a whiff of paint fumes.

A pretty woman with tired eyes and auburn hair answered. "Yes?"

"Mrs. Trotter?"

"Yes."

"I'm here to see your husband."

"Can I tell him what it's about?"

"I need to talk to him about an insurance document I'm supposed to sign."

"Couldn't this wait until he's back in the office?"

"I'm sorry, no. He said it was important."

Carl Trotter stepped into view. "I've got it, honey." He pushed past her onto the porch and pulled the door shut. "What the hell do you want now?"

Cash squared his shoulders, seeing that he would need to take a direct approach. "I'll get right to the point. You told me you were at your son's Little League game the night that Griff Turner died. I checked the league's website. There was no game."

Trotter's face reddened. "There was no *official* game. The other team didn't have enough players, so they had to forfeit. The coaches divided the boys up for a scrimmage. They played for about an hour and then we went for pizza."

Cash stared open-mouthed. Of all the responses he had imagined, this one hadn't made the list. "How do I know you're not making that up?"

Trotter tensed and Cash braced for a physical assault. Instead, Trotter pushed open the front door and called out, "Rhonda, would you come here?" When she appeared, he said, "Mr. Ramsey was asking me about Liam's game the other night. What was the final score? I can't remember."

"Oh," Rhonda said, her face lighting up. "Six to four, Liam's team won. He got two hits. It wasn't a real game, though."

"And what did we do after the game?"

"We went to Tony's for pizza."

Trotter trained a sour look at Cash. "Satisfied?"

"Then I brought the kids home, and you went back to your office." She looked at Cash. "He got home pretty late. I think it was after midnight. I didn't even wake up when he got in."

Trotter put a hand on Rhonda's shoulder and nudged her back through the doorway. "That's enough, honey. I'll take it from here."

When Rhonda was back in the house, Cash said, "Why did you go back to your office?"

"Get the hell off my porch."

"Can I just ask—"

Trotter shoved Cash hard enough to knock him off balance. "Next time I see your face, I'm calling the cops. Understand?"

Cash grabbed Trotter's shirt and pinned him against the front door. "Listen, you son of a bitch, I know you're hiding something. And when I find out what it is, I'll be back." He let go of the shirt and, without a backward glance, marched down the sidewalk certain of one thing. Trotter had lied to his wife about going back to the office. And if that was true, where the hell had he been?

31

Novak took a deep breath and fought the urge to hurl his glass against the wall. Reining in his temper, he gritted his teeth and said into the phone, "Why the hell isn't this guy in jail yet?"

Throughout the many years he had known Novak, the man on the other end of the call had endured many such fits of rage from his friend. Experience had taught him it was best to wait a few seconds before replying. Once Novak's breathing quieted, he said, "The bastard ran, that's why. Can you believe it?"

"Hell, yes, I can believe it. Nobody wants to be arrested."

"Good point. But nobody can hide forever."

"You'd better be right." Novak downed the rest of his bourbon. "Because he's stirring up a shitload of trouble out there on his own."

"Speaking of trouble," the man said, "he went to see Trotter again, this time at his house."

Novak refilled his glass from the ever-present bottle on the card table. Maybe another swallow or two would calm his nerves. "Shit. What did he want?"

"He thought he caught Trotter in a lie. Some bullshit about a Little League game his son played in. Trotter told him he was full of crap."

"Did he buy it?"

"Seemed to. Then Trotter told him to fuck off and not come back or he'd call the police." The man paused. "Only thing is, Trotter's wife blabbed that he went somewhere after that."

"Shit."

"I know. He should have left that woman a long time ago."

"Did he get a plate number?"

"No, the guy's not stupid. He parked around the corner."

"Both times?"

"The first time they were in Trotter's office. They never went outside."

"Carl's not going to crack, is he?" Novak said, rubbing his forehead.

"No. He's rock solid."

"We could always cut him out."

"What good would that do? He'd still know everything."

Novak blinked. Trotter was their friend, but friendship had its limits. "You know the old saying, 'dead men tell no tales.'"

"What the hell, Barry? He's got two kids."

"They'd still have their mother."

"I said no. Don't even think about it."

"All right. But just so you know, if push comes to shove, everybody's expendable. Understand?"

"That would include you."

"Yeah, right," Novak said after another swallow of bourbon. "But I know I won't break."

"Trotter won't either. Neither will I."

"What about the widow?"

"Would you stop? We're not killing anybody else."

A long silence ensued. At length, Novak said, "Not unless we have to."

32

Cash waited until one in the morning before he darted down the alley past the pizza joint and entered Erfurt Park. The county courthouse loomed large, but no light shone from its windows. Only the hoot of an unseen owl disturbed the otherwise empty night.

He came armed with a flashlight and Edie's map. After following the crushed granite path to the park's gazebo, he veered right. A gentle slope led toward Randolph Creek, fifty feet distant. According to Edie, the body had been found lying face up, arms and legs laid out like DaVinci's Vitruvian Man. Cash had no difficulty locating the site, as numerous feet had stomped a ten-foot circle of flattened grass not far from the gazebo. Either Steve didn't try to find the spot very hard or he possessed limited powers of observation.

Cash squatted at the edge of the circle and played his flashlight across the grass. A dark spot caught his eye. He looked closer and saw a red splotch smearing the blades: blood. He stood and walked in a slow, methodical spiral toward the circle's center but saw nothing else of significance. Reversing himself, he searched ever-expanding concentric circles until he reached the thick vegetation along the creek. Turning to his left, he focused the flashlight beam on the bushes and made his way another fifty feet. He then retraced his steps and patrolled the area fifty feet beyond his starting point. He was about to give up when he caught a flash of color among the brambles. Forcing his way through the vines, he came upon a wadded-up paper napkin. He used a stick to pick it up and carry it back to the clearing.

Cash smoothed the crinkled napkin with the stick. With the aid of the flashlight, he was able to make out a border of brown and orange leaves around a tan square. An irregular red splotch darkened the center. Suppressing an urge to shout, he pulled a plastic sandwich bag from his pocket and maneuvered the napkin into it. A thrill shot through him. He had finally caught a break.

***

After leaving Erfurt Park with the bloody napkin, Cash returned to the brewery for a few hours of fitful sleep. He awoke at six, fetched Steve's truck, and headed toward Frida Simmons's house. On the way, he recalled a time around his eighth birthday when his parents went to a party and left him and his siblings in Frida's care. When they came home an hour late, Frida was annoyed. She explained that she was an early riser, and she had accepted the job only because she knew she'd be home by ten. Cash's dad apologized and gave her an extra ten bucks.

Cash suspected that, despite the early hour, Frida would already be up. The first gray streaks of dawn were lightening the sky when he arrived at her modest ranch house. Across the street was the elementary school, closed for the summer. He parked in the school lot and plotted his approach.

The house's windows were dark. Either Frida had already left for work or she was still asleep. A light flicked on. Cash slipped out of the truck, hurried to the front porch, and rapped on the door. A chair scraped a tile floor from inside. Light footsteps padded toward him. A woman's voice called out. "Who is it?"

"Frida, it's Adam Cash."

The deadbolt clicked and Frida cracked the door open. When she saw Cash, she pulled it all the way and said, "Damn, Adam. What are you doing here? They're looking for you."

"I know. Can I come in?"

She stepped aside so he could slide past her into the living room. After shutting the door, she led him back to the kitchen, where a steaming cup of coffee was waiting on a table beside an iPad.

"Sit down. Want some coffee?"

He found an empty chair. "No, thanks."

She dropped into a seat and wrapped her hands around the coffee mug. "You're putting me in a bad spot."

"I'm sorry. I need your help."

"With what?"

"Finding Griff Turner's killer."

"Go on."

He explained, taking her through his movements on election day. The confrontation with Turner at the Firewheel. The library. Turner's argument with Bill Carpenter at the pizza place. Getting drunk at the Dizzy Dillo with Clovis Ward. Falling asleep on the courthouse lawn. Edie driving him home. "I'm telling you, I was just as surprised as you must have been to hear Griff was dead. I've been trying to figure out who did it, but I'm getting nowhere."

She sipped her coffee. "Where are you staying?"

"It's better if you don't know."

"Good point. What do you want from me?"

"I need to know what evidence they think they have against me."

She set the cup down and leaned back in her chair. "That's asking a lot."

"I know. I wouldn't ask if I wasn't desperate."

"It could cost me my job. Even worse, I could go to prison."

What could he say? She was right on both points.

She rubbed her eyes. "Remember how you used to beg me to make chocolate chip cookies when I babysat you guys? You have that same look on your face now." She paused. "Tell you what. Ask me specific questions. Maybe I'll answer, maybe I won't."

"Thanks. Did they really find one of my flyers in his mouth?"

"Yes."

"Were my fingerprints on it?"

"No."

"Did you really find the murder weapon in my car?"

She paused. "Yes."

Cash heard the hesitation in her voice. "What?"

"There was a beer bottle. I didn't see it at first. Then I was called away for a couple of minutes. When I got back, I found the bottle wedged up under the driver's seat."

"Who called you away?"

"Vicky, that kid in the sheriff's office. She said a deputy told her to have me check my car for a missing file."

"Which deputy?"

"She didn't say."

"Did you have it?"

"No."

"What makes them think the bottle was the murder weapon?"

"There was blood on it. The type matches Griff's. We're waiting on DNA testing."

"My fingerprints were on it, too."

"Right. Funny thing, though. The blood was on the bottom of the bottle, suggesting that someone had held it by the neck and swung it like a club. Your fingerprints were only on the label and body. The neck was clean."

"What brand of beer was it?"

"Bud Lite."

Cash reached into his pocket and came out with the plastic bag containing the bloody napkin. "I found this in the park not far from where y'all found the body. Can you check to see if that is indeed blood?"

She looked miffed that the crime scene hadn't been thoroughly searched. "Sure, but it won't hold up in a courtroom."

"We're not in a courtroom. Like I said, I'm just trying to get at the truth."

She took the bag. "Okay. How will I let you know the results?"

"I'll check back with you."

"By the way, Griff wasn't killed in the park."

Cash twitched in surprise. "What?"

"The body was moved. I found postmortem staining on his chest and abdomen. That's caused by blood pooling in dependent areas after death. After a while, the blood clots, and no more flow takes place. The body was found face up. So, somebody moved it after the blood had coagulated and could no longer pool. Also, the amount of blood I found at the scene seemed inconsistent with the wounds I saw. Scalps bleed a lot. There just wasn't that much blood at the park."

Cash recalled a lecture at Sam Houston State on postmortem lividity. He had paid close attention, thinking the information would someday be useful. That day had arrived. "So, if the body was moved, where was he killed?"

"I don't know. But wherever it was, there should be a lot of blood. If it hasn't been cleaned by now, that is."

Cash stood. "Thank you."

She led him to the door and gave him a quick hug. "Good luck, Adam. I want to believe you."

"Thanks. I'll be in touch."

33

The only time Santos remembered a vehicle being stored in the department garage was when Griff Turner raced to get his new Jeep Gladiator under cover during a sudden hailstorm. The garage mainly functioned as a place to search vehicles in connection with a crime. It was monitored by two video surveillance cameras, one in each bay. The feed was stored on a hard drive maintained by the county's IT expert, Mandy Wilson. Santos had never met Wilson but had spoken to her on the phone countless times.

"Okay, I see that file. Now what?" Santos said into his phone.

"Double-click to open it up."

Santos picked up on the impatience in her voice. "Come on, Mandy. We can't all be computer experts."

"You don't have to be a computer expert to know how to open a file."

Santos suppressed an urge to say something he'd regret. He needed her cooperation, not only to access the surveillance database but with other possible computer-related issues down the road. "It's open."

"Scroll down to find the date you're interested in."

He spun the mouse wheel. "Got it."

"Double-click."

He did.

"What do you see?"

"Let's see ... basement, conference room, lobby—"

"Farther down."

"Here it is. Garage. Thanks, Mandy."

"No problem."

Santos ended the call. He saw a group of files on the screen labeled one through four. Assuming that each file represented a six-hour block of time and that the start time would be midnight, he opened the third one. A video player popped open. The time stamp read 12 00 00. He knew from experience that the system used military time. This file, therefore, started at noon. He clicked the play arrow.

An image of the empty garage appeared. Santos clicked on the fast-forward double arrow and watched until he saw the bay doors open. He fast-forwarded another few minutes and a tow truck appeared with Cash's Ford Fiesta. The driver backed into the garage, lowered the Fiesta, unhooked it, and left. The door leading to the main building opened, and Frida Simmons stepped out. She walked over to the Fiesta and opened the trunk.

Frida spent a few minutes searching the vehicle. Then Vicky entered the garage. A nice girl but gullible. She and Frida held a brief conversation, after which Frida strode outside, clearly annoyed. Vicky disappeared back into the building.

The recording experienced a brief flicker, and then Frida was shown back inside the vehicle. "What the hell was that?" Santos muttered. He backed up the timeline and watched again. Frida went outside, the brief flicker, and, like magic, she was back in the Fiesta. Santos rewound the clip and watched again, this time paying attention to the time stamp. At the flicker, the numbers jumped from 12 21 36 to 12 25 42. Just over four minutes were missing.

He watched Frida continue her search. Soon, she extricated herself from the car, fetched a short dowel from a nearby workbench, and climbed back into the vehicle. Moments later, she reappeared, this time supporting an upside-down beer bottle on the dowel. A Bud Lite bottle. The reputed murder weapon.

Santos leaned back in his chair and let out a long breath. Had somebody doctored that video? He called Mandy.

"This is Wilson."

"Mandy, it's Gabe. I have a question. Would it be possible for someone to erase part of these videos?"

"No. You can't edit the files. The only thing you could do would be to delete it altogether."

"And the time stamp. Is that time elapsed or the actual time?"

"The system has an internal clock, so it's the actual time the video is being shot."

"I'm seeing a time gap on the one I'm interested in."

"The only way for that to happen would be for someone to switch off the camera and then switch it back on."

"Do those cameras ever malfunction?"

"I suppose it's possible. But I've never had any complaints."

"Okay, thanks."

Santos ended the call. What accounted for the time gap? It seemed an unlikely coincidence that a malfunction would occur at the precise moment that Frida left the building. That meant someone had intentionally turned the camera off. Why? Santos could think of only one reason.

34

Steve shook his head and said, "So you're stuck."

"For now." Cash's gaze took in the old fermentation tanks. "It's hard to carry out an investigation from the basement of a brewpub."

"Give me something to do."

"I need my own phone. Can you get me a burner?"

Steve looked like he didn't know how to do that. "Yeah, I guess."

"You'll probably have to go to San Antonio. Be sure and pay cash."

Now he seemed more curious about how it was done. "My day is pretty free. I can go later this morning."

"I'll need some money, too. Three hundred should do."

"You're going to pay me back, right?"

"You still owe me that from lunch in Del Rio."

Steve produced a wry smile. "Good point."

"What I keep coming back to is the extortion," Cash said, scratching his chin. "The killer has to be somebody who was tired of paying it."

"I don't know," said Steve. "It pissed me off, but not enough to risk going to prison for the rest of my life. It really wasn't all that much money."

"If that's the case, why did he bother?"

"I was paying five hundred a month. Pocket change in the overall scheme of things. But what if there were ten others paying the same rate? That's five thousand bucks a month."

"Still not life-changing."

"No. But it would make life a lot easier."

Cash bit his lip. "Bill and Ted were only paying three hundred a month."

"Son of a bitch. Why did they get a break?"

"I don't know. Who else do you think was paying?"

Steve shrugged. "I'm not sure. I didn't know about Bill and Ted."

"Something's just not adding up. Turner had to be involved in something dirtier than shaking down business owners for lunch money."

"Drugs?"

"Maybe, but I don't have any evidence of that yet," Cash said, thinking. "I'm heading back to the gun range tonight. Maybe I'll get lucky and find something that will explain why Griff spent so much time there."

"Good idea." Steve headed for the stairs. "I gassed up the truck for you."

"Great. Can I ask one more favor?"

"What?"

"Do you have a ski mask?"

***

"The guy's a ghost," Noteboom said. "Nobody in town has seen him."

Ward took a long pull on his Coke bottle and glared across the desk. "I don't believe in ghosts. Somebody knows where he is."

"If they do, they're not talking."

Ward downed the last drop of his Coke and set the bottle on the desk with an emphatic thump. "Coke in a glass bottle. The way God intended it to be drunk."

"Is it really better?"

"You bet it is. It's made in Mexico. They use real sugar instead of that corn syrup crap."

"Should a sheriff be using Mexican coke?"

Ward rolled his eyes at the lame joke. "Getting back to the business at hand, somebody's helping him. I've already talked to his girlfriend. She claims she hasn't seen him."

"Who's his girlfriend?"

"Edie James."

"I don't think they're together anymore."

"Who gives a shit? There's his baby mama, too. Bernadette something."

"Fenster."

"Yeah."

"You want me to talk to her?"

"No, I'll do that."

Noteboom shot his boss a puzzled look. "So, what do you want me to do?"

"I gave Vicky a few of his campaign flyers the other day. Go get them from her. Then you, Deke, and Gabe show his picture around town and find somebody who will admit to seeing him. He can't hide forever."

"Gee, that sounds exciting."

"Just do as you're told."

"What are you going to do?"

Ward opened a small refrigerator behind his desk and pulled out a bottle. "Me? I'm gonna have another Coke."

***

Cash arrived at the gun range a few minutes before the nine o'clock closing time. He counted four vehicles in the lot, all pickups. He pulled around to the back of the building and killed the engine. Before exiting the truck, he slid Steve's ski mask over his head. At the back side of the building, he spotted a lit door that looked like it might lead to the room with the TV. As he crept up to it, he noticed a mounted security camera and was glad he had covered his face.

To Cash's surprise, the door was unlocked. He turned the knob cautiously and light-stepped into the building. He found himself in a small, dark space cluttered with stacked boxes. He paused to allow his eyes to adjust to the low light and made out another door six feet farther in. Loud shouts and peals of laughter filled the room beyond. The distinctive odor of marijuana smoke filled his nostrils.

Cash eased the door open to see the familiar garage-sized room furnished with three sofas facing the opposite wall. A pornographic film played on the wall-mounted TV. A man and woman occupied each couch. The two couples closest to the TV were watching the film. It was their laughter that Cash had heard through the door.

The man on the couch closest to Cash had his head tilted back and his eyes closed. A joint dangled from his lips and his arms rested along the top of the couch. A woman knelt in front of him with her head between his legs.

The woman's head jerked up and down several times. The man tensed and let out a soft moan. The woman lifted her head and said something to the man. He handed her the joint. She climbed up into his lap, her naked breasts dangling before him. Cash now could make out her red hair, pointed chin, and oversized ears. It was Bernadette. Mother of his child. Drawing hard on the joint, she looked past the man, spotted Cash, and screamed.

Cash slammed the door shut and spun around to make his escape. A woman's call sounded from outside the building. The outer door flew open and a couple stumbled in. Cash tried to push his way past the man and woman, but they blocked his way. "Who the hell are you?" the man said, slurring his words.

Someone yanked the inner door open, and two men rushed into the small space. They grabbed Cash and dragged him into the TV room. The newly arrived couple trailed behind.

The lights came on. The people in the room stood bunched together and stared at him. Cash recognized Bernadette, who had donned a T-shirt, and Pete Klein, but no one else. Pete said, "Get his ski mask off." Before Cash could react, a hand yanked it from his head. Cash withered under the glare of the unfriendly faces. Spotting the shocked expression on Bernadette's face, he gave her a barely perceptible head shake.

"You're that guy that was here earlier," said Pete, tripping over his words.

Cash backed toward the door, but Pete and another man rushed him. He stopped them by pulling his Ruger and pointing it at them. They glared at him with bloodshot eyes. Surveying the crowd, Cash saw that they were all stoned. "Hands where I can see them," he said. "I'm not here to rob you. I just want to know what the hell's going on."

"What does it look like, dumbass?" said a heavyset man. "We're watching porn with these pretty ladies."

Cash caught the eye of one of the women. "It's good money, honey," she said, stretching out the last two words and giggling.

He turned to Pete. "Why did Sheriff Turner spend so much time here?"

Pete laughed. "Because he was one horny son of a bitch. What's it to you?"

Cash edged toward the door. When a man circled as if to block him, he pointed the gun and said, "Get back over there." The man shuffled back to stand with the others.

Cash said, "I'm leaving now. Don't come after me. The first person that comes outside gets a bullet, understand?" Remembering the security camera and wishing to avoid leaving a record of his visit, he extended his hand to the man holding the ski mask. "Let me have that."

The man handed it over. Cash pulled it over his head. "I mean it. Don't come after me. Just go back to your party."

Cash backed into the small anteroom and leaned against the door. After a last glance at Bernadette, he slipped through the doorway and sprinted for the truck. As he climbed into the driver's seat, he heard the metal door of the building open. He fired the engine, floored the accelerator, and raced out of the parking lot. In the rearview mirror, he saw Pete stagger around the corner. The stoned man shouted something unintelligible and keeled over sideways. Cash kept his foot on the gas until he was out of sight.

35

Cash slept in the next morning. He woke up at six, but rolled over and went back to sleep. The thought of facing another day as a murder suspect was too depressing. Now it was ten-thirty and he still lacked any desire to get up. He stared blankly at the fermentation tanks and wondered if he should turn himself in and stake his chances on finding a good lawyer.

Voices sounded upstairs. Steve's and one belonging to a woman. Probably a server coming in early. The voices stopped. Footsteps thudded in the stairwell.

Steve stepped into the basement. "Rise and shine, sleeping beauty."

"Go away."

"Come on, man. You've got to get up. Someone is here to see you."

"Who?"

"You're not going to believe this. Bernadette."

Cash bolted out of his sleeping bag. "Shit. How did she know where to find me?"

"She didn't. She said you once told her to come to me if she needed you but didn't know where to find you. By the way, it would have been nice of you to let me know I was the stand-in baby daddy."

"Sorry. I've been meaning to tell you. What does she want?"

"She wants me to tell you she's sorry for last night. What the hell is she talking about?"

Cash closed his eyes, wondering how much he should tell Steve. "I saw her at the gun range."

"What was she doing there?"

"I crashed a pretty wild party. Booze, porn, oral sex ... and Bernadette."

"Oh. What do you want me to do? She doesn't know you're here."

Should he see her? Had she come to blackmail him? Threaten to rat him out to Pete Klein and his gang of stoners if he didn't give her some money? After what he saw, he should be the one blackmailing her. But maybe he should learn the reason for her visit. "Sure, send her down."

Steve produced a cheap flip phone from his pocket and tossed it to Cash. "Before I forget, this is for you."

"Thanks. I owe you."

"Yeah, I'm keeping track." He disappeared up the stairs. Moments later, Bernadette appeared in the doorway. She had cleaned herself up. Fresh clothes, tidy hair, even a touch of makeup. She looked nice. Nothing like the woman bouncing up and down in that guy's lap last night.

"Hello, Cash."

"Hey, Bernadette." They eyed each other for an awkward moment. "What can I do for you?"

"I wanted to tell you I'm sorry about last night."

Cash didn't know how to respond. "What the hell was going on?"

"Pete throws these parties. He pays me to come. I'm not a hooker if that's what you're thinking. He says all I have to do is show up. What I do at the party is up to me."

"So, what I saw ... you wanted to do that."

She hung her head. "I was pretty high."

"Who were those other women?"

"I don't know. Friends of Pete's, I guess."

A heavy silence enveloped the room, broken at length by Bernadette. "You don't have to worry about Emma. Momma was with her all night. I'd never leave her alone." She paused, her eyes glistening with tears. "I love her, Cash. I want to be a good mother."

"Then maybe you ought to stop hanging out with those lowlifes."

"I know. I'm not going back."

"Smart choice."

Yet that wasn't the reason she had come looking for him. "There's something else."

"What?"

"You were asking about Sheriff Turner last night. Why?"

"You know he's dead, right?"

She nodded.

Cash saw no harm in telling Bernadette about his current predicament. In a small town like Pinyon, she'd find out soon enough. "Clovis Ward thinks I killed him. I didn't. I need to figure out who did."

"Why did you come to Pete's place?"

"I heard that Turner spent a lot of time there. I thought if I knew why, it might give me a clue about the identity of his killer. Any ideas?"

"No, he came to those parties for the same reason as the other men, to get high and fool around."

"Did you ever see him or anyone else at those gatherings do anything illegal?"

"Sure. They smoked weed all the time."

"Something more serious than that."

Bernadette didn't answer right away. When she spoke, her words came out slowly. "There's this guy, he'd come with the sheriff sometimes. I don't know his name. They always just called each other 'Cuz.'

Last week they got into a big fight. The guy offered one of the women some pills. Sheriff Turner saw it and took the bottle from him. He said something like 'Not in my town, you're not.' They were yelling at each other. The other guy said 'Don't worry. Novak's got it all figured out.' But that just made the sheriff even madder. He told the guy he'd arrest them if they didn't stop. That's when they started hitting each other."

"What happened then?"

"Pete and another guy broke it up. The sheriff took me out to his car for a while. When we came back, the party was going on as usual."

"Did he say anything in the car?"

She looked at the floor. "We didn't do much talking."

Cash paced back and forth. Who was "Cuz?" What was in the pill bottle?

Bernadette cleared her throat. "I guess I better go."

Cash walked over to her. Surprising even himself, he gave her a quick hug. "Thank you."

"You're welcome."

Cash resumed his pacing.

"Cash?"

He turned.

"Once you find the killer, you can come see Emma anytime you want."

He smiled at her. "Thanks."

"Well, see you around."

When Bernadette was gone, Cash used the burner phone to make a call. He knew the number by heart.

"Noble County sheriff's office. This is Vicky."

"Vicky, this is Cash." She said nothing, but he heard her gasp through the phone. "Are you there?"

"Yes. What do you want?"

"I know you can't talk now. When will you be home today?"

"I'm going over at lunch to check on my cat. She's been sick."

"Good. Not your cat. Good that you'll be home. What's your cell number?"

She gave it to him.

"Thanks. Please don't tell anyone I called."

***

Cash forced himself to wait until a few minutes after noon to call Vicky again. She answered on the first ring. "Hello?"

"Hey, Vicky, it's Cash."

"What do you want?" She sounded nervous.

"Do you remember telling Frida Simmons to check her car for evidence yesterday?"

"Yes."

"What was that all about?"

"Nothing, really. I was just relaying a message."

"Who asked you to make that call?"

She didn't answer right away. "Did I do something wrong?"

"No. I just need to know who asked you to do it."

There was a long silence before she replied. "It was Judd."

"Judd Noteboom?"

"Yes."

"Thanks, Vicky."

"Did you do it?"

Cash drew a long breath. At least she was giving him the benefit of the doubt by asking. "No, it wasn't me."

"I didn't think so. Well ... I've got to check on my cat."

"Hold on. Can I call you again if I need to?"

"Okay. But only if you promise to take me dancing someday."

"Vicky, you're barely eighteen." She didn't answer, and Cash sighed. "Okay. Someday."

36

The county office building faced the sheriff's department across the street. The one-story limestone and white brick structure housed several departments, including the appraisal district, county clerk, district attorney, planning department, and county treasurer. County medical examiner Frida Simmons also had an office in the building, and Deputy Gabe Santos was roaming the halls in search of it.

Santos had never been in the building. Hired six months ago by Sheriff Turner, he spent most of his time serving subpoenas, enforcing property seizures, supervising prisoners in the county jail, if there were any, and patrolling county roads for traffic violators. Although he enjoyed the job, he had expected a taste of excitement from time to time. A robbery, a livestock theft, a drug bust, a crime that went beyond graffiti at the high school or a married couple waking their neighbors by screaming at each other. Nothing that exciting had ever happened since he'd been on the job.

Until now. Sheriff Turner's murder had electrified Noble County. The case was on everybody's lips, from the mayor on down to the high school kid loading hay bales at the feed store. At first, everyone wanted to know who had done it. Now they demanded to know when the acting sheriff would apprehend his primary suspect, the murder victim's election opponent, Adam Cash. So far Ward's hard-charging approach had yielded no results. People were getting restless.

Santos had no doubt that they would eventually find Cash. But was Cash indeed the culprit? Ward's main piece of evidence, the beer bottle with Cash's fingerprints on it, was likely a plant. And Ward kept harping on the fact that he had seen Cash drinking beer at the Dizzy Dillo, so the bottle found in Cash's car could have come from there. But people didn't usually walk out of a bar with a beer bottle.

They still didn't know where the murder had taken place. For Ward's theory to hold up, Cash would have had to carry the bottle from the bar to that location. After the murder, he would have had to take it back to his car. Why would he do that? Who would be stupid enough to kill someone and dump the murder weapon in his car? Especially something as disposable as a beer bottle? Santos remembered Cash well enough from army days to know the man had more sense than that.

These questions bothered Santos enough for him to seek answers himself, no matter what Ward said. Ward seemed to have closed his mind to the possibility that anyone but Cash could have killed Griff Turner. Santos conceded Cash might have, but he also wanted the department to get it right. If Cash was innocent, he didn't want the man who had saved his life to rot in prison for a crime he didn't commit. That was why he wanted to talk to Frida Simmons.

He found her office at the end of a hallway, one of two branching off from the central lobby. The door stood open. Santos rapped on the doorframe and peered into the room to find Frida going through a file. He marveled at her immaculate desk. Other than the file, the only other objects on it were a telephone and a potted aloe vera plant.

Frida looked up. "Yes?"

"Ms. Simmons, I'm Deputy Gabe Santos."

"I remember you from the briefing. What can I do for you?"

"Can I come in?"

She waved him to a reception chair across the desk from her.

"I'd like to talk to you about the investigation into Sheriff Turner's death."

"What would you like to know?"

Santos chose his words carefully. "At the briefing, you brought up a couple of points that would have to be explained by a prosecutor."

"I did. As you know, Chief Deputy Ward wasn't impressed."

"That's why I'm here. I'm just wondering if there's anything else that implicates Adam Cash as the killer."

Frida shook her head. "Nothing I know of."

"Is that beer bottle really the murder weapon?"

"Ward seems to think so. I'm not so sure. Like I said at the meeting, the orientation of the prints is wrong. Also, the degree of skull fracture would suggest that a much heavier object was used."

"Something else bothers me. I looked at the surveillance video when you were searching his car. You left the garage for several minutes."

"I did. Somebody sent me on a bullshit mission to look for an evidence bag in my car."

"There's a gap in the video."

She arched an eyebrow. "What do you mean?"

"Right as you were leaving the garage, the video cuts off. When it comes back on, you're already back in the car."

The medical examiner's eyes narrowed as the implication sank in. "Somebody could have turned off the camera and planted that bottle."

"That's what I'm thinking. Let me ask you, do you think Cash did it?"

Now it was Frida's turn to be cautious. "I only present the evidence. It's up to you guys to figure it out from there."

"I know. It's just ... I hear you've known Cash a long time."

"Almost since he was in diapers."

"So, you watched him grow up. Did he ever do anything that would suggest he would become a murderer?"

She stared at him with unblinking eyes. "Absolutely not."

"I thought you might say that. I served with him in Afghanistan. That place hardened a lot of folks. Made them callous to the suffering they saw every day. That didn't happen to Cash. He wanted to help people."

Frida's voice softened. "He was the sweetest kid. Nice and polite. Yes ma'am, no ma'am, that sort of thing. People liked him. Not just other kids, but adults too."

"What about now?"

"I don't know. I don't see him that much. He's only been back in Pinyon a short while. He went straight from the army to Sam Houston State. I've run into him a few times here and there, but I can't say that we're close."

"I see. You know, we're going to catch him sooner or later."

"I'm aware of that. Know what I think?"

"What?"

"When you do, I wouldn't stop searching for the killer."

37

Cash couldn't get Bernadette's words out of his mind. "The other guy said, 'Don't worry, Novak's got it all figured out.'" The only Novak in Pinyon Cash knew of was Barry Novak, owner of Barry's Gelato Palace, which operated out of a narrow brick building tucked in between the chamber of commerce and the pharmacy. Rumored to be from Fort Worth, Novak had opened the place less than a year ago. Everyone loved his gelato, but Cash thought it odd the place was open only two days a week. How could a business survive with such limited hours?

In the alley behind the gelato shop stood the ruins of a house that had burned down twenty years ago. An hour after sunset, Cash squatted behind a pile of rubble that was once its chimney. From what Bernadette had told him, Novak was involved in something that riled Griff Turner enough to cause a fistfight between him and his cousin. Maybe it also got Turner killed.

Cash trained a pair of binoculars cadged from Steve on the gelato shop's rear entrance. No lights and no security cameras. He spotted none on the pharmacy or chamber of commerce building either. Life in a small town.

Staring through the binoculars, Cash consoled himself with the thought that at least this time he knew what he was looking for. The van Bill and Ted had used to bring their TVs from the gelato shop to their restaurant. They had borrowed it from the man who sold them the TVs. Given that the man had been meeting with Novak, perhaps he was the same man Turner had fought with.

An hour into his vigil, all Cash had seen were two dogs in the alley sniffing trash cans. He stood to stretch his aching legs. Something fluttering overhead spooked him. He looked up to see a bat's wings merge into the darkness.

A vehicle turned into the alley, prompting Cash to drop back behind the chimney rubble. It rolled past the pharmacy and stopped behind the gelato shop. The engine shut off and a man exited through the driver's door. He produced a set of keys, unlocked the door to the building, and disappeared inside.

Cash peered through the binoculars and identified the vehicle as a white cargo van. The fender had a dent identical to the one he had seen on the van at the pizza restaurant. It was the same van.

Cash crouched lower as two men came out of the building. It was too dark for him to make out their faces. One man propped the door open. The other opened the rear door of the van and hopped in. Metal clinked against metal. The man in the van barked a command and three women emerged from the vehicle. The men led them through the shop's rear door.

Unintelligible conversation drifted out of the building. A man's voice boomed, "Sit down. ¿*Comprende?*"

Several minutes passed without the men reappearing. Cash decided to risk inspecting the back of the van. He darted from cover and made his way to the vehicle. Inside, he saw a narrow wooden bench on either side of the cargo space. Three large eye hooks spaced two feet apart poked up from each bench. Short chains dangled from the eyehooks. Cash leaned in for a closer look. They weren't chains; they were handcuffs.

Cash heard voices in the doorway and froze. One of the men reappeared in the alley. There was no way Cash could run without being seen. He backed up several steps, turned around, and bent over with his hands on his knees.

"Hey, what are you doing?" the man said.

Cash didn't look up. He made a retching noise and staggered a few steps.

"Are you okay, buddy?"

He put up a hand, palm out, and retched again.

"Had one too many, eh?"

He nodded and took several deep breaths.

Dismissing Cash, the man got into the van. A second door slammed, and Cash knew the man's partner had joined him. Reeling as if drunk, Cash stumbled down the alley. As the van rolled past him, he turned his back to it and bent over. It rounded the corner and disappeared.

Cash straightened and checked his watch. Nine-thirty. Bill and Ted should still be up. Perhaps they could explain the handcuffs.

***

The pizza shop owners lived together in a house near their restaurant. As Cash approached it, he noticed a light shining through the living room window. At least one of them was awake. Judging by the lights in other houses on the block, so were some of the neighbors. To minimize the risk of being seen by one of them, Cash slipped around to the back of the house and rapped on the door. Recalling Bill's gun at the restaurant the other night, he pulled his Ruger.

"Who is it?" Bill said from the other side of the door.

Instead of answering, Cash knocked hard enough to rattle the door in its frame. When Bill pulled it open a crack, Cash pushed it in and charged into the house. Bill stumbled backward, catching himself on the kitchen table. Cash rushed up to him and shoved the pistol under his chin.

Ted appeared in the doorway. Spotting Cash's gun, he raised his hands and said, "What the hell?"

Cash said, "Let's all go into the den."

He had them sit side by side on a threadbare sofa. Keeping the gun trained on them, Cash lowered himself into an easy chair. "All right, boys, tell me what's going on."

They exchanged confused glances.

Bill said, "What the hell are you talking about?"

"I want to know about the guy who sold you the TVs. Who is he?"

"I told you, we don't know."

"Bullshit. What's his name?"

"Why don't you go fuck yourself?" said Bill. "You have no right to charge in here with a gun asking questions."

Cash pointed the gun at his chest. "They can put that on your tombstone, Bill. Killed by a guy with no right to be there. Now, who is this guy?"

Bill thrust out his chest. "Go ahead, tough guy. Shoot me. A defenseless man sitting in his own home."

Ted put a hand on his partner's knee. "Easy." He looked at Cash. "Bill's telling the truth. We don't know his name. We were told it would be best not to ask."

"By who?"

"Griff Turner. That said, we do know he's with Browning Electronics in Boerne."

Cash studied their faces. Seeing no telltale signs of lying, he said, "Did you notice what's in the back of that van?"

Ted said, "Nothing, really. A couple of benches."

"What about the handcuffs?"

A bewildered look spread across Ted's face. "Handcuffs? I don't know what you're talking about."

"Me either," said Bill.

"There were three women in the back of that van. I think they were kidnapped."

"Good Lord."

Ted said, "Honest to God, Cash, we don't know anything about that."

"How did you find this guy?"

"We didn't. Turner did. Last week he came in for a pizza—free, of course—and I mentioned we needed new TVs. The next thing we know, this guy shows up." He paused. "Can you put the gun away?"

"In a minute. What did he look like?"

Bill described him. Tall, well-built, thick head of brown hair. Around forty years old. Cash thought it could be one of the guys at the gelato shop.

"One last question. What are you leaving out?"

They looked at each other. Bill said, "Not a damned thing."

"Come on, you guys are hiding something."

"We might as well tell him," said Ted. "What's he going to do, arrest us?" He looked at Cash. "We bought some weed from the guy, too. That's why we don't know his name. He wouldn't tell us. Said he wants to stay anonymous."

"But you said he's Griff Turner's cousin."

"That's right. Turner blabbed that fact."

"Did Turner know about the weed?"

"He did. He got some from the guy, too. His was free. Just like his pizza."

Cash slid the gun into its holster. "All right, gents. I'll let you get on with your evening. But if I find out you lied to me, I'll be back."

"Maybe, maybe not," Bill said, still annoyed by the jolt of fear Cash had given him. "Clovis is still looking for you."

38

Cash used Steve's laptop to learn that Browning Electronics was owned by a man named Andrew Browning. An internet search for the name brought up only one hit, a Facebook site featuring several photographs of Browning holding up a fish he had just caught. Cash hadn't gotten a good look at either man at the gelato shop, but thought Browning resembled Bill Carpenter's description of the man who sold him the televisions.

Barry Novak had a higher profile. A biography on the gelato shop website said he had earned a degree in finance from Texas Tech University, followed by a law degree at the University of Texas. His earnings from a ten-year career at a "prestigious" law firm in Fort Worth allowed him to retire early to pursue "investment opportunities." These paid off well enough for him to establish two gelato shops, one in Fort Worth and one in Pinyon. He also owned an electronics store in the Fort Worth suburb of Saginaw.

Why Pinyon? Cash wondered. Why would a big-city lawyer with no apparent connection to the Hill Country bother selling gelato in a small, out-of-the-way Texas town? And how could a savvy business owner justify a shop that was open only two days a week?

Maybe Novak owned a ranch in Noble County. He wouldn't be the first rich out-of-towner to buy a chunk of Hill Country land on which to play cowboy. But a search of the county property records turned up only his ownership of the building on the square. Nor could Cash find any social media sites for the man.

Cash mulled over the coincidence of both Browning and Novak owning an electronics store. Cash didn't believe in coincidences. He checked the time on the laptop screen. Almost midnight. Time for a few hours of sleep before he hit the road for the electronics store in Boerne.

***

Browning Electronics proved to be a small store in a nondescript strip mall along Highway 87. Cash cruised past it without stopping and then drove through Boerne's historic downtown to reach a Walmart Supercenter a mile beyond. He purchased a box of powdered donuts, a pint of chocolate milk, and a magnetic vehicle-tracking device. Back in the truck, he devoured the snack before driving back to the electronics store. He was early, so he pulled into the parking lot to wait.

Twenty minutes later, the white panel van with the dented fender turned into the lot, circled behind the building, and disappeared. Soon after that, the lights in the store came on. A tall, thin man with dark hair appeared behind the glass door. Cash figured it was Andrew Browning. He unlocked the door and flipped a wall switch. An electronic "Open" sign flickered before settling into a steady red glow.

Cash got out of the truck and walked to the shop. When he opened the door, an electronic beep sounded. Browning saw him and smiled. "If there's anything I like, it's an eager customer."

Cash returned the smile. "I'm looking for a TV. I heard you were the guy to see."

"I am indeed. Can I ask who referred you?"

"Griff Turner."

Browning's smile faded. "Griff Turner? I don't believe I know him."

"How about Barry Novak? Or Bill Carpenter?"

"Mister, I don't know what you're talking about."

Cash came closer. "Are you sure about that? From what I hear, you and Turner are cousins. And I saw you behind Novak's shop up in Pinyon last night."

Browning retreated behind a nearby counter. Placing his hands on the glass, he said, "I'm afraid I have to ask you to leave."

"Look, I'm not here to make trouble. I'm just looking for a deal like you gave Carpenter and Hubbard."

"I don't want any trouble either. That's why I'd like you to leave."

"Come on, dude." Cash pasted a smile on his face. "It's just a couple of TVs. I'm a friend of Griff's."

Browning crossed his arms. "Griff Turner is dead."

Feigning regret, Cash said, "Yeah, that sucks. I hear he was murdered." When Browning said nothing, he added, "How about it? For Griff's sake?"

"I'll tell you what," Browning said, slipping a hand into his pants pocket and coming out with a phone. "You've got thirty seconds to get out of here before I call the police." He turned on the phone and held it up, ready to punch in a number.

Cash threw up his hands. "All right, all right. Geez, Bill said you'd be cool, but I guess he had that wrong."

"Guess so."

After Cash left, Browning placed a call, but not to the police.

"What do you want?"

"Some guy just came into my shop wanting a special deal on a TV."

"Big deal. I don't give a shit about your TV business."

"He said he wanted the same deal Bill Carpenter got."

A long silence passed. "What did he look like?"

"About six-two. Brown hair, cut short. No mustache or beard. Built like a jock."

"Shit. I think I know who that is."

"What do you want me to do?"

"Nothing. When are you coming back up here?"

Browning began pacing the floor. "Listen, maybe we ought to lay low for a while."

"Grow a pair, you son of a bitch. You can't back out now."

Browning screwed his eyes shut and thought of the warning from Kessler. "You're right. I'm just nervous, is all. I'll be back tomorrow tonight with a couple more."

***

After Cash left the electronics store, he drove two blocks and stopped at a coffee shop, where he bought a latte and a cinnamon bun and found a seat by the window. Reviewing his morning so far, he told himself that Browning and Novak had to be dirty. Turner had been as well, although Browning and Novak must have crossed a line that the sheriff wouldn't.

Cash finished the latte, left Steve's truck at the coffee shop, and walked the two blocks back to Browning's. As he drew near, he veered behind the building and crept up to the white van. After pulling the magnetic tracker from his pocket, he ducked behind the rear fender, felt for a smooth surface, and pushed the tracker against it. He heard the click as the magnet latched onto the metal. Satisfied, he jogged to the end of the building and returned to Steve's truck.

Cash settled into the driver's seat and closed his eyes. He replayed the encounter with Browning in his mind. The guy was hiding something. The tracking device gave him a chance to discover what it was. The next time Browning showed up in Pinyon, he'd be ready.

A sharp rap at the window jerked him from his thoughts. Cash looked to his left and his heart stopped. A Boerne policewoman peered in at him through the glass. He lowered his window. The world seemed to close in on him as he steeled himself for whatever came next.

The woman held up a small paper bag. "You forgot something."

The cinnamon bun. Cash could breathe again. He reached for the bag. "Thank you."

"I saw you leave without it. When you didn't get into your truck, I decided to wait until you came back. Any longer and I might have eaten it myself."

"I got back just in time, then."

The woman laughed. "Yes, you did. Well, have a good one."

"You too."

The policewoman left. Cash tossed the bag on the seat and exhaled a long breath. He closed his eyes and waited for his heart rate to slow. Once it did, he started the truck and headed back toward Pinyon. A smile crept onto his face. For the first time since going into hiding, he saw a glimmer of hope.

39

Bernadette loved animals. Dogs were her favorite, but anything that walked on four legs held a special place in her heart. At the moment, she was trying to calm a frightened mutt as her boss, Dr. Elizabeth Manor, prepared to give it an injection. The animal was small but strong and feisty. Some kind of terrier mix.

"You worry about the head and I'll take care of the rest," said Dr. Manor. "Just don't let him bite you."

"Oh, he doesn't bite," said the dog's owner, a frumpy woman with gray hair and a missing front tooth. "Brutus would never bite anyone."

Noting the frightened expression on the animal's face, as well as the sharp teeth an inch from her face, Bernadette wasn't so sure. She redoubled her hold and said, "It's okay, Brutus. You'll be fine."

Dr. Manor jabbed the needle into the dog's neck, pushed the plunger, and yanked the needle out. "All done."

Bernadette released the dog and patted its head. "Such a good boy."

"See," said the owner. "Brutus is a sweetheart."

A man's voice reached them from the lobby. Bernadette couldn't make out all the words but thought she heard her name. The door to the exam room opened and Dory, the receptionist, stuck her head in. "There's someone here to see you, Bernadette."

"Who?"

"I don't know. They're from the sheriff's department."

Bernadette looked over at her boss. Dr. Manor said, "Go on. I can take it from here."

As she followed Dory to the lobby, Bernadette rifled through her memory, trying to guess why a sheriff's deputy would visit her. Was it about the parties at Pete's? She hoped not. With her heart pounding in her chest, she approached the men and said, "I'm Bernadette."

"I'm Chief Deputy Ward," the tall one said. He gestured at the other uniformed man. "This is Deputy Noteboom."

"What's this about?"

"Is there someplace we can go to talk?"

Dory said helpfully, "Room three is empty."

Motioning for the two men to follow, Bernadette headed toward the empty exam room. When they reached the door, Ward put up a hand and said to his colleague, "Wait here."

Bernadette stepped into the room. Ward followed and shut the door. "What's going on?" she said, her voice trembling.

Ward said, "You're not in trouble. I just have a few questions about Sheriff Turner's murder. Did you hear about that?"

She nodded.

"We believe Adam Cash might be the sheriff's killer. We need to find him."

"Adam killed someone?" Bernadette said, feigning surprise as she raised a hand to her mouth.

"It would appear so."

"I don't know. He doesn't seem like that kind of person."

"They never do. Do you know where he is?"

She looked away. "I'm sorry, no."

"Are you sure?"

"Yes, I'm sure."

Ward studied her face, his eyes narrowing to slits. "It's against the law to lie to me."

"I know."

"And you have no idea where he is."

"No." After a moment's silence, she added, "I really don't."

Ward crossed his arms and adopted a sterner tone. "Let me lay it out for you. I think you're hiding something. And if that's the case, you'd be committing a serious crime. I'd have to arrest you."

Bernadette stared at the floor and said nothing.

"You have a baby, don't you? A little girl?"

She nodded.

"What do you think will happen to that baby if you go to prison?"

"I guess my momma would take care of her."

"Not true," said Ward. "Child Protective Services would step in and take her away. They'd put her in foster care. Maybe even put her up for adoption. You'd lose her forever."

Bernadette knew he was lying. She had a friend who had given up a baby for adoption. They had made her sign her name countless times before it was final. They had to have a mother's permission before allowing an adoption to go through. Unless the mother was abusing or neglecting the child. And she wasn't. She was taking good care of Emma. She would never do anything to hurt her.

"Mr. Ward. I mean, Sheriff Ward—"

"Chief Deputy."

"Sorry. Chief Deputy Ward, I'm telling you the truth. I don't know where he is. I haven't seen him since last week when he came by to visit the baby. He said he wanted to spend the night sometime so he could get to know her better, but I said no. That was before the sheriff was killed."

"Not long ago, Sheriff Turner told me he met you one night over at the gun range. He said it was quite a pleasant experience, that you two had a real nice time together out in his car."

Bernadette's face flushed crimson.

"I'm guessing you'd like to keep that information between you and me. Am I right?"

The implied threat pushed a button in Bernadette. She straightened her back, thrust out her chin, and said, "I don't care what you say. I don't know where he is. Now please go."

The outburst seemed to surprise Ward. He took a half step back. "All right. I hear you loud and clear." He spun around, ripped the door open, and marched away.

Out in the parking lot, Noteboom said, "How did it go in there?"

"Not good," Ward said with a grunt. "She wouldn't tell me shit. She's hiding something."

"How do you know?"

"She avoided eye contact, seemed overly nervous. Then she got defensive and threw me out of the room."

"So, what now?"

"I want you to watch her. Follow her if she goes anywhere. If my hunch is correct, she'll eventually lead us right to him."

40

On the drive back to Pinyon, Cash remembered a loose end he needed to tie up. He turned off the highway at the next gas station. Using the burner phone, he made a call.

"Noble County sheriff's department. How can I help you?"

"Vicky, is that you?"

"Who is this?"

"Adam Cash. Don't say anything. I just need a phone number."

"Okay."

"Can you get me the cell number for Frida Simmons?"

"Hold on a second."

Cash heard her tapping on a keyboard, and then she came back on the line.

"Got something to write with?"

"No. Just give me the number."

She recited it to him.

"Thanks."

"Don't forget you promised to take me dancing."

Cash had hoped she wouldn't remember his earlier promise. "I won't." He ended the call and tapped in Frida's number.

"Frida Simmons."

"Frida it's me, Cash. I mean Adam. Are you in a place you can talk?"

"Give me five minutes and call me back."

He stuck the phone in his pocket and checked his wallet to see how much cash he had left. Fifty bucks. With time to kill, he pulled the truck over to the gas pump. He told the clerk inside he wanted forty dollars' worth of gas and handed over two twenties. Spotting several copies of the *Boerne Star*, he laid another dollar on the counter.

Back in the truck, Frida answered his call on the first ring.

"What's up?"

"Can anybody hear you?"

"No. I'm out in my car."

"What did you find on that napkin I gave you?"

"You were right. It is blood."

"Do you know what type?"

"Human."

Cash rolled his eyes. "No, I mean, what's the blood type?"

"Oh, A negative."

"Does that match Griff Turner's?"

"Yeah. Where did you find this thing?"

"Never mind. Thanks."

He poised a finger to end the call when he heard Frida say, "Whose phone are you using?"

"It's a burner."

"Can they trace your location with it?"

"No, it doesn't have GPS. The best they could do is get a general location. Of course, somebody would have to tell them the number for that."

"I won't say anything. But if they find you and take the phone, my number will be in the call history."

Cash winced. "That's right."

"Please don't call again."

"Frida, I—"

"I have to go." The line went dead.

***

Back in Pinyon, Cash parked behind the brewery and hurried into the building. He wanted to talk to Steve, but the brewpub was already open, so he didn't dare show his face upstairs. He settled onto his sleeping bag with the *Boerne Star* and waited.

A half-hour later, Steve came bouncing down the stairs. "You're back," he said. "Have you made any progress?"

"Yeah, maybe. I need you to do something for me."

"What?"

"Check out all the cafes, restaurants, fast-food joints, and coffee shops in town."

"What am I looking for?"

"I found a napkin in the park where Turner's body turned up. It has his blood on it."

Steve scoffed. "You want me to look for napkins? Seriously?"

"I want you to look for a particular type of napkin. This one was light tan, with brown and orange leaves around the edges."

"Oh. Okay."

"Put Edie on it, too. You guys can divide and conquer."

"What are you going to do?"

Cash picked up the newspaper. "I'm going to work a crossword puzzle."

41

Andrew Browning's van remained in Boerne overnight. From the electronics shop, it traveled 1.2 miles to an address on Graham Street. Cash pulled the address up on Google Maps and saw a small limestone house surrounded by a six-foot cedar fence. Browning probably lived there.

Cash lay on his sleeping bag, contemplating his next move. The gun range and pizza restaurant had turned out to be dead ends. But Browning was bringing women to Pinyon in handcuffs. Griff Turner was Browning's cousin. He had threatened to arrest Browning for something they fought about at the gun range. Is that what got Turner killed?

Then there was the napkin with Turner's blood on it. An unknown person had murdered Turner and moved his body to Erfurt Park. A bloody napkin was left behind.

The identity of the second man behind the gelato shop remained a mystery. It would remain a mystery at least until the van returned. And Cash couldn't very well search the town's cafes and coffee shops for the napkin. Steve and Edie would have to manage that. Therefore, all he could do now was wait for their report.

***

The van was on the move. After leaving the electronics shop, it threaded its way through Boerne to reach Interstate 10 and head south toward San Antonio. After a fifteen-minute stop in the Alamo City, it reversed direction and returned to Boerne. Cash expected it to stop at Browning's store, but instead, it bypassed the town and made for Junction. Cash assumed its destination was Pinyon, so he readied himself for another stakeout. He shed his Dallas Cowboys T-shirt for one that was solid black. For the hundredth time since going into hiding, he checked the load in his Ruger and shoved the weapon back into its holster. An extra clip went into his pocket. He fished his pocket-sized Maglite out of his backpack and clicked it on. It cast a strong, unwavering beam. He was ready to go.

Feeling his stomach rumble, Cash downed two granola bars and the last of his apples. He checked the Ruger one last time. Patting his pocket for the Maglite, he headed out into the night.

Keeping to the shadows cast by the streetlights, Cash made his way to the park entrance and entered the alley behind Novak's place. Arriving at the ruins of the house directly behind the shop, he spotted a panel van parked in the alley. Was he too late? No, the fender was intact. Also, Browning drove a white van. This one was tan.

Cash crouched in the same spot he had spied from the other night. A misting rain began falling. He wished he had brought a hat. The rain intensified, soaking his T-shirt until it clung to his skin. A light breeze kicked up, and he shivered from the sudden cold.

Headlights appeared at the end of the alley. Cash peered through the weeds as a white van approached. Tires crunched gravel as the vehicle swung around and parked beside the first van. The driver doused the headlights and dropped onto the pavement. Cash recognized Andrew Browning. He ducked his head as Browning turned in his direction. Cash's staring must have alerted him. Moments later,

Cash heard the shop's back door swing open and shut. When he peered over the top of the rubble pile, Browning was gone.

The building's back door squeaked open and a man stepped outside. It was too dark for Cash to make out the face, but the enormous frame and muscular build told him it was somebody he hadn't seen before. The man swung open the back door of the van and peered inside. Browning joined him. "Bring them inside," said the larger man. He retrieved several fast-food sacks from the van's front seat and disappeared back into the building.

Browning hopped into the van. Metal clinked against metal. He reappeared and motioned with his hand. "Come on. *Andale*."

Stretching their legs and rubbing their wrists, two women emerged from the vehicle. Browning gestured, and they followed him into the building.

Cash stood up and hurried to the shop's rear. Drawing his Ruger, he took hold of the door handle and tugged. Without making a sound, the door swung open a few inches. He put an ear to the gap and heard muffled conversation. Easing the door open just wide enough to accommodate him, he slipped through the opening. He held his breath as the door clicked back into place. The muffled conversation continued.

Cash found himself in a narrow hallway. Up ahead, he could see a sliver of the shop's dining area. No people were visible. A closed door with a sign reading "Rest Room" stood to his left. To his right was the kitchen, dark and empty. He tiptoed down the hall until he could see Browning and the tall man seated at a small table. Both men munched a cheeseburger. Two cardboard boxes sat on the table, each one filled with pill bottles. The two women sat at another table, heads down, hands in their laps. Untouched bags of food sat in front of them.

Browning said, "Where's Judd?"

"Taking a dump."

"Did you tell him to use the air freshener this time when he's done?"

"I'm not sure he knows how to use a spray can."

They both laughed.

Judd? Could that be Judd Noteboom? It was time to get some answers. Heart thumping against his ribcage, Cash stepped into the room. The tall man looked up. His puffy face and large gut suggested this wasn't his first cheeseburger.

Noticing the confused expression on his companion's face, Browning spun around in his chair. His eyes popped wide as he recognized Cash. "You!"

"Do you know this guy?" the tall man asked.

"He was in my shop. He wanted me to give him the same deal we gave Bill Carpenter."

The tall man smirked and lifted his gaze to Cash. "You must want a TV real bad."

Keeping the gun aimed at the men, Cash took another step into the room. He nodded at the boxes of pill bottles. "What is that?"

Browning said, "I'll tell you what it is. It's none of your fucking business."

"Easy, Andy," said the tall man. "Let's see what our uninvited guest wants." He shrugged at Cash. "So? What can we do for you?"

Cash said, "Are you Barry Novak."

"Who's asking."

"Never mind. Are you?"

"I am. Who are you?"

"Who's Judd?"

"A friend."

"Is it Judd Noteboom?" When there was no answer, he said, "You kidnapped those women, didn't you?"

Novak laughed. "You're one nosy son of a bitch, aren't you?"

"Was Griff Turner part of this?"

"Part of what?"

Cash gestured at the women. "This. Human trafficking."

"Again, not really your business. Come to think of it, I can't think of a good reason for us to sit here and let you interrogate us."

"Because I'm holding the gun, asshole."

Novak stood. "The thing is, I don't think you're going to use it."

Cash pointed the gun at the big man's chest. "Sit down. And keep your hands where I can see them." Novak sat. "I want the man who killed Griff Turner. You're going to tell me who that is."

Novak arched an eyebrow. "I know who you are. You're the guy they want for killing the sheriff."

"Who killed him, damn it?"

"Cash, isn't it? Is that your first or last name? Never mind, it doesn't matter. As for Turner, you're barking up the wrong tree. So why don't you do yourself a favor and get the hell out of here before you get hurt?"

"If it wasn't one of you, just tell me who it was. That's all I want."

"I guess you're just going to have to kill us." He fingered the metal napkin holder on the table. "Because we're not telling you shit."

Cash glanced at the two women. He couldn't leave them with Novak and Browning. "Ladies, come with me. I'll get you out of here."

Novak said, "Nice try, but they don't know a word of English."

As Cash's eyes flitted between the two men, a commode flushed from behind the closed bathroom door. When Cash glanced in the direction of the noise, Novak grabbed the napkin holder and flung it at him. Cash ducked, but Novak produced a gun from his waist and fired, the bullet blasting out a chunk of drywall inches from Cash's head. Before Novak could fire again, Cash fled into the hall, arriving just as the bathroom door cracked open. He yanked it shut and burst through the back door into a driving rain. As he ran, he heard Novak shout, "Tell Judd to watch the women."

Cash raced toward the park. Twenty feet behind him, Novak fired a shot that whistled overhead.

Panting, Browning said, "Cut it out. This isn't Fort Worth."

"Shut the fuck up."

"I'm telling you, man, keep it up and the whole town will be on us."

Cash sped into the park and passed the gazebo. He turned to see Novak and Browning round the corner and sprint after him. He felt confident he could kneel and pick them off but shooting them would complicate his quest to clear his name. Maybe even destroy it altogether. He darted through the state park gate at the rear of Erfurt Park and turned right, toward the riverbank. Maybe he could lose his pursuers in the thick vegetation that had been his childhood playground.

Another shot rang out and Browning shouted something unintelligible. Spotting the familiar sycamore tree that marked the entrance to the otherwise impenetrable thicket, Cash hooked to his left and followed the narrow path to the river. He heard Novak swear as he and Browning stumbled about looking for a way in.

Cash reached the water's edge. He holstered his pistol and, taking care not to splash, stepped off the bank and into the river. Massive raindrops pelted his head and face as he pushed away from shore. Using a silent breaststroke, he swam toward the opposite bank. If he could put enough distance between himself and his pursuers, he would disappear into the inky darkness.

Another minute of swimming brought Cash to the opposite bank. Grabbing a cypress root to keep the current from pulling him downstream, he turned to check on his pursuers. He saw a man—he thought it was Browning but couldn't be sure in the dim light—burst through the bushes and trip, falling face-first into the mud. Another man, presumably Novak, emerged behind him. Ignoring the first man, he peered up and down the shoreline. The first man climbed to his feet and held a brief conversation with his companion. Cash heard their hoarse whispers but couldn't make out the words. The men turned and plunged back into the thicket.

Cash hauled himself out of the water. A stiff breeze was blowing, but he ignored the chill and focused on what he had learned. Barry Novak and Andrew Browning were trafficking immigrant women. Presumably, Browning brought them up from Boerne in his van. Novak then took them to Fort Worth. Given the boxes of pill bottles Cash saw, the pair might also be moving illegal drugs.

Cash slogged back to the brewery. He regretted leaving the women behind, but what he would have done with them? He promised himself that, in addition to proving his innocence, he'd find a way to break up this trafficking ring.

Back at the Packsaddle Cash activated Steve's laptop and checked on Browning's van. It was already heading back toward Boerne. He figured Novak was already on his way to Fort Worth. Pondering his next move, he changed out of his wet clothes and dropped onto his sleeping bag. He closed his eyes, but sleep eluded him. He had a possible motive for the sheriff's death, and those two men were evil enough to do it. But how did a dummy like Judd Noteboom fit into the picture?

42

Co-owning a small-town pizza restaurant fulfilled Bill Carpenter's wildest dream. Five years ago he never imagined that one day he'd have such good fortune. Bill had never held a job longer than two years, hopping from one menial position to the next, never making more than just enough to pay the rent, buy food, and stock the refrigerator with cheap beer. On the other hand, he had never gone hungry or slept without a roof over his head. He would have told anyone who asked that he was content with his lot in life. But was he happy? No.

Then he met Ted Hubbard. Ted was a go-getter. To Bill, he seemed always to be reaching for the next rung of the ladder. Ted had started out by working as a mechanic in his uncle's motorcycle repair shop in San Marcos. By the time the older man's heart condition forced his retirement, Ted had saved enough money to buy him out. A year later, he sold the business and used the proceeds to earn a finance degree from Texas State University. After graduation, he scored a job in the billing department of Central Texas Medical Center and began dabbling in online day trading. The latter proved successful enough for him to quit his hospital job, move to Pinyon with Bill, and buy the pizza restaurant.

They met at a Halloween party given by a mutual friend. Bill came dressed as Peter Pan, Ted as a pirate. Ted pulled a hand into his sleeve and introduced himself as Peter Pan's nemesis Captain Hook. Bill found that hilarious. The two of them spent the evening together, swapping stories and lustful glances. After the party, Ted invited Bill to his house for a drink. They spent the night in bed and had been inseparable ever since.

These days Bill would say that not only was he content, he was happy as well. He and Ted lived in a comfortable house. They owned and operated the pizza restaurant together. Pizza was Bill's favorite food. He could have all he wanted. As much as he liked pizza, he liked beer even more. He could have all he wanted of that as well. Bill was in heaven.

Ted didn't share Bill's fondness for beer. On the nights that Bill started drinking, Ted would close the restaurant, go home, and go to bed. Bill would click on a TV in the restaurant dining room, take a seat at the bar by the beer taps, and drink himself into a stupor. He might smoke a little weed, too. Then he'd stumble to a cot in the back office and fall asleep until morning.

This was one of those nights. Ted had gone home, and Bill found a Texas Rangers game on TV. By the time the game ended, he had worked his way through six pints of beer. After relieving himself of what felt like a gallon of urine, he crawled onto his cot.

A loud pounding on the front door woke him up. Still wobbly from the beer, Bill rose and took his gun from the desk drawer. He crept down the hall into the dining room and saw two women banging on the window. Staggering toward them, he shouted, "What the hell are you doing?"

The women began chattering in Spanish. Bill didn't understand a word, but they looked desperate, so he unlocked the door. They burst inside. Startled, he raised his gun. They fell to their knees, pleading.

"Ladies, ladies," said Bill. "What's going on?"

Their pleading intensified.

He lowered the gun. "I'm not going to hurt you. Do either of you speak English?"

"Help. *Por favor*," said one of the women.

"Help you with what? Jesus Christ, it's late."

The front door swung open, and a man charged inside. Bill's mouth fell open. "Noteboom?"

Ignoring Bill, Noteboom pointed a gun at the women. "Let's go," he shouted. "Back outside."

The women screamed and huddled behind Bill.

Bill said, "What the hell are you doing? Who are these women?"

Noteboom aimed his gun at Bill's face. "Stay out of this, Bill. Set your gun on that table."

"First, tell me what the hell you're doing here."

"Put the goddamned gun down."

"Put yours down first."

With a quickness that caught Bill by surprise, Noteboom lunged forward and grabbed one of the women by the hair, knocking her hair clip to the floor. The woman screamed.

Bill's neck flushed hot. The son of a bitch had broken into his restaurant and was giving him orders? Pushing women around? Making them scream? Screw that. He shook his head to quell the lingering beer-induced dizziness. "God damn it, Noteboom, get the hell out of my restaurant."

They glared at each other. Bill's breathing quickened as the world seemed to close in on him. So what if Noteboom had a gun? He had one, too. Noteboom was an intruder. He was defending his territory.

Bill jerked his hand up and fired. His shot went wide and smashed into a television, sending a spray of glass and plastic particles onto the counter. Noteboom fired as well, and the bullet struck Bill in the middle of his chest. As his vision darkened, Bill squeezed the trigger again, but his arm was dropping as if weighted with lead. His shot buried itself in the floor. Eyelids sagging, he sank to his knees. The last thing he saw before slipping away was the mounted javelina snarling at him from behind the bar.

43

Cash rummaged through his bag of groceries and found two granola bars and a banana. The chocolate milk was long gone. He peeled the banana and took a bite. Footsteps sounded overhead, then on the stairway. Steve rushed into the basement. His breaths came in quick gasps. "Bill Carpenter's dead."

Cash blinked. "What?"

"Somebody broke into his restaurant last night and shot him. Ward and his guys are over there now. They've got it blocked off while they wait for Frida."

"Who found the body?"

"Ted. He's pretty shook up."

Poor Ted, Cash thought. His relationship with Bill was an open secret in Pinyon. Cash had heard an occasional negative comment around town, mostly from those he knew to be evangelical Christians, racist rednecks, or both. Could this be a hate crime? As strongly as he disagreed with certain people making homophobic statements, he couldn't picture any of them resorting to murder.

"I need to talk to him."

"It will have to be later. He's over at the restaurant right now. I imagine Ward is grilling him. You could call him on your burner. I have his number in my contacts."

"With Ward there? No way."

"I mean later. I'll keep watch and let you know when he leaves."

"Don't forget you're looking for that napkin."

"You know I have a life, right?"

"You know I'm looking at life in prison, right?"

"Calm down. I'll get it done."

***

"Looks like a robbery gone bad."

Santos raised an eyebrow. "Hubbard said nothing was stolen."

"That he's willing to admit," Ward said, his eyes fixed on Bill Carpenter's corpse.

"What does that mean?"

"What if he was dealing drugs? Maybe he stiffed somebody, and they didn't like it."

"Should we get Hubbard back here and ask him?"

"No, don't bother. He's a mess right now."

"What do you suggest we do?"

Ward shrugged. "There's not much to go on, is there? We found the front door unlocked. Our perpetrator came in, got caught by Carpenter. The guy shot him and left. End of story."

"We could dust for prints."

"That's Frida's job. She can pull the bullet too. See what kind of gun it came from."

"Maybe there are footprints outside."

Ward sauntered toward the front door. "I'll tell you what. You go take a look and let me know what you find. I'll be back at the office writing up the report."

***

An old clock hung on the basement wall near the stairwell entrance. It reminded Cash of the ones from his days at Pinyon High School. Black rim, white face, plain numbers. He had spent a lot of time in school staring at those clocks, waiting for the bell to ring. Now he stared at the one in Steve's basement, wondering how long he should wait before calling Ted Hubbard. A week was probably too soon. He'd give it an hour and a half.

Ted answered on the fourth ring. "Hello?"

"Ted, it's Cash."

There was a long silence. "What do you want"?

Cash drew a deep breath. "First, let me say how sorry I am to hear about Bill. You must feel terrible."

"Did you have anything to do with it?"

"Why would you say that?"

Cash heard Ted's scoff through the phone. "Think I've forgotten you holding a gun on us in our living room?"

"Ted, I swear, it wasn't me. I'm wondering if this might be related to Sheriff Turner's death."

"Why would you think that?"

"Are you somewhere you can talk?"

"I'm at home."

"Are you alone?"

"Now that Bill's gone, yes."

Cash chose his next words carefully, not wanting to irritate Ted enough for him to hang up. "There aren't a lot of murders in Pinyon, are there?"

"Not until now."

"Exactly. What are the odds we'd get two in a week? Unless they're connected, that is."

"Maybe you're right. Still, I can't see a link."

"Nothing was taken, right?"

"Right."

"Could there have been something in there you didn't know about?"

"Like what?"

Cash hesitated. He knew his next sentence could end the phone call. "Could Bill have been selling drugs?"

"Hell no." Ted's anger was clear. "He hasn't touched that shit in years."

"Sorry. I'm just thinking out loud. Did you find anything out of the ordinary when you came in this morning?"

"No ... wait a minute. There was a hair clip on the floor."

"A hair clip? Couldn't that have been dropped by a customer?"

"Sure. But I swept last night before I left. Seems like I would have found it then."

Cash thought back to seeing the women at Novak's place. Browning and Novak had left them behind when they chased him out of the shop. Maybe the women escaped and fled to the pizza joint. Whoever had been in the shop's bathroom could have followed them there. Had either of them been wearing a hair clip? He couldn't remember.

"What was Bill doing at the restaurant so late?"

Ted explained about Carpenter's late night drinking sessions.

Cash said. "Sounds like he was just in the wrong place at the wrong time."

"It was just bad luck?" Ted's voice was cracking.

"I'm really sorry."

"Cash, who did this?"

"I have an idea, Ted, but I need more proof. Believe me, I want to find the bastard as much as you do."

44

Steve sighed and said, "I'm sorry, Cash. I struck out. Most places just had white napkins. A few had logos, like the Dairy Queen and Subway. Nothing with leaves."

"That's okay. Thanks for trying."

Cash sat with Steve and Edie on dining room chairs that Steve had carried down to the basement. Edie placed a hand on Cash's knee and said, "Why don't you turn yourself in? Get yourself a good lawyer and beat this thing."

Cash shook his head. "Even if I got off, a cloud would always be hanging over my head. People would look at me and see the guy accused of murdering their sheriff. There's no way I could stay in this town."

"That sounds harsh."

He ignored the comment. "Where did you look?"

Edie counted the places off on her hand. "The Firewheel, of course. Also, the Dillo, Bessie's Coffee, both gas stations, the catfish place by the Valero. I even checked the hardware store. I remembered they've got a coffee pot behind the counter."

Cash nodded at Steve. "And you?"

"I checked all the fast-food places."

"Why am I not surprised? Which ones?"

"Subway, Chicken Express, Sonic, and the Dairy Queen."

That seemed to cover every place in town. The napkin was his best—no, his only—piece of physical evidence and so far it had gotten him no closer to solving the crime. "What do you guys know about the gelato shop owner? His name is Barry Novak."

"Not much," said Steve. "I've only seen him once. He came in and had a couple of beers. I introduced myself and we shook hands. That's about it. Big, scary-looking guy."

Edie said, "I've never met him. As far as I know, he's never been to the Firewheel. I had gelato at his place once, but a high school kid served me."

Steve's phone buzzed with a text. He glanced at it and stood up. "I have to get back upstairs."

Cash watched Steve go with a sinking heart. Would he ever be able to show himself in Pinyon again? He smiled at Edie and said, "Thanks for trying."

As they stood up, Edie stepped in close. "Don't give up."

"Thanks."

She smiled, and Cash felt his knees go wobbly. Would she ever fail to have that effect on him?

Noticing his weakness, Edie caressed his hand. They stared at each other so long Cash had to resist the urge to fall into her arms. She lifted her head and pecked his lips, sending an electric shock down his spine. As she turned to leave, she said, "I'm rooting for you, cowboy."

45

Bernadette dipped the tiny spoon into the jar of mashed green beans and brought it to her daughter's mouth. The child squealed with delight, latched onto the spoon, and licked it dry. "You're a bottomless pit," Bernadette said. Her phone rang and she stuck the spoon back into the jar. "Sorry, baby, I'll get back to you." She picked up the phone and held it to her ear. "Hello."

"Bernadette, it's Steve. I wonder if you could do something for me."

"What?"

"It's really for Cash. He's out of food."

"Is he broke?"

"No, but he can't access his money. If he uses a credit card or ATM card, they'll find him. And I'm swamped. The Lowe's over in Junction wants ten cases of pale ale, and I don't have it canned yet."

"Oh. What do you want me to do?"

"Could you go to Lowe's and pick some stuff up? I can tell you what to get."

"You run a restaurant. You don't have food there?"

"He wants some things I don't have."

"Like what?"

"Granola bars, chocolate milk ..."

"I can't afford to be buying him food," Bernadette said.

"I'll pay you back. I'll even throw in an extra twenty bucks."

Twenty bucks? She could always use a little extra cash. "Okay."

"Great. I'll text you a list."

***

Bernadette tossed the bag of apples onto the conveyor belt and said, "That's it."

The checker, an ex-classmate named Kelly, said, "Weren't you just here yesterday?"

"Momma needed some things."

Kelly scanned the last item on the belt. "She must really like chocolate milk. I didn't even know it came in gallon jugs."

***

"Here's fifty bucks," said Steve as he handed Bernadette several bills. "Thirty for the food and twenty for you."

"What about gas money?"

"Gas money? You live, what, three blocks from the store?"

"I had to drive here, too."

Steve frowned but handed her another five.

"Thanks." She pocketed the money. "Has he found the sheriff's killer yet?"

"It's probably best if we don't talk about that."

"Oh, okay. Bye."

Steve scooped up the groceries and headed for the stairwell. Bernadette crossed the Packsaddle's empty dining room and pushed through the door to reach the sidewalk. As she climbed into her twelve-year-old Hyundai Accent, she failed to notice the man in the late model Ram 2500 pickup truck parked a half block away. She fired up the Hyundai's engine and sped off.

Seated in the Ram, Deputy Judd Noteboom muttered, "Bingo." The corners of his mouth curled up to form a smug grin as he watched the Hyundai disappear. He reached for his phone.

46

Clovis Ward couldn't decide if he wanted to see the woman or not. On the one hand, he needed to question her. On the other, their first face-to-face encounter in a decade would be awkward. As Ward eased the squad car to a stop in front of the suburban ranch house, he decided he hoped that she was home. That would at least satisfy his curiosity.

A long-forgotten tingling sensation tickled Ward's gut as he marched up the sidewalk. He rang the bell and stepped back so he'd be visible through the peephole. Heavy footsteps thudded inside the house. That could only be Del, the woman's husband. Damn. Well, he needed to talk to him, too.

The door swung open. A fifty-year-old man with a slight paunch and gray-flecked hair stood before him. A tense moment of silence crept by. Ward opened his mouth to speak, but the man stepped forward and swung a roundhouse punch that just clipped his chin. The chief deputy staggered but stayed upright.

"What the hell?" Ward said, rubbing his chin. It had been a glancing blow. Enough to hurt, but not that much.

The man glared and puffed up his chest as if ready for more. "I told you I'd kick your ass the next time you came to my house."

"You do see this uniform, don't you?"

"Go ahead, big shot. Try and arrest me."

"God damn it, Del. I'm here on official business."

Del scoffed. His body relaxed, but his icy stare remained. "You know you're in Austin, right? That's a long way from Pinyon."

Ward raised his hands in a gesture of peace. "I just want to talk to you."

"All right. Talk."

"Can I come in? Or do you want your neighbors calling you about the sheriff on your porch?"

"You're not a sheriff. You're a deputy."

"Acting sheriff. That's one of the things I want to talk to you about."

Del hesitated. Ward resisted the urge to shove the man into the house and barge in after him. His patience was rewarded when Del jerked his head and said, "Five minutes."

Del led Ward into a sunken living room with furniture that looked as if it had been delivered yesterday. Ward took in the leather couch, walnut coffee table, and seventy-five-inch wall-mounted TV. "Looks like the HVAC business has been good to you."

Del settled into a lounge chair. "I can't complain."

Ward waited for an invitation to sit, but none came. Ignoring the snub, he removed his hat and dropped onto the couch.

"Okay, what do you want?"

"It's about your son. Adam." That got the bastard's attention.

"Is he okay?"

"He's fine. Unfortunately, Griff Turner isn't."

"What are you talking about?"

"Somebody killed him a few days ago." Ward paused to search for the right words. "The evidence we've collected so far suggests that Adam may have done it."

Del stared at Ward as if he had just sprouted a second nose. "You're out of your goddamn mind. Adam wouldn't kill anyone. At least, not without a good reason."

"I know this is hard to believe. It's just—"

"Hard to believe?" Del said, his voice rising. "It's bullshit. You've got the wrong man."

"Like I said, we have firm evidence that Adam is the perpetrator."

"What evidence?"

Ward explained about the bottle with Cash's fingerprints.

"How do you know it's the murder weapon?"

"There were traces of blood on it. Griff's blood."

"Hell, that doesn't prove anything. Maybe he found it after the fact. Maybe that's why his prints are on it."

"I'm sorry, Del, but we found it in his car. And he's gone on the run. We've been looking for him for several days."

"Let me get this straight," Del said, his brow wrinkling in disbelief. "You want to arrest my son for murder?"

"Have you seen or heard from him lately?"

"Answer my question."

"Yes." Noting the look of disbelief on Del's face, he added, "We want to arrest Adam for murder."

Del took a deep breath. "Something doesn't add up. I think you're chasing the wrong guy."

Ward kept quiet. He had expected this response. There was nothing to be gained by arguing.

Out in the foyer, the front door opened and closed. A woman stepped into the living room and froze. Sparkling eyes, petite figure, and brown hair that bounced with every step. Ward felt his heart skip a beat as his gaze wandered over her face and body. He recalled the feel of her fingers caressing his chest, her moist lips against his, her tongue tickling his ear. The endearing gasps that slipped from her mouth during the act. Her head on his shoulder afterward. The intoxicating aroma of that thick, curly hair.

"Hello, Janet," Ward said.

"Clovis." Her eyes flitted to her husband.

Del said, "Have a seat."

She scooted an ottoman next to her husband's chair and sat down. Her lips pressed into a thin line as she cast a wary glance at Ward. "What's going on?"

Del cleared his throat. "Clovis thinks our son killed Griff Turner."

Her lips parted. Bright red lips. Ward had always loved that color on her. "Griff Turner is dead?"

Ward said, "He is."

"I'm sorry to hear that. First Carter, now his son."

"That kid was always a bully," said Del.

Janet said, "And you think Adam killed him? That's impossible."

"That's what I've been saying," said Del, bitterness in his voice. "It's a load of horse manure."

Ward locked eyes with Janet. Hers were as gorgeous as ever. "I'm sorry, Janet. It's true."

"I don't know what to say. Adam never hurt anyone."

"I have to ask. Have you been in contact with him recently?"

"No. I, uh, the last time we spoke was about a week and a half ago." She fell silent, puzzling through this strange visit. "You've got it wrong, Clovis. Adam's not a murderer."

"He's in danger, Janet. I need to find him." His thoughts shifted to Cash's siblings: Reid, an Austin musician, and Emily, a pediatric nurse. "Would he be in contact with his brother or sister?"

"You leave them out of it." Her voice was cold. "I have nothing else to say. Please go now."

"Did you hear what I said? Don't you care about him? Don't you see he needs help?"

Janet leaped from the ottoman. "Don't I care about my own son? What kind of idiotic question is that? I've asked you to leave. Now I'm telling you. Go."

Ward rose. "If there's something you're not telling me, you're committing a crime."

"Fuck off, Clovis," Del said, jerking himself out of the lounge chair. "Now get the hell out of our house."

Ward's jaw tightened. He glowered at Del. A dumb son of a bitch like him didn't deserve a woman like Janet. "You're making a big mistake." He looked at Janet, and his gaze softened. What he wouldn't give for one more night with her. "What do you think, Janet?"

Janet strode past him to the front door. She yanked it open. "Goodbye, Clovis."

As he passed her, he studied her face for any vestige of the tenderness he remembered. There was none.

Outside, Ward got behind the wheel of his squad car and swore. He promised himself he'd make them pay for their hostility. Even Janet. She should have left that bastard Del when she had the chance. His phone rang. He fished it from his pocket and held it to his ear. "Ward."

"How did it go with the parents?" It was Noteboom.

"How do you think? It was a real shitshow."

"Well, I've got some news that should cheer you up."

"What?"

"I found him."

47

Janet slammed the door shut. Del stood transfixed, his mind trying to process the fact that his son was wanted for murder.

"What are we going to do?" Janet said.

Del began pacing. "That son of a bitch. This is payback for you dumping him ten years ago. I can't believe you ever slept with the guy."

"Let's focus on the present, shall we?"

Del didn't want to scour the past any more than she did. "You're right. We've got to think about Adam."

"Why hasn't he called us?"

"Didn't you hear what Clovis said? He went on the run. If he used his phone, they'd be able to find him."

"So where is he?"

Del resumed his pacing. "Adam's a fighter. And he's not stupid. The only reason he'd have run is that he's innocent and he wants to clear himself. So where would he go?"

"He'd have to stay in Pinyon to clear himself."

"Right. Otherwise, how could he solve the crime?"

"Maybe he's at the ranch. Not in the house but hiding somewhere in the woods."

"He can't work from the woods. It's too far from town."

Janet snapped her fingers. "I know. Do you remember that fight you two had when he was in high school?"

"Yeah. He drove off and said he wasn't coming back."

"He was gone for two days. Where did we find him?"

Del's face brightened as he caught Janet's drift. "He was holed up with Steve Jenkins."

"Right. He's at the Packsaddle."

***

"Son of a bitch," said Ward, almost dropping his phone. Of course. Steve Jenkins. Cash's old high school buddy. Why hadn't he thought of that?

"Is something wrong?"

"Did you see him?"

"No. I've been following Bernadette, like you said. She just took two bags of groceries into the brewpub. She came out empty-handed."

"Maybe they're for somebody else."

"Who? Jenkins runs a restaurant. He's not getting his supplies from Lowe's."

"Good point."

"What do you want me to do?"

Ward drummed his fingers on the squad car's steering wheel. Noteboom couldn't go in by himself. He needed backup. Either Conrad or Santos was likely nearby, but Ward wanted to be the one to arrest Cash. That would go a long way toward proving to the county commissioners that they should appoint him sheriff. Noteboom would have to wait. "Get Santos over there. Put him on the back door and you stay out front. Wait for me. I'll be there as soon as I can."

"You're over three hours away."

"I'll drive fast."

"What if he leaves?"

Ward slammed a fist into the steering wheel. "Then follow him, damn it. I want to be there for the arrest. Am I clear?"

"Yes, sir."

"Good. Keep me posted."

***

Del Cash made it to Pinyon in record time, just under three and a half hours. After cruising past the peach stand at the edge of town, he slowed to a stop at Pinyon's only traffic light. Correction, there were two now, another one having been installed near the Tractor Supply a few years ago. Still not enough to give him any regrets about leaving the place. Why his son had been so hell-bent on coming back here remained a mystery.

He turned left onto Mesquite Street, and his heart stopped. At the far end of the block, parked in front of the Packsaddle, was a sheriff's squad car. Its lights flashed in a sickening rhythm, reminding Del of a ticking time bomb about to explode. He was too late. Clovis Ward had beaten him to the punch. With his gut roiling, Del backed his Ford Taurus into an empty spot, switched off the engine, and watched.

Santos paced the alley behind Packsaddle Brewing, agonizing about his role in Cash's impending arrest. He harbored significant doubts about his fellow veteran's guilt, but he had to admit they had no leads on another suspect. Yet what about all the unanswered questions? How had the supposed murder weapon gotten into Cash's car? Why had the body been moved? Where had the murder taken place? They had searched Cash's house and found nothing suggesting it as the location. Ward and Noteboom searched Griff Turner's house and also came up empty. Other than Bill Carpenter's claim that Turner had been in his restaurant, they didn't even know where the sheriff went the night of the murder. And now Carpenter was dead of a gunshot wound.

That was another sticking point. Carpenter's killer remained on the loose. Ward's lackluster investigation into the restaurant owner's murder was hard to explain. Shouldn't they be going after that killer as hard as they were going after Cash?

Santos continued his pacing. Something was wrong. They were arresting a man, Santos's former comrade-in-arms, on flimsy evidence. He couldn't defy his boss, but he had to do something to derail this train. As he stuck his hands into his pockets, he felt something. It gave him an idea.

***

Judd. Cash was backtracking on his earlier guess. It could be a last name, like the famous mother-daughter singing duo. Yet that was unlikely. If it was a first name, that was Noble County Deputy Judd Noteboom. Would that mean the deputy was involved in the human-trafficking scheme? If so, maybe he had killed Bill Carpenter. And if Noteboom had killed Bill, it wasn't too far of a stretch to suspect that he'd also murdered Griff Turner.

Such thoughts tormented Cash as he lay on his sleeping bag. Trying to put the pieces together while stuck in the basement of Steve's brewpub was like trying to read a book from across the room.

He sat up and pulled on the Ariat Rancher boots that his parents had given to him as a graduation gift a year ago. He wondered when he would see his mother and father again. Would it be for a home-cooked meal around the kitchen table in their Austin home? Or through a plexiglass window at the Noble County jail?

Loud voices from upstairs caught Cash's attention. Steve was arguing with someone. A woman spoke up and a booming voice told her to butt out. Clovis. He was here, and it didn't sound like he was ordering a beer.

Cash grabbed his Ruger. Taking care to keep quiet, he hurried up the stairs. Out in the taproom, Steve and Clovis continued their argument. Cash crept down the hall toward the back door. With slow, careful movements, he nudged it open and stepped outside. The door clicked shut. A man said, "Don't move, Cash." It was Santos.

Cash turned, still holding the Ruger but keeping it pointed at the ground.

"Set the gun down," Santos said.

"Gabe, I didn't kill him."

"Right now that doesn't matter. Please put the gun on the ground."

Keeping his eyes on Santos, Cash lowered his hand and released the gun. He struggled to come up with a plan. After everything he had been through, it couldn't end like this.

"Kick it toward me."

Cash did so.

"Now turn around."

Santos moved in with a pair of handcuffs. Cash flinched as he slipped the cuffs on and pulled them shut.

Cash said, "This is a mistake, Gabe. I was set up. You've got to believe me."

"I'm inclined to, but right now I've got to take you in."

The Packsaddle's back door burst open. Clovis Ward and Judd Noteboom, guns drawn and aimed at Cash, charged into the alley. Ward said, "Adam Cash, you're under arrest for the murder of Sheriff Griff Turner."

Cash glowered at Ward but said nothing.

Ward recited the Miranda warning, then said, "You've been hiding here the whole time, haven't you? Your friend Steve is in a shitload of trouble. Your baby mama too."

"You know this is bullshit."

"What I know is that we finally have our man. Santos, get him to the squad car."

Santos grabbed the handcuffs with one hand and Cash's arm with the other. As he was being frog-marched to the car, Cash felt the deputy press something into his hand. "This might help," Santos whispered.

Cash closed his fingers around the object. It was a paperclip. A spark of hope flashed in his chest. Yes, the paperclip could come in handy. What's more, Santos was trying to help.

***

Del's shoulders sagged as his son was led to the squad car in handcuffs. Clovis Ward led the procession. Del had a brief fantasy of leaping out of the car and wiping the smug look from the bastard's face. Yet that wouldn't keep Adam out of a jail cell.

Behind Ward came Judd Noteboom, trotting along like the butt-sniffing lapdog he had always been. Some people were natural leaders, some were natural followers, and others, like Noteboom, were loathsome toads eager to follow the boss's orders, no matter how twisted they *were*.

A deputy Del had never seen before was carrying on a whispered conversation with Adam. Something that filled his son's face with determination and a lack of fear. The boy wasn't giving up. If Adam wasn't conceding defeat, Del told himself, he wouldn't either.

The deputy eased Adam into the back of the squad car. Ward climbed behind the wheel while Noteboom got in on the passenger side. Del slumped into his seat as Ward drove past. Once certain he wouldn't be seen, he pulled onto the street and followed.

48

Cash sat in the back, sealed off from his two favorite people, Ward and Noteboom, by the polycarbonate partition. Gloom enveloped him like a fog bank, but the feel of the paper clip kept him from total despair.

Noteboom laughed, "This makes things a lot easier, doesn't it?"

"Shut up," said Ward.

They rode the rest of the way to the sheriff's office in silence. Ward and Noteboom flanked Cash roughly and led him into the lobby. Vicky looked up, and her flash of recognition instantly transformed into concern.

Ward led Cash to a chair against the wall and nudged him into a seated position. He looked at Noteboom and said, "Watch him. I'll get started on the paperwork."

Ward disappeared down the same hall Cash had followed to his failed interview with Griff Turner. After all that had happened, the interview seemed like a lifetime ago. Cash squirmed in the chair, trying in vain to find a comfortable position with his arms cuffed behind his back. "Come on, Judd. Are the cuffs still necessary?"

"Protocol," Noteboom said gruffly. He sauntered over to a coffee machine behind Vicky's desk. As he poured himself a cup, some of the dark liquid sloshed onto his pant leg. "Damn it," he said, setting the cup down.

Cash watched Noteboom take a napkin from a stack next to the machine and use it to blot his pants. He recognized its pattern: a decorative border of brown and orange leaves surrounding a solid tan center. It was identical to the bloody napkin he had found at the park. He now had no doubt that Browning's Judd was Deputy Judd Noteboom.

Noteboom tossed the soggy napkin and dropped into a leatherette armchair. He sipped his coffee and glanced at Cash.

Vicky said, "I'm sorry you were arrested, Cash."

"Shut up," said Noteboom. "He killed the sheriff."

***

Cash fingered the paperclip in his hand. When he was in college at Sam Houston State, he purchased a set of police handcuffs at a campus garage sale. Curious about how magicians extricated themselves while cuffed, he looked up a YouTube video on the subject. With a little practice, he was soon able to open the locked cuffs using either a paperclip or a bobby pin. The skill had won him several bar bets.

Cash scooted forward in the chair to give himself room to maneuver. Noteboom glanced up before returning his attention to the magazine in his lap. Keeping a wary eye on Noteboom, Cash shifted the paper clip to his dominant right hand. With his left thumb and pointer finger, he straightened out the first bend of the clip and inserted the tip into the keyhole. He then bent the tip to a right angle and pulled it free. After working the tool back into the keyhole, he felt for the ratchet that engaged the cogs on the cuff itself. By twisting the paper clip, he was able to push the ratchet against the lock spring just enough to disengage the cogs. The cuff popped open with a soft click.

He was free, but now what? Keeping his arms behind his back, he stood and said, "Come on, Noteboom, these cuffs are killing me."

Noteboom said, "Sit down." When Cash didn't, Noteboom got up and strode toward him. As he started to push Cash back into the chair, Cash swung a fist that connected solidly with Noteboom's jaw. The deputy flew backward as Vicky stiffened in her chair and gasped. Cash charged and punched Noteboom again, sending him sprawling onto a desk. As Noteboom tried to pull himself up, Cash hit him one more time, knocking him out cold.

Cash heard a door slam down the hall. He raced out of the lobby and onto the sidewalk. His head swiveled all around as he tried to come up with a plan. Ward wouldn't be far behind.

Across the street, Del snapped to attention at the sight of his son bolting through the doorway. He leaped from the Taurus and hollered, "Adam! Over here."

Cash spotted his father and froze. What the hell was he doing here? Yet he had no time to figure out why. He dashed across the street and scrambled into his father's car. Del dropped back behind the wheel and fired up the engine. As he roared onto the highway, Cash said, "What's going on, Dad?"

"I should ask you the same thing! Where should we go?"

"I don't know. Just drive."

Del floored it and raced out of town. Cash said, "I didn't kill him, Dad."

"I know you didn't. That's why I'm here."

A mile later, Cash pointed ahead to an unpaved road intersecting the highway and said, "Turn there." After they had gone another hundred yards, Cash said, "Stop the car."

"We can't, son. They'll be coming."

"I don't want them to catch me with you."

"We've got a lead on them."

"Dad! Stop the damn car!"

Startled by his son's outburst, Del braked to a hard stop. "What now?"

"I'll think of something." Cash opened his door. Looking back at his father, he said, "Thanks, Dad."

"You bet."

As the door slammed, Del called out, "I love you, son."

"I love you, too. Now get the hell out of here."

49

Cash was free, but where could he go? Certainly not back to the Packsaddle. That hideout was burned, probably along with his relationship with Steve. He only hoped that Ward wouldn't come down too hard on his friend.

What about Bernadette? During their last encounter, she had seemed to soften to him. But she had Emma to care for. She wouldn't risk an arrest that would result in separation from her child. Plus, he had been captured just a few hours after she brought him groceries. Had she betrayed him to Ward?

His parents were out. That would be the first place Ward would look. Anyway, how would he get to Austin?

Steve's house? Forget it. Steve had already risked enough. Santos? His support could only go so far. Cash couldn't ask him to risk not only losing his job but going to prison.

That left Edie. Would she take him in? Like Bernadette, she was a single mother with a child to care for. But Edie's boy was older, meaning that he might be able to stay with a friend for a few days. And the last time he had seen Edie, she had kissed him. A brief kiss, yes, but didn't that indicate she harbored feelings for him? He sure as hell hoped so.

Cash fished the paper clip from his pants pocket. He unlocked the other cuff. He started to toss the handcuffs but, thinking he might find a use for them later, stowed them along with the paper clip.

No matter where he planned on going, Cash knew he first had to get out of sight. Behind him was a field of prairie grass fenced with barbed wire. A line of cedar trees began a hundred feet on the other side. Cash twisted the fence wires together and snaked his body through. He knew he could make it back to town by keeping away from the road and working his way through the trees. Then a new thought hit him.

50

Cash knew the lay of the land. He knew all the country around Pinyon. As a kid, he had hiked, ridden horses, or driven UTVs all over town. He'd fished the river, swam in every creek, scaled every hill, and climbed every tree. He'd hunted deer, turkey, and Indian arrowheads. He had even found an impressive spearhead, which his father convinced him to donate to the county museum. It was displayed with a card bearing his name.

Within a hundred yards he encountered Calf Creek, a seasonal waterway that dumped into the Nolina River. He knew the creek cut through a corner of Noteboom's three acres. He followed it to a hill where he had once camped with a group of middle-school friends. The creek circled the hill and dropped into a ravine thick with greenbrier. The thorny vines tore into Cash's clothes and flesh as he pushed his way through, leaving rips in his jeans and a few painful scratches on his arms.

When he came to a barbed wire fence crossing the creek, he knew he had reached Noteboom's property. He crawled through it and emerged from the last tentacles of the greenbrier. The brick house rose fifty yards away, its metal roof shaded by two towering live oak trees. A dirt road sliced through the field to a dead end in front. He couldn't see any vehicles, either in front or in the attached carport.

Cash jogged across the field, keeping alert for any hint of an approaching vehicle. He crept up to a front window and listened for the sound of a TV or radio. He heard nothing. No car, no noise in the house: Noteboom was probably still out cold. After the beating Cash had laid on him, he was probably at the county hospital. Cash permitted himself a slight smile. The bastard had it coming to him.

As he crept to the front door, Cash was alerted by something odd about the gravel walkway between the road and the house. The dry pebbles crackled under his feet, but he heard a different sound, too, as if something wet lay underneath. He bent down and brushed a patch of pebbles aside. The ground was damp. He glanced at the house and saw a coiled hose fifteen feet away. Had Noteboom used the hose to wash something from the footpath?

Cash stood to his full height and surveyed a slow circle around the damp spot. There, a dark stain a foot beyond it. He leaned down and scooped up another handful of pebbles. Holding them up for a close view, he noticed rust-colored stains on most of the stones. He scraped at one with his nail. The color flaked off with little effort. The residue under his nail resembled dried blood. Unless Judd handed out regular whoopings at his house, something wrong had gone down here.

The front door was locked. Stepping past a five-gallon paint bucket of rusty garden tools, Cash made his way to the backyard. There, he had more luck. The back door opened but was stopped by a security chain. He returned to the paint bucket and rummaged through it until he found a reel of fishing line. He made a loop in one end and, reaching through the crack in the door, attached it to the chain's slider. After pulling it tight, he looped the other end over the top of the door and tugged it toward the hinges. Then he closed the door. By pulling on the line he was able to pop the chain from the slider. Released from its restraint, the door opened.

Noteboom was a bachelor, no doubt, to judge by the appearance of the den. A well-worn lounge chair in the middle of the room faced an enormous wall-mounted television. Below the TV was an ash-filled hearth. Empty beer cans and an overflowing ashtray covered an end table next to the chair. Two baskets of dirty laundry and a jumble of fishing poles propped in a corner completed the look. A nauseating stench of old tobacco smoke fouled the air.

Cash crossed the room to inspect the hearth. He probed the cold ashes with a finger but touched nothing solid. At the edge of the ash pile, he found scattered bits of partially burned paper. He picked one up and saw it was the corner of a napkin. Just enough of it remained for him to make out an orange leaf. He sifted through the ashes and found three similar remnants.

Cash passed into the kitchen, where he found stacks of dirty dishes teetering in the sink. Dirty pots and pans on the stove. Empty pork and bean cans and ramen packages cluttering the counter. An overturned cereal box spilling its contents onto a grease-stained dining table.

He opened a cabinet door to find a Glock G19 handgun sharing space with several dusty spice bottles. Only in the house of a deputy. After checking the magazine—it was full—he pocketed the gun and returned to the den. Down a hall were three bedrooms and a bathroom. The hall bath surprised him with its relative cleanliness. Cash guessed that Noteboom didn't use it much. The primary bedroom contained only an unmade bed and a chest of drawers. Clothes littered the floor. The walls were bare. The bathroom displayed more evidence of the slob that he had come to see. Cash fought an urge to retch when he glanced at the commode.

One of the two remaining bedrooms was empty. The other contained only a gleaming mahogany gun cabinet. Behind the glass of its upper section, Cash saw a shotgun and two deer rifles, one of which was fitted with an impressive scope. The lower section held a pistol and several ammunition boxes.

Cash was glad to find the cabinet unlocked. He would have hated to damage such a fine piece of furniture to get at the guns. He took out the pistol, which he recognized as a Ruger GP100. He smiled at the old-school look of the six-shot cylinder and matching six-inch stainless-steel barrel. The modern black rubber grip contrasted with the Wild West look of the weapon. At just under three pounds, it sat heavy in his hand.

After loading the Ruger, Cash checked to make sure the other guns in the cabinet were empty. He then hid them in the closet. Returning to the den, he selected a hunting magazine from a pile on the floor and settled into the lounge chair to wait.

51

Cash didn't have to wait long. Halfway through reading an article on wild hogs, he heard a vehicle rolling over the packed dirt out front. He ditched the magazine, picked up the Ruger, and swiveled to face the front door.

The vehicle's engine died. Heavy footsteps crunched gravel and a key turned in the lock. The door swung open. Key in one hand and fast-food bag in the other, Noteboom strolled inside. Cash raised the pistol and said, "Hello, Judd."

The deputy stared at Cash until recognition set in. His eyes flitted around the room as if looking for a means of escape.

"Come on in," Cash said. "Is that Whataburger? My favorite."

Moving with leaden feet, Noteboom took another step and shut the door. "That's my gun."

"It's a nice one. I hope you don't mind me borrowing it."

"What do you want?"

Cash laughed. "That's rich. What I want is to go back in time before I was framed for a murder I didn't commit. Seeing as how I don't have a time machine, I want you to confess and clear my name."

"You're full of shit."

"You know I'm not."

Noteboom nodded toward the kitchen. "Can we go sit at the table? I'd like to eat this before it gets cold."

"Just sit on the floor."

After considering not to give in, Noteboom sat. "Now what?"

"Now you can eat your burger and tell me how you did it."

Noteboom withdrew his meal from the sack: a burger, fries, and a large drink. He unwrapped the burger and took a bite. Speaking with his mouth full, he said, "You're just making things worse for yourself. I didn't kill Turner."

"There's blood out on your walkway."

"That's deer blood. I shot one a couple of days ago."

"You hunt out of season?"

He shrugged.

"So, if I were to call Frida Simmons and ask her to test that blood, you'd have no objection."

Taking another bite of the burger, Noteboom said, "Sure, but there's no need for that. I don't think you know what you've stepped in here."

"Why don't you enlighten me?"

"Why don't you go fuck yourself?"

Cash jerked the gun to his left and squeezed the trigger, causing Noteboom to flinch. The bullet smashed into the TV, sending a shower of glass and plastic onto the rug.

"Hey, man, that's a brand-new TV!"

"What's it to you?" Cash said, pointing the Ruger back at Noteboom. "You can get another one cheap from your friends Barry and Andy."

Noteboom blanched at the mention of the names. "I don't know what you're talking about."

"Sure you do. I visited your buddies at Novak's place the other night. I heard them talking about you. Apparently, you were in the bathroom taking a dump."

"Goddamn it, I don't know who you're talking about."

Cash fired again, this time aiming over Noteboom's head and putting a hole in the front door. "After this, I start shooting arms and legs."

"All right, already, I know them. I was in Boerne a while back and bought that TV you just ruined from Browning."

"There are a lot of places to buy a TV. Why did you go to his shop?"

"Griff told me to. He said Browning would give me a good deal."

"How did Griff know Browning?"

"I don't know." When Cash aimed the Ruger at Noteboom's leg, the frightened man said, "I swear, I don't. I think they were cousins or something."

"How does Novak fit in?"

"Please don't shoot me. I swear to God I don't know."

"Who were those women I saw?"

Noteboom didn't answer.

"Did you kill Griff Turner?"

"I thought you did," Noteboom said with a scoff. "Hell, we found the murder weapon in your car. Your prints were all over it."

"You mean the beer bottle that you planted?"

"You're so full of shit."

Cash was getting fed up with the attitude, but he kept his cool. "I reviewed the tape. Several minutes are missing. Someone turned the camera off right after you sent Frida Simmons on a wild goose chase."

Noteboom scoffed. "I don't know how that thing works. And I didn't send Frida anywhere."

"Did you kill Bill Carpenter?"

"You're out of your mind."

"Hubbard found a hair clip from one of those women near Carpenter's body."

Noteboom's eyes twitched, but he said nothing.

Cash bit his lip. "Admit it, Judd. That's Turner's blood on the sidewalk. You killed him."

Noteboom took a long, hard look at Cash. "You've got it all wrong." When he received no response, he climbed to his feet. "I'm going into the kitchen to eat at the table. So, if you'll excuse me—"

"Don't bother. I found the Ruger."

Noteboom froze.

"Give me your phone."

"Fuck you."

More attitude. "I swear I'll put one in your kneecap."

He hesitated, then fished out his phone and tossed it to Cash.

"Now your keys."

He tossed them to Cash. "So you're adding auto theft to your murder charge?"

"Turn around and put your hands behind your back."

Noteboom complied. Cash stood up, fished the handcuffs from his pocket, and cuffed one of Noteboom's wrists. As he attempted to attach the other, the deputy made a quick spin and swung the loose end of the handcuffs into the side of his head. Cash staggered as stars danced before his eyes. Noteboom swung again. Cash ducked, and the blow bounced off his collarbone, sending a spasm of pain shooting down his arm. Noteboom drew his arm back for another swing, but Cash charged and drove him against the wall. Pressing the barrel of the Ruger into his cheek, he said, "You're trying my patience, Deputy."

Still wobbly, Cash hauled Noteboom across the room to the shattered TV. "Put your hands up by that wall mount." When Noteboom complied, Cash locked his hands together above the flexible arm. Given the size of the TV, the cuffed man wouldn't be able to extend his arms far enough to free himself.

"In an hour or two, I'll let somebody know to come turn you loose."

"Come on, man, I gotta take a piss."

Cash stuck the Ruger in his belt. "That's hardly a problem in this dump. Do it on the floor. It will improve the smell of this place." He strode to the front door. "This isn't over."

Noteboom curled his lips into a wicked sneer. "You're goddamned right it's not."

52

As Cash drove Noteboom's Ram pickup back to town, he decided he had no intention of notifying anyone about the deputy's predicament. At least not anytime soon. Let the bastard sweat.

He entered town and started for Edie's house. On the way, it occurred to him that if he was going to use it as a hideout, he couldn't park the Ram there. Skirting the square by two blocks, he drove to the Tractor Supply on the south end of town and steered the truck into a space between two other pickups. After exiting the vehicle, he circled the building toward an empty field out back. Once there, he paused to contemplate his next move.

Noteboom was lying. Cash could feel it. The son of a bitch had killed Griff Turner and had likely shot Bill Carpenter as well. He was also up to his ass in human trafficking. The case he was drawing up all made sense, but Cash needed proof. He'd try Mia Turner again.

***

By keeping to less traveled streets, Cash made his way on foot back across town to Mia's house. Though it was a workday, he wasn't surprised to see her car in the driveway. Real estate agents kept irregular hours. Thankfully, Carl Trotter's Nissan Sentra was nowhere in sight.

Cash strode up the walk to the front door. This time he wouldn't knock, as he had no intention of allowing Mia to refuse him entry. He turned the knob and pushed. The door opened. He pulled his Ruger and stepped into the house, closing the door behind him.

The first thing he noticed was that the ancient oak floor was in dire need of refinishing. Its poor condition surprised him, as the rest of the room appeared fresh and tastefully decorated. He tiptoed across the living room, stopping when he heard footsteps from another part of the house. He darted into the hall and glimpsed Mia slipping into a bedroom. Dashing after her, he charged in just as she pulled a handgun from a dresser drawer. "Put it down, Mia," he said. "I've got one too."

Mia hesitated, but then heaved a sigh and let go of the gun. It clattered as it fell back into the drawer. "What the hell, Cash? You broke into my house."

She wore a modest blouse and those form-fitting jeans he had seen her in before. God, she was something to look at. Cash pushed that thought from his mind and said, "I want some answers."

"About what?"

"About a lot of things. Griff's murder to start."

"Why would I know anything about that?" She spat the last word out as if he had asked her to explain quantum mechanics.

"Mia, I know he mistreated you, but surely you don't want his killer to go free."

She tossed her head and sat on the edge of the bed. "Sometimes I think he got what he deserved."

Cash lowered the Ruger. "I hear he hit you."

She turned her head and said nothing.

"I know about Carl."

"He told me."

"He believed me when I said I didn't kill Griff."

"That sounds like him." She swiveled her legs onto the bed and pushed back against the headboard. "So, who did?"

"I think it was Judd Noteboom."

"Could be. Noteboom's an ass. He never liked taking orders from Griff."

"Mia, if I'm going to prove anything, I need some answers."

"Then hurry up and ask me some questions. I'm showing a house in half an hour."

"I know Griff was extorting money from several businesses in town."

That made her laugh. "How do you think we got this place? He called it his 'pay to play program.'"

"I think he may have also been mixed up with two guys named Andrew Browning and Barry Novak. They're trafficking illegal immigrants." He thought of the boxes of pills he had seen at Novak's. "Maybe drugs, too."

Her face exploded in horror. "No. Griff would never have put up with that. He could be a son of a bitch, but he wasn't cruel. And he hated drugs. Don't you know his sister died of an overdose?"

A vague memory pinged. "I remember that."

"He was fifteen at the time. He told me once that anybody caught selling drugs in Noble County should be shot. If there was a drug trade in Pinyon, Griff would have known about it. And he certainly wouldn't have kept quiet about human trafficking."

"Maybe he found out what they were doing, and they wanted him out of the way."

"I hadn't thought of that." A tear rolled down her cheek. "Griff loved being sheriff. He wanted to do a good job. Like his dad. Everybody loved his dad and Griff wanted people to love him, too. He did a lot of good, you know."

Cash saw no point in reminding her that the extorted business owners might not see it that way.

"If I were you," she said, "I'd start looking at the people Griff arrested over the years. I'll bet he pissed somebody off enough for them to want revenge."

For the first time, Cash noticed her bruised and swollen left hand. A white band around her ring finger showed where her wedding ring had been.

"What happened to your hand?"

She glanced at it and flexed her fingers. "I was so upset when they told me about Griff that I punched a wall."

"And your ring?"

"My fingers are swollen, so I had to take it off. I've got it in my jewelry box."

"Mia, I'm sorry about his death. That must really hurt."

The sadness drained from her face. "Not as much as the bastard's fists."

53

Ward leaned across the conference table and glared at Santos. "How the hell did he get loose?"

Santos had no regrets about what he had done, but his pulse quickened anyway. "I don't know. I had him in handcuffs."

"I know he was in handcuffs. The question is, why didn't they hold him?"

"I wish I could tell you."

Ward's face went red. "What a colossal fuckup. Our chief murder suspect escapes from the damn *sheriff's* office."

Santos said nothing. He had known this was coming, and he understood he could do nothing but let Ward's anger run its course.

"Maybe you didn't put the cuffs on right," said Ward, his temper losing steam.

"No, I snapped them into place. And I tugged on them to make sure."

Conrad said, "He beat the hell out of Noteboom when he escaped."

"Gave him a concussion at the very least," said Ward. "We'll add that to his charges."

"He won't see sunshine for a long time."

Santos said, "If we can catch him."

Ward tilted his head back and eyed his two deputies with grim determination. "We'll catch the son of a bitch." He directed a fierce look at Santos. "And when we do, let Deke put the cuffs on."

***

Cash hustled away from Mia's house as fast as he could. Mia had called Ward on him the first time, and he couldn't be sure she wouldn't do it again. He hurried over the bridge spanning the river, then trod a faint footpath leading down the embankment to the water's edge. From there he followed the river to the state park, where he slipped into his childhood hiding place to give himself a chance to think.

If Mia was right, Sheriff Turner's moral flexibility stretched as far as petty extortion, but no further. Not far enough to turn a blind eye to human trafficking and pill smuggling. If Turner was Browning's cousin, as Noteboom had said, it made sense that he knew about the TV discounts. Noteboom would have met Browning through Turner. But how had Barry Novak become involved? Despite owning the gelato shop, the man had a low profile in Pinyon. Cash had never seen him around town, but Noteboom apparently had. Or maybe Browning had been Noteboom's link to Novak.

Cash needed to do some research and, for that, he needed computer access. It was time to go to Edie's.

***

During Cash's unsuccessful run for sheriff, Edie had once sent him to her house to pick up a box of campaign flyers. When he asked her if the door would be unlocked, she told him about a key she kept hidden under a birdbath in the backyard.

Edie lived on a quiet street of modest houses that abutted the middle school. Since it was summer, Cash had no concerns that anyone would see him as he cut across the grounds to reach her house. He tried to look as if he belonged as he strode up her driveway and through the six-foot cedar gate into her fenced backyard. Cash felt shielded enough behind it that he didn't worry about nosy neighbors spotting him as he upended the birdbath. But there was no key.

Where else might she hide one? He checked all the obvious places he could think of: under the doormat, behind the air conditioner, or taped to the porch light. He couldn't search the front of the house for fear of being seen. That left only one option: breaking in.

The back door was locked, as he had expected. So were the kitchen window and the smaller bedroom window. His last chance was the tiny bathroom window in between the den and kitchen. He was in luck. Edie had left it open.

He found a hand trowel by the birdbath and used it to pry off the bathroom's screen. The opening was tight, but he managed to squeeze through headfirst, propping his arms on the commode seat as he wriggled his legs through. After closing the window, he walked into the living room and sat on the sofa. Before him was the wall-mounted photo of Edie and her son Luke. The boy had the same dark eyes and oval face as his mother. Edie beamed as she held him. Such a beautiful woman, Cash mused.

It pained him to think of what he gave up when he joined the army. He had asked Edie to wait, but she said that, while she could wait for a husband, she wouldn't wait for a boyfriend. The response stung. He hadn't wanted to lose her, but the notion of the lifetime commitment represented by marriage frightened him. He told her she should find somebody else. Fine, she said. And she did.

His name was Randy Howser. Edie met him shortly after his arrival in Pinyon to set up a medical practice. She chose to ignore the fourteen-year difference in their ages when she married him. Three years later, Luke was born. Not long after that, Randy cheated on her with a server at the Firewheel. She forgave him for that but two months later she caught him in bed with a local rancher's wife. She filed for divorce. He took a job in San Antonio. They hadn't seen each other much since.

Cash wondered how any man married to Edie would see a reason to stray. He wished he hadn't been so fearful of commitment when he left for the army. But the kiss gave him hope that the final chapter had yet to be written. If he could just clear his name, all he needed was another chance. This time he wouldn't screw it up.

54

Barry Novak drained the glass of Michter's and picked up his phone. It was time for those yahoos in Pinyon to put the matter of Griff Turner's death to rest. When Noteboom had told him of the apprehension of their chief suspect, the poor slob who lost the election to Turner, Novak thought they had. But Noteboom was quick to add that the guy had escaped. Not only escaped but escaped with Noteboom in the room. At the sheriff's office, no less. Unbelievable.

Thinking back to that night at the gelato shop when the guy burst in with a gun, Novak could see how he could escape custody. The man had courage and conviction. It was no wonder that Noteboom had been bested. Hell, the weasel had been stupid enough to allow those two women to escape the shop. That led to him shooting the restaurant owner, an act that brought unwanted attention to them all.

Novak tapped in a number and waited. After four rings, his contact in Pinyon answered. "What do you want?"

"I want you to fix things."

"I'm working on it."

"Listen, if this isn't wrapped up soon, Kessler is bound to find out what's going on. I don't think I need to tell you how unhappy he'd be to know of a loose cannon like that."

"For God's sake, calm down. Nobody's telling Kessler shit."

"I'm just saying that this thing has to be stopped. Now. I want that guy Cash taken care of. Am I clear?"

There was a long pause before Novak heard the man say, "Loud and clear."

***

Cash's heart fluttered when he heard Edie's car pull into the driveway. The door opened, and Edie and Luke stepped inside. She saw him but closed the door casually. Her expression didn't change. "Good to see you, cowboy," she said.

She rushed to him and gave him a lingering hug, one that Cash wished could go on forever. "Oh, my God," she said. "I heard they caught you. Everybody's talking about it. How did you get away?"

He started to tell her, but she put up a hand. "Hang on, let me set Luke up with a snack." When she returned, she pulled him onto the couch. "Okay, let's hear it."

He explained about hearing Ward upstairs at the Packsaddle, grabbing his gun and sneaking outside, being caught by Santos, and being driven to the station by Ward and Noteboom. He told her about the paper clip but omitted the part about getting it from Santos. If she didn't know about his involvement, she couldn't inadvertently give him away. He mentioned seeing the napkin and explained its significance. He concluded by telling her about picking the handcuff lock, immobilizing Noteboom, and hitching a ride with his father.

"Your father was there? Why?"

"I don't know. We didn't get a chance to talk."

"How did you pick the lock on your handcuffs?"

"It's actually pretty easy." He explained how he had done it. "And it doesn't have to be a paper clip. Any short piece of bendable metal will do. A bobby pin, for example. I'm surprised it doesn't happen more often."

"Huh. I've seen that in the movies and always thought it was impossible. You'll have to show me sometime."

He smiled wryly. "Let's hope it's a skill you'll never need."

"Did you come straight here?"

"Not exactly…" He filled her in on the events at Noteboom's house.

"Judd Noteboom killed Griff Turner? Wow."

"Yeah. But I've got to prove it."

"You will." She stood. "Are you hungry? I've got leftover spaghetti and meatballs. It's Luke's favorite."

"Sounds great."

They ate at her dining room table. When they finished, Edie bathed Luke, dressed him, and read him a story until he fell asleep. While she was reading, Cash peeked in on the two of them and gave himself another mental lashing for losing her ten years ago.

Edie returned to the den and sat on the couch next to Cash.

"You're a good mother," Cash said.

"I do my best." Her knee brushed his. He hoped it was no accident. "What are you going to do now?"

"I was hoping I could stay here for a bit."

"What about Luke?"

"Do you have any friends he could stay with?"

She thought about it. "I guess I could ask Julie."

"Julie Needham? Your friend from school?"

"Yeah."

"I didn't know she was still in Pinyon."

"Married with two kids."

"While you're calling her, can I use your computer?"

***

After logging in, Cash performed another internet search of Barry Novak. He discovered nothing new. Next, he tried Judd Noteboom. Not much there either, just the fish pictures on social media and his bio on the Noble County website. Noteboom had been hired by Griff Turner's father five years back. He was born in Kerrville, raised on a Kerr County ranch, graduated from the University of Texas at San Antonio, and moved to Pinyon to take the deputy job. He was single and enjoyed fishing and hunting.

"Yeah, and you're a total slob," Cash muttered under his breath.

He leaned back in the chair and stretched. Edie kept her laptop on an antique rolltop desk in her bedroom. Her queen-sized bed lacked the mountain of decorative pillows that his mother favored, a nod to practicality that Cash appreciated. Her dresser top was devoid of clutter, as was the desk. Cash wondered how anyone could be so neat. It was a refreshing change from Noteboom's house and, to a lesser degree, his own.

He started to enter another search term when he glimpsed Clovis Ward's name in a sidebar of the sheriff's department site. He clicked on it. Ward's biography mentioned a childhood in Menard, a town fifty miles north. He had begun his higher education at Angelo State University on a football scholarship and transferred to Texas Tech for his junior year. He graduated with a degree in finance and was a member of the fraternity Sigma Alpha Epsilon.

A cog clicked in Cash's brain. Didn't Barry Novak graduate from Texas Tech? Cash opened another window on the laptop, performed a search on Novak, and confirmed that he had. His degree was in finance, as was Ward's. Cash checked Novak's age against Ward's. Novak was 43; Ward had just turned 44. Given the similar ages, it seemed likely they had attended Texas Tech at the same time. Their pursuit of the same degree must have brought them together on campus.

Cash performed another search using "Barry Novak" and "Sigma Alpha Epsilon" as search terms. He found a site for a fraternity reunion five years earlier attended by Novak. On it was a group photograph of Novak and other alumni. Standing next to Novak was Clovis Ward.

More puzzle pieces locked into place. Clovis Ward and Barry Novak knew each other from their time at Texas Tech. Novak and his fraternity brother Ward concocted a plan for Browning to deliver kidnapped women to Pinyon. From there, Novak would take them up to Fort Worth. Cash could only guess what he did with them there. Ward met Andy Browning through Browning's cousin, Griff Turner. He recruited Browning to procure the captives in San Antonio and bring them to Pinyon. With his finger on the pulse of Hill Country law enforcement, Ward brought a level of security that their operation otherwise lacked. Either Noteboom found out and forced his way into the operation, or Ward brought him in for logistical help. Griff Turner wasn't in on the deal. He learned of it and threatened to shut it down. Ward and his cronies killed Turner to prevent that. They hadn't planned on killing Bill Carpenter but were forced to when Carpenter stumbled onto the runaway women in his restaurant.

Cash sat back and smiled. He was detecting his way out of his nightmare, after all. What he needed was physical evidence connecting either Ward or Noteboom to the murders. He'd found the blood on Noteboom's walkway, but if Noteboom had any sense, he'd take care of that as soon as somebody let him loose from the handcuffs. He could also inspect the truck parked at Tractor Supply. Maybe it had been used to transport Turner's body to the park. That reminded him. By now the truck was likely the only vehicle in the parking lot. Somebody would eventually report it to the sheriff's department. He had to move fast.

Cash remembered Ward approaching him at the Dizzy Dillo. Ward could have had his pick of bottles that Cash had drained. He could have given one to Noteboom, who then planted it in Cash's car.

Edie padded into the room and interrupted his thoughts. "I talked to Julie. She'll keep Luke for a few days. I'm going to take him over there now."

"Great," said Cash. "After that, we have an errand to run."

55

When Cash and Edie arrived at Tractor Supply in Edie's Prius, he saw several vehicles left in the parking lot. He had forgotten that Tractor Supply stayed open until seven. There were three pickups, Noteboom's and two others.

It began to rain. Just a mist at first, then a drizzle that became a downpour. "Are you sure you're okay with this? I did steal this truck," Cash said.

Edie said nonchalantly, "I don't want to see you go to prison."

"Okay, then. I'll wait a couple of minutes, and then meet you back at your house."

"Sounds good."

"Don't forget to have the garage ready."

She delivered a light punch to his arm. "Give me some credit." He could tell she was enjoying this. A high-stakes game in the little town of Pinyon.

After Edie left, an idea struck Cash. He had removed the battery from Noteboom's phone after leaving the deputy handcuffed to his television mount. He replaced it and scrolled through Noteboom's texts until he found a conversation with Ward. Cash was disappointed to see nothing incriminating. He tapped out a message and sent it to Ward:

Cash knows it was us.

Within moments, a reply from Ward appeared.

How?

Cash typed:

I don't know.

Another instant reply:

Where are you?

Realizing this was as good a time as any to get Noteboom out of the handcuffs, Cash typed:

My house. We need to talk.

Ward replied:

Be there soon.

Cash removed the phone's battery, wiped it and the phone, and tossed both out the window into some nearby weeds. Minutes later, he pulled Noteboom's truck into Edie's garage. Inside the house, he heard Edie call out from her bedroom and found her perched on the bed, untying her shoes. She ripped them off one by one and dropped them to the floor. "It feels good to get these off."

"Should I sleep on the couch?" Cash asked.

Edie came close enough for him to feel her warm breath on his face. She stroked his arm and gazed into his eyes. Her scent triggered a chill that tickled his spine. Anticipation gathered momentum, and he inched his head toward hers, waiting for her to tell him to stop. She didn't. Their lips touched.

Edie thumped a finger against his chest. "The couch? No, I've got a better idea."

***

After his best night of sleep in a week, Cash cooked migas for breakfast. Edie was out of salsa and cilantro, but Cash rated neither of those items as critical. As long as he had eggs, tortillas, cumin, and cheese, he could make it work. Besides, his mother always said that migas was a Spanish word for "whatever you have in the refrigerator."

Halfway through their breakfast, someone knocked at the front door. Cash flinched. Edie said, "It's okay. You stay here and I'll take care of it."

She padded into the den and opened the door to see Deke Conrad. "Good morning, Deke. What brings you around so early?"

Conrad peered past her. "Can I come in?"

"I'd rather you not. Luke's been on a rampage and the place is a pigsty."

He knitted his brow, not expecting that answer. Tamping down the drum beating in her chest, she said, "Is there something I can do for you?"

"You haven't seen Cash lately, have you?"

"No."

"Has he been in touch with you?"

"Sorry, no."

"Do you mind if I come in and have a look around?"

Edie crossed her arms in a calculated show of impatience. "As a matter of fact, Deke, I do. Like I told you, the house is a mess and I'm getting ready for work."

He looked undecided. Did he see through the lie?

"All right, I'll get going then. If you do hear from him, you'll let us know, right?"

"Of course."

When she returned to the kitchen, Cash stood up. "I should go. I've already gotten Steve in trouble, and I don't want anything to happen to you."

She pulled him in tight and hit him with a prolonged kiss. "You're not going anywhere, cowboy. Got it?"

Feeling his favorite friend stirring below, he said, "Got it."

They resumed eating. Edie said, "What's the plan today?"

"Last night I sent Ward a text from Noteboom's phone that made him sweat enough to set up a meeting. By now he'll have gone to see Noteboom and cut him loose. He'll also know I took the truck and that it was me who sent the text."

"So, what good did it do?"

"It'll shake him up. He'll know I'm on to him. I'll let him percolate on that today while I take a closer look at Noteboom's truck. Do you have any rubber gloves?"

"Aren't your fingerprints already on it?"

"Yeah, but no sense in adding more."

She got up, opened the cabinet under the sink, and pulled out a pair of rubber gloves. Tossing them to Cash, she grinned and said, "While you're at it, go ahead and clean the bathroom."

56

Taking baby steps, Vicky eased her way into the conference room, balancing four cups of coffee on a legal pad. Moving with all the speed of a sloth, she set the makeshift tray on the table.

"Nice job," Santos said. "You didn't spill a drop."

"Thanks," Vicky said with a smile. "Would anyone like cream or sugar?"

"No, they wouldn't," Ward said, waving her out of the room. "You can get back out front."

Stung by Ward's abruptness, Vicky slunk away. Santos watched her go, wondering why his boss had to be such an ass.

Ward made sure the door was shut behind her. Returning to his seat, he looked at Santos and said, "Learn anything around the square?"

Of course I didn't, Santos thought. *Cash isn't stupid enough to hang around there.* "He's not at the Packsaddle or any of the stores. Nobody has seen him."

Ward swore under his breath and directed his gaze at Noteboom. "What did he say when he left your house yesterday?"

Noteboom lifted his head. His mouth hung open and his eyes had a distant look. A purple bruise colored one cheek. "Sorry. What?"

"Pay attention, damn it. I said, did Cash say anything to you yesterday that might give us a clue about where he went?"

"No. Just some bullshit about him being innocent."

"That leaves you, Deke."

Santos noticed the slight smile creasing Conrad's face and his heart sank. The dumb son of a bitch had found something. Conrad said, "I think he's at Edie's. I didn't see anything through the door, but she wouldn't let me in the house. Also, it rained last night and there were muddy footprints on the driveway that were too big to be hers."

"Hot damn. I knew that's where he'd end up."

"You want us to go get him?"

Ward squinted as the wheels turned in his mind. "No, I want you and Santos out on the highway. We're getting complaints about speeders on the offramp. A few tickets should put a stop to that."

"You want us to patrol the highway?" Conrad's disappointment was obvious.

"Am I not speaking English?"

A heavy silence settled over the room. Santos broke it by saying, "Will there be anything else?"

"No, you guys get going. Noteboom and I will handle Cash."

**

A yearning gripped Cash as he watched Edie leave for work. Wouldn't it be a slice of heaven to see her off every morning? Share breakfast with her, discuss the upcoming day over coffee, kiss her goodbye when one of them left. But two big questions loomed large to puncture that dream. Did she feel the same way? And was he going to prison?

Her passion in bed last night had seemed clear enough. But Cash had gained enough experience over the years to know that passion and love are two different beasts. As he examined his feelings, he believed both emotions simmered within. Hers remained a mystery. A mystery he intended to solve.

Cash returned his thoughts to the immediate matter at hand—proving his innocence by proving the guilt of Clovis Ward and Judd Noteboom. The texts from Ward would appear suspicious to an unbiased person, but they wouldn't be enough for an indictment, much less a conviction. For that, he needed physical evidence. Unless something turned up in Ward's house, the truck provided his best opportunity of finding it.

He needed to talk to Frida Simmons. If things went his way, she would be the one to search the truck. But it was too early for that. She'd need an official order to perform a search, and he couldn't approach Ward or Noteboom for one. Maybe Deke Conrad or Gabe Santos? Contacting his old army friend would be risky, so he'd wait on that for now. And Conrad was an unknown.

How to contact Frida? She told him not to call again and, anyway, he had no phone. Noteboom's phone was in the Tractor Supply parking lot and Cash's burner had been confiscated at his arrest. What about an email? She might not see it for hours, or even until the next day. And an email would leave an electronic trail that could be traced back to Edie, and hence to him. But what choice did he have?

He returned to Edie's bedroom. As he sat down at the desk to use the computer, something caught his eye that he hadn't noticed before. A telephone. Edie still had a landline!

He found Frida's phone number on the Noble County website. She picked up on the first ring.

"Frida Simmons."

"Frida, it's Cash. Can you talk?"

"I told you not to call me."

"I know who killed Turner."

There was a long silence. "Who?"

"Ward and Noteboom."

"How do you know?"

Cash gave her what he knew, concluding with the blood at Noteboom's house. "He's probably washed it off by now, but I have his truck."

"You took his truck? Where is it?"

"I don't think I should tell you that just yet."

He heard her exasperated sigh come through the phone. "Adam, I can't search it if I don't know where it is."

"I'll tell you soon enough. In the meantime, you should know that I've driven it. My prints will be all over the cab."

"That could be a problem."

"Should I wipe it?"

"I guess it doesn't matter. After all, Noteboom knows you took it."

"Okay. Anything else you'd recommend?"

"Yeah. Don't get caught."

***

Santos banged a hand against the steering wheel, startling Conrad enough for him to drop his bag of Fritos.

"Damn, Gabe, what the hell?"

"This is bullshit."

Conrad plucked corn chips from his lap and put them back in the bag. "What's bullshit?"

"Ward should have taken us with him."

"Come on, dude. What's easier than sitting in the car waiting for speeders to go by?"

"Don't you think it's weird that Ward didn't want us to go with him to arrest a potentially dangerous murder suspect?"

"What makes you think he's dangerous?"

"I don't. But Ward thinks he is. Cash has Noteboom's gun."

"You don't think he'd shoot anyone, do you? This is Adam Cash."

"Exactly. I don't think he killed Sheriff Turner. I think this is a personal vendetta of Ward's."

Conrad laughed. "Yeah. He doesn't want any witnesses when he blows him away." In a more serious tone, he added, "Except Noteboom."

A light bulb clicked on in Santos's brain. Noteboom. He and Ward were working together. Why else would Cash have gone to Noteboom's house? "Ward sent us here to get us out of the way."

"I don't know. Maybe Cash went to Noteboom's to get a gun."

"If that's all he wanted, he wouldn't have waited for him to come home."

"Weird."

Santos turned the key in the ignition.

"What are you doing?" Conrad asked.

"We're going to Edie's."

57

Cash had to work to get his fingers into Edie's gloves. He felt silly slipping them on, given that his fingerprints were already all over Noteboom's truck, but he wanted to keep the damage to a minimum. He climbed into the vehicle's cab. Where should he go now? He didn't want the truck to be found in Edie's garage. He had a flash of an Exxon station—that was nearby. He'd take it there.

The only other vehicle at the station was a tan sedan being filled up by a harried-looking mother with two screaming children in the car. Cash parked as far as possible from the woman and, after tossing the keys onto the floorboard, got out of the truck. As he started to close the door, he caught sight of an odd object behind the seat and froze. Amid a jumble of tools, fast-food bags, and empty soft drink bottles lay a hammer. Taking care not to touch anything, he leaned in to inspect it. It was a claw hammer, with a steel head and black rubber grip. A streak of red ran across the hammer's face. A single black hair an inch long was stuck to it.

Cash felt as if a huge weight had been lifted from his shoulders. If that was indeed Turner's blood and hair on the hammer, he had found his physical link between Noteboom and the murder. He slipped off the rubber gloves and stuck them in his pocket. A short walk later, he was back at Edie's house.

He called Frida.

"Hello?"

"There's a bloody hammer in the truck. I parked it at the Exxon station."

"Wow, okay. What now?"

"Can you let Gabe know?"

"I'll call him right now."

***

Racing back to town, Santos felt his phone buzz in his pocket. He fished it out and glanced at the screen.

"Who is it?" said Conrad.

"Frida Simmons." He killed the call and pocketed the phone. "It can wait."

***

It was just getting dark outside when Cash went into the kitchen to fix himself a ham and cheese sandwich. He found some milk in the refrigerator but no chocolate syrup. Disappointed, he carried everything to the table. He was sitting down to eat when a stray noise outside caught his ear. Footsteps? Maybe.

He put down the sandwich and crept into the den. It was quiet. He must have imagined the footsteps. Pulling back the curtain just enough to peek outside, he almost fell over when he saw Clovis Ward staring back at him. He was running for his Ruger when a bullet smashed through the window and into the opposite wall. An instant later, he heard banging at the back door. Someone else was trying to get in.

Cash heard the back door blast open just as he reached Edie's bedroom. He snatched the Ruger from the nightstand and listened. Someone had entered the house. Given that he had seen Ward through a front window and the noise had come from the back, he assumed it was Noteboom.

He snatched a paperback book from Edie's desk and slipped into the hall bath. From there, he tossed the book across the hall into Luke's bedroom. It hit the wood floor with a loud thump that he hoped would fool Noteboom. Footsteps sounded in the hall. Just as they reached the bathroom, Cash leaped out and, wielding the Ruger like a club, smashed it into a man's face. Noteboom. The deputy staggered but didn't fall. He raised a pistol, but Cash grabbed his gun arm and pushed up as a shot exploded next to his ear.

Noteboom used his fist to deliver a vicious blow to Cash's ribcage. Ignoring the searing pain, Cash drove his adversary against the wall, dropped the Ruger, and pounded his face over and over until the battered man slumped to the floor. When he was down, Cash swung a booted foot into his head.

Glass shattered in the living room. That meant Ward was in the house. As Cash tried to roll Noteboom over to retrieve his gun, a bullet blasted the sheetrock inches from his head. He dove into the bathroom, slammed the door shut, and locked it.

Heavy footsteps thudded in the hall. "I see two guns out here, Cash. I'm betting one of them is yours. Which means the only thing you're holding in there is your dick."

Cash didn't answer. He glanced at the bathroom window behind him, the same window he'd used to get into the house. Why the hell had he closed it? He was trapped.

"It wasn't supposed to go like this," Ward shouted through the door. "You could have beaten a murder rap. Christ, the evidence was so thin you could see through it. Now I've got you on breaking and entering, assaulting a law officer, and auto theft. I can't ignore that."

"So, you're going to arrest me? That shot you took says otherwise."

"That was just a warning. Come on out. We'll talk it over."

"I know it was you and Noteboom that killed Griff Turner."

Laughter from Ward. "Now all you've got to do is prove it."

The doorknob jiggled. Cash dashed to the window. It was locked. He found the latch and released it. Two shots blasted through the door as he leaped to the commode and propelled himself through the window. He hit the ground rolling as another shot shattered the glass above his head. Footsteps sounded to his left. Was it Noteboom? He scrambled to his feet and started to run when a shouted command froze him.

It was Deke Conrad. Legs spread in a shooting stance, his hands holding a pistol aimed at Cash. Someone pushed through the bathroom window behind him. Cash spun around to see Ward climbing to his feet and raising his gun.

"I've got him covered," Conrad shouted. "Get some cuffs on him."

Ward jerked the gun in Conrad's direction and fired. The deputy swayed, a confused look on his face, blood gushing from his abdomen. He slumped to the ground and lay still.

Ward swung the gun back toward Cash. "So long, Cash."

A gunshot rang out, kicking up grass at Ward's feet. Santos! Standing just inside the gate next to Conrad. Ward raised his gun. He and Santos fired simultaneously. Santos jerked backward as Ward's shot struck his arm. Ward spun a half-circle, bright red blood streaming down his thigh.

Ward tried to bring his gun to bear on Cash, but Cash executed a perfect tackle to bring the big man down. He punched Ward in the face, eliciting a loud grunt. Ward struggled to lift his gun, but Cash struck him again and the weapon slipped from his hand. He hit him one more time and Ward went still.

"Get off of him!"

Cash looked over to see a bloodied Noteboom shove Edie through the gate. What would it take to put that guy out of action? And when had Edie come home?

Edie tripped and dropped to her knees. Noteboom hauled her up by the hair, eliciting an angry shriek. He put a gun to her head and stepped behind her to shield himself from Cash.

"Get off him. Now!"

Cash grabbed Ward's gun and climbed to his feet. "Let her go, Noteboom."

Noteboom pointed the gun at Cash. "Come closer."

Cash took a step.

"Closer." His arm shook.

Noteboom blinked in an unsuccessful attempt to clear blood from his eyes. He wiped his face but still seemed to be having trouble seeing through the blood. "I swear to God, I'll blow her fucking head off if you don't get your ass over here."

Still on the ground, Ward shouted, "Shoot him, Judd." Cash backed up to bring Ward into view. The chief deputy had climbed to his feet and was limping toward Noteboom. "God damn it, shoot him!"

Noteboom fired. The bullet whizzed past Cash and thudded into the cedar fence beyond. Military instincts kicking in, Cash dropped to the ground and took aim, but couldn't risk a shot without hitting

Edie. Noteboom fired another wild round. Moving as fast as his injured leg allowed, Ward said, "Let's get the hell out of here."

Cash shouted, "Let her go, Noteboom. I'll shoot Clovis."

Ward picked up his pace. Noteboom pressed the barrel of his gun beneath Edie's jaw. He fired a parting shot at Cash and, dragging Edie with him, followed Ward through the open gate onto the driveway.

Cash sprinted after them. A bullet smashed into a gatepost and sprayed splinters into his face. Throat dry, heart pounding against his ribs, he dashed onto the driveway. At the curb, Ward was climbing into the driver's seat of a squad car parked in the street. Noteboom shoved Edie into the back seat, jumped in, and yanked the door shut. The engine turned over and, tires screeching, the car sped away from the house. Cash raced to the street but could only watch as the red taillights disappeared around a corner.

Cash stood transfixed, unsure of his next move. Remembering Conrad and Santos lying wounded in the backyard, he ran back through the gate and reached Santos first. Even in the fading evening light, he could see the pain on his friend's face. "Are you okay?"

"Hurts like a mother," Santos said through gritted teeth. "Call an ambulance. I'm about to pass out."

"I don't have a phone."

"There's one in my pocket."

Cash fished out the phone. After placing the call, he checked Conrad. The deputy was alive but unconscious. As Cash applied pressure to the wound, Santos said. "Did they take Edie?"

"Yes."

"Go after her. I'll take care of Deke."

"You're about to pass out."

"Help is on the way. Call Ward. He's in my contacts."

Cash found the number and made the call. Ward answered. "Something tells me this isn't Deputy Santos."

"Where are you?" Cash said, fury in his voice. "What do you want?"

"I want your ass in a jail cell."

"You meant to kill me."

"I'll kill your girlfriend if you don't do what I say."

"What do you want me to do?"

"Come to the department. Alone and unarmed. I don't want to hurt her, so don't make me have to."

Edie's voice came through the speaker. "Don't do it, Cash! He'll kill you!"

"Shut up!" said Ward. There was a long silence before he came back on the line. "You get your ass here to the station if you ever want to see her again."

"I'll get there as fast as I can, but I don't have a car."

"Hang on." Cash heard muffled conversation between Ward and Noteboom before Ward said, "It's a fourteen-minute walk. At fifteen minutes, I pull the trigger."

Trying not to sound desperate, Cash said, "Don't hurt her. I'm coming." He started for the gate.

"Where is he?" Santos hollered.

Without breaking stride, Cash called out. "Sheriff's office."

"I'll come with you!"

"You can barely walk. Just wait for the ambulance."

Cash hustled back out front, to Edie's Prius. The driver's door was open. Noteboom must have surprised her when she pulled up.

Cash knew the car had a push-button start, and that Edie kept the key fob in her purse. If he was lucky, she had left the purse in the car when Noteboom grabbed her. Sure enough, there it was, a brown leather flap bag in the passenger seat. He climbed behind the wheel, closed the door, and pushed the button to start the car.

He drove fast. As he slowed to turn onto Main Street, he heard the wailing sirens of an ambulance coming toward him. The time spent waiting for it to round the corner and pass him felt like an eternity.

A block from the station, Cash slowed to a stop and got out of the car. He knew he had arrived well within Ward's allotted time and wanted to scope out the situation before confronting the two kidnappers. He shoved Ward's gun into his belt and strode toward the building. No lights were on inside. Noteboom leaned against a wall by the entrance.

Cash marched toward him. The deputy turned and raised a pistol. "Hold it."

Cash stopped. "Where is she?"

"She's with Ward."

"I know she's with Ward. Where the hell is he?"

Noteboom pointed at a nearby bench. "Sit down and shut up. You'll see him soon enough."

Cash sat.

Noteboom positioned himself in front of Cash. Without warning, he swung a fist into Cash's face, smashing his nose and sending blood spurting onto the sidewalk. The pain was agonizing, but Cash did his best not to give Noteboom the satisfaction of letting it show.

Noteboom said, "Stand up, you son of a bitch. Put your hands in the air."

Cash obeyed the order. Noteboom jammed the gun barrel into his back. With his other hand, he performed a quick search that turned up Ward's gun.

Cash spit blood. He couldn't breathe through his nose. "You're a helluva lawman, Noteboom. You should always search your prisoners first before punching them."

"Shut up."

A phone rang in Noteboom's pocket. He pulled it out and pressed it to his ear. "Yeah, he just got here. We'll be right over." After returning the phone to his pocket, he waved the gun. "Let's go. Around to the parking lot. I'll follow."

Cash started down the sidewalk. Without looking back, he said, "She'd better be okay."

"Or what?"

"Or I'll kill both of you." He meant it.

"Yeah? How the hell are you going to do that?"

They reached the parking lot. It was empty except for a squad car.

"Get in the back."

Cash climbed in.

Noteboom pushed the door shut. He circled the car and got in the driver's seat.

For the second time in two days, Cash was on the wrong side of a squad car polycarbonate screen. Dread roiled his gut while blood trickled from his nostrils. He leaned to one side to let it drip onto the seat. "Where are we going?" he asked, catching sight of Noteboom smirking at him in the rearview mirror.

Noteboom switched on the ignition. "Your funeral."

58

Noteboom drove past the courthouse and turned onto a residential street. Cash said, "We're going to Griff's house? Why?" The deputy said nothing. He pulled into the driveway next to Ward's squad car and killed the engine. He got out, taking care to keep his gun trained on Cash, and opened the back door of the car. "Let's go."

Noteboom shoved Cash into the house and shut the door. Stepping past his prisoner, he turned and trained his gun on Cash.

Cash's dread gave way to fear when he saw Edie at the dining room table, hands cuffed in front of her. Ward filled the chair beside her, gun in hand, a pained expression on his face. Wincing, he rose.

Cash said, "Edie, are you all right?"

"For now."

"Where's Mia?" Noteboom asked.

"Who knows?" Ward said. "Probably over in Junction banging Carl."

Ward limped toward Cash and fixed him with a glare. Without warning, he slammed a fist into Cash's gut, doubling him over. As his diaphragm regained movement, Ward said, "You were right. I never did like you."

"The feeling's mutual."

"You know why your daddy hates my guts? Because ten years ago me and your hot mom were banging each other like rabbits. She is one fine piece of ass."

Cash found it impossible to process this information. Clovis Ward and his mother? No wonder his father hated the son of a bitch. He indicated Edie. "She isn't part of this. Let her go." The words came out in quick gasps.

"Not a part? No, I'd say she's in pretty damn deep. You can thank yourself for that."

Cash gulped for breath and stole another glance at Edie. She was holding something. A bobby pin. She hadn't forgotten their talk about the handcuffs. He needed to stall for time. "I found the hammer Noteboom used to kill Turner."

"How many times do I have to tell you?" said Noteboom. "It wasn't me."

"Shut up, Noteboom," said Ward.

Cash looked at Ward. "You did it?"

Ward shook his head and scoffed. "Turner was one dumb son of a bitch. He was happy with the nickels and dimes he got from squeezing people like your buddy Steve. If he had come in with us, he could have made a fortune. But no, he was above all that. Stupid bastard."

Cash stole a glance in Edie's direction and saw the bobby pin bounce on the floor. His heart sank as Edie bent over to retrieve it. He had to buy her time. Looking back at Ward, he said, "So, you killed him."

"What the hell else was I supposed to do? Turn my back on easy money? All because of that hypocritical asshole? Not a chance."

Cash let out a cynical chuckle.

"What's so funny?"

"I can see how a dumb fuck like Noteboom would get mixed up in this. But you've been a cop for how long? Fifteen, twenty years? Have you always been a piece of shit?"

That was going too far. Ward grunted and raised the gun. "Time to take care of business."

Cash tensed. A glance past Ward showed Edie still struggling with the handcuffs. Ward seemed happy enough to brag about how clever he was. Cash said, "Why bring me here? Why Griff's house?"

"Makes things neat and tidy. You hated the sheriff, so you killed him. Now you're back to finish off his wife. Who knows, maybe she saw you kill her husband. Lucky for her, she's not home. Also lucky for her, we came along to save the day."

"Who will believe that?"

"Everybody. Look at us. I'm shot and we're both beat to shit. It took everything we had, but in the end, we got the bad guy."

An audible click sounded from Edie's lap. Ward turned just as she leaped from her chair and threw a vicious right into his jaw. Cash simultaneously lunged at Noteboom. The deputy fired a wild shot that sailed past him. Cash decked him with a roundhouse punch, then charged Ward. He grabbed the chief deputy's gun arm and pushed it upward as Edie delivered a savage kick to his wounded leg. Ward screamed and twisted away. With a flash and a deafening bang, he fired a shot that exploded next to Cash's ear. Edie kicked again and Ward dropped to his knees, giving Cash an opening to swing a booted foot into his abdomen and drive the air from his lungs. Ward collapsed, wheezing and fighting for breath. He attempted to raise his gun hand, but Cash stomped on his arm, bent down, and pried the gun from his grasp.

A gunshot from behind caught Cash by surprise. He was preparing to fire back when he saw Noteboom, gun slipping from his hand, blood spewing from his chest, topple like a tree. His body crashed into the floor, twitched, and went still.

Heart pounding, Cash looked up from Noteboom's body and saw Santos in the doorway. The deputy lowered his gun and said, "Got the son of a bitch."

With a groan, Santos slumped against the door frame. As blood oozed freely from his wounded shoulder, he slid to the floor. Cash pressed Ward's gun into Edie's hand. He nodded at Ward. "If he moves, shoot him." Rushing to Santos, he said, "What the hell are you doing here? Why didn't you go to the hospital?"

"A good soldier doesn't leave his buddy behind. You ought to know that."

"How did you find me?"

He shrugged. "All the squad cars ... have GPS."

"You saved my life. Edie's too."

Santos tried to grin, but it came across more as a grimace. "Now we're even."

59

Santos grimaced as he reached for a water cup beside his hospital bed. Bringing it to his mouth, he drank as if he had just stumbled in from the desert. "How's your nose?"

Cash put a finger to his bruised and swollen face. Noteboom had thrown a powerful punch. "Hurts like hell."

"And Deke?"

"He'll be okay. They had to take out a section of his small intestine, but thankfully, no vital organs were hit. The bullet just missed his spinal column, so he's lucky in that respect. The doctor said he should make a full recovery." Cash glanced at Santos' heavily bandaged left arm. "How's the wing?"

"I'll let you know once the pain meds wear off."

"Are they letting you out of here anytime soon?"

Santos grinned. "Not for a while. There are still a couple of nurses I haven't flirted with yet." He placed the cup back on the bedside table, triggering another pained expression. "What's up with Ward and Noteboom?"

"Noteboom's dead. Ward will be discharged later today and go straight to the Kimble County jail. So far he's keeping his mouth shut."

"Kimble County?"

"Noble County law enforcement is stretched a bit thin at the moment."

Santos was back to being all business. "Not for long. I'll be back soon."

"What about the nurses?"

"They have my number."

They heard a tap at the door and Frida Simmons came in. "Hey, guys."

"Hey, Frida," said Santos. "What brings you here?"

"I came to check on you, dumbass. But I also wanted to give you an update." She glanced at Cash. "You should hear this, too."

Cash said. "What did you find in the truck?"

"Just that hammer. It had both Ward's and Noteboom's prints on it, so I'm not sure who used it to kill Turner."

"It was Ward."

"Doesn't really matter. Ward's going down no matter what, especially once I get DNA results back on the hair you found on the hammer. That should confirm it's the murder weapon. You're lucky you found it, by the way, because the blood on Noteboom's sidewalk isn't human."

"He said it was from a deer."

"For once he was telling the truth."

Not all clues led in a straight direction. "I broke into his house because I thought it was Turner's blood."

"Cash, they knew you were close. That's why they tried to kill you."

"Yeah, but something's not adding up. We still don't know where those women came from. Or where they are now."

"You'll figure it out. You got your phone back, right?"

Cash slipped it out of his pocket. "Yeah."

She pulled out her own phone and tapped the screen. "I'm texting you Fred Uecker's number. He's one of the county commissioners."

"What does he want with me?"

She smiled, delighted to tell him. "He wants to offer you a job."

Cash's phone dinged. He glanced at the screen and said, "I'll give him a call."

"Gabe, I'm glad you're doing well," Frida said. "I've got to run. I'm having my floors redone."

"Thanks for coming by."

When Frida had left, Santos said, "I wish I was a rich doctor and could afford new floors."

"New floors . . . ?" said Cash. A vivid image bloomed in his mind. Where the murder must have taken place. A last puzzle piece fell into place.

"What?"

"Nothing. I gotta go call Uecker."

Five minutes later, Cash sat in his car with his phone to his ear. "Uecker," a voice said.

"This is Adam Cash."

They spoke for less than a minute. When Cash ended the call, he exhaled a long breath and looked at himself in the rearview mirror. "Hello, Deputy."

60

Rhonda Trotter heard the doorbell ring and shouted, "Can you get that?" She didn't hear any answer, so she assumed Carl had. When it rang again thirty seconds later, she tossed the shirt she was folding and headed downstairs. Passing through the den, she saw her husband slumped on the sofa. A baseball game was playing on the TV. "Good grief, Carl, didn't you hear the doorbell?"

He didn't answer.

Rhonda pulled the door open and gasped in surprise at the sight of two Junction police officers. One said, "Good afternoon, ma'am. Are you Rhonda Trotter?"

"I am."

"Is your husband home?"

"Yes. What is this about?"

"We need to talk to him."

She waited for the officer to elaborate. When he didn't, she looked over at her husband and said, "Carl, it's the police. They want to talk to you."

He stood up and she could tell he had already looked to see who they were.

"Baby, is something wrong?"

"I'm sorry."

"Sorry for what?"

Trotter stepped past Rhonda to face the officers. "I'm Carl Trotter."

As Trotter was being led away in handcuffs, Rhonda shouted after him, "What the hell did you do?"

***

Mia Turner entered the lobby of the Noble County Sheriff's Department for what she assumed would be the last time. The thought gave her no feelings of regret. Being a sheriff's wife had brought her no joy. Her husband's long hours, phone calls at all times of the day or night, and his swaggering self-importance served as constant irritants. Compounding that were his unpredictable rages, during which the verbal abuse sometimes became physical. She never should have married the guy.

Vicky looked up from her keyboard. "Hey, Mia. Are you here for his things?"

"Yes, Cash called and asked me to come by."

Vicky rose and gestured for her to follow. She led her down the hall into an interview room, where several sealed cardboard boxes lined the floor.

"Am I a suspect?" Mia said with a nervous laugh.

"It's the only place we had to store his stuff. They're repainting his old office."

Mia picked up a box. "Can you help me carry these to the car? I hurt my hand."

"Somebody wants to talk to you first," Vicky said, sweeping out of the room.

Mia headed toward the doorway, but Cash appeared out of nowhere to block her way. "Hello, Mia."

"Cash, thank God. Can you carry these boxes for me? I've got a—"

"Hurt hand. I know."

She waited for him to move. When he didn't, she said, "Do you mind?"

Cash stepped inside and shut the door. "Have a seat," he said, gesturing. When she didn't react, he took the box from her and pulled out a chair. With a puzzled look on her face, she lowered herself into it.

Cash took the chair on the other side of the table. He clicked on the same recording machine Clovis Ward had used with him.

"What are you doing?"

"We still need you to clear up a couple of things. This will only take a minute."

"I don't understand. You're not with the department."

"Actually, I am. The county commissioners hired me as a deputy. Acting Sheriff Santos would conduct this session, but he's still in the hospital."

Mia said nothing.

"Do you understand that this conversation is being taped?"

"I guess. I still don't know what's going on."

"Could you state your full name for the record?"

"Mia Elizabeth Turner. Come on, Cash, what's—"

He cut her off to give his own name and the date. When he was done, he said, "How's that hand?"

She raised it and flexed the fingers. "It's getting better. Just a nasty bruise, the doctor said."

"I see you still aren't wearing your ring."

"What's the point? I plan on selling it."

Cash produced an evidence bag from his pocket. Inside was a wedding ring. "I can't let you do that. At least, not yet."

"What are you talking about? That's mine." She reached for the bag, but Cash pulled it back.

"It's also evidence. I searched your house while you were out on a call this morning. Don't worry, I got a warrant first. I left a copy on your dining room table." He tapped the bag. "I found this in your jewelry box, just like you said."

She wrinkled her nose. "You searched my house?"

"Frida ran an RSID test on residue we found in the prongs. It's human blood."

"What's an RSID test?"

"It's how to tell human from animal blood." He gave the evidence bag another tap. "My guess is it will turn out to be Griff's, but we won't know that until the DNA results are back."

She didn't respond, but the pace of her breathing picked up.

He gestured at her bruised hand. "It's not like in the movies, is it? Hitting someone."

"I don't know what you're talking about."

"Must have been a helluva blow, to break both his jaw and your hand."

"What's that supposed to mean?"

"Right." His phone dinged with an incoming text. He glanced at it and shifted topics. "Something Frida Simmons said yesterday got me thinking about the floor in your house. Why would you have such a beat-up floor in an otherwise beautiful home? It's a simple question, one you already know the answer to. Until recently, it had carpeting over it. I saw the threads under the baseboards. Beige. Must have gone well with the furniture."

Her defiant look melted.

"So, I asked myself, why take up the carpet? It could be a coincidence. Maybe you're just redecorating. But the carpet is missing in only that one room. A professional would have finished a job that small in one day. You, or somebody with you, ripped that carpet out in a hurry because there was something on it that you needed to get rid of. Like blood. Griff's blood. Of course, that carpet is long gone, buried beneath a ton of garbage at the landfill, I'm sure. Fortunately, Frida Simmons just sent me a text about evidence she found in your Highlander. She's searching it right now, out in the parking lot. Guess what. There are beige carpet fibers in back."

Mia thrust out her chin. Her eyes blazed with newfound determination. "I know what you're trying to do. You're trying to set me up as Griff's killer. Well, I didn't do it and you can't prove that I did."

Cash tapped a finger on the table. "You might not have done it, but you were there. And you helped cover it up. Tell me, who held him while you broke his jaw? Clovis? Noteboom? Carl Trotter?"

"Carl didn't do anything."

"You might as well come clean. I dug a little deeper on your boyfriend Carl. I remembered seeing a Texas Tech sticker on his car next to another one I didn't recognize. Know what it is? It's the logo for Sigma Alpha Epsilon. Do you know who else was in Sigma Alpha Epsilon? Barry Novak and Clovis Ward. It took some digging, but I found a picture of the fraternity from twenty-five years ago. Guess who's in it? Barry, Clovis, and Carl."

He paused to give her a chance to respond. Her lower lip trembled, but she kept quiet.

"Give it up, Mia. Your husband found out about the human trafficking. He confronted his cousin Browning about it at the gun range. They had a fight. Browning told the others that Griff wouldn't bend. They made a plan. One that you approved of, sick as you were of

Griff's beatings. After the election night victory party at your house, they jumped him. Clovis cuffed him and sat him down. You broke his jaw with your fist. Ward crushed his skull with a hammer. He had Noteboom try to frame me by planting a beer bottle with my prints on it in my car. He didn't plant the hammer because there was nothing to connect it to me. And he knew he'd be in charge of the murder investigation, so he figured blaming it on me was a slam dunk.

"You're full of shit."

"You called Carl. Or maybe he was already there, celebrating the reelection of the man whose wife he was screwing. The three men stuffed Griff into the squad car—there's blood in the trunk—and dumped him in the park. Oh, and Carl's prints are inside the squad car. That's how I know he helped. Poor Carl. What a man won't do for a pretty face. Anyway, they put the carpet in your trunk for disposal later. Then everybody got together and decided to make me the fall guy. Or maybe that was the plan all along."

He stopped to catch his breath. Mia stared at her hands and sank even lower in her chair. "I'll get a lawyer that will tear that theory apart."

"Be my guest. But you should know that Carl already talked. The folks in Kimble County called me right before you got here. Carl says they had been planning to get rid of Griff after it became clear he wouldn't stand by and let them use Pinyon as a human-trafficking way station. Oh, and did I mention the oxycodone? It's what they were using to keep the women they kidnapped from causing trouble. Carl helped them steal it. He had a friend at Santa Rosa Hospital who was tipping him off about incoming drug shipments. She's being arrested as we speak. Anyway, with your help, Ward and Noteboom killed Griff. When they looked for a way to cover their tracks, there I was, the sore election loser who threw a punch at the sheriff earlier in the day, standing there with a big fat target on my back."

Cash clicked off the recorder and stood up.

"Here's the sad part. You were right about one thing. Like you said, Griff wanted to do good. And it got him killed."

Mia hung her head. "Turn it back on. I'll tell you what I know."

61

While Mia Turner was spilling her guts, Barry Novak was having lunch with a rich client at the Cast Iron Restaurant in downtown Fort Worth. The client, a recently fired oil company executive suing his former employer for breach of contract, was droning on about his victimhood and Novak was having trouble paying attention. He kept glancing at his phone, waiting for it to ring. He had left Clovis Ward seven messages already this morning, demanding a callback. Why the hell hadn't he responded?

The executive's voice pierced Novak's reverie. "Barry, are you okay? Did you hear me?"

Novak looked up. "What?"

"I said, have you heard from their lawyers yet?"

"No ... not yet."

"Don't you think they should have responded by now?"

Novak vaguely eyed his sixty-dollar steak and said, "Yeah, I guess so."

"You guess?"

He shoved the plate away and stood up. "I'll be right back."

Before his client could react, Novak left the table and marched to the men's room. He pulled out his phone and made a call. It went to voice mail. "Goddamn it, Clovis, where the hell are you? Call me back." As he returned to the table, he froze at the sight of a Fort Worth police officer talking to his client. The oil exec said something to the cop and pointed toward the bathrooms. Barely able to breathe, Novak strode swiftly to the restaurant exit. He passed through the velvet entry ropes and swung left toward the lobby. Out of nowhere, another officer appeared and grabbed his arm.

"Are you Barry Novak?"

"Yes."

"Mr. Novak, you're under arrest."

***

They found two women in Novak's basement prison. A Spanish-speaking Fort Worth police officer interviewed them. The women had fled gangs in their home country of Guatemala. They were seeking a better life in San Antonio, where a smooth-talking man promising employment imprisoned them instead. He kept them for two weeks, using that time to get them hooked on oxycodone.

Another man then took custody of them. This man handcuffed them in the back of a van for a drive to an unknown town, where they were transferred to another van that brought them to Fort Worth. They had been in Novak's basement for a week. He had raped them daily.

The Fort Worth police turned the case over to the FBI. Its agents ran into a brick wall when Novak lawyered up and refused to talk. The Spanish-speaking Fort Worth officer uncovered Novak's ownership of the gelato shop in Pinyon and phoned the Noble County sheriff's office. Cash took the call.

62

Browning squirmed between the two unsmiling men flanking him in the back seat of the utility vehicle.

The one with bad breath said, "Be still."

Enrique, the driver, said, "There's nothing to worry about, Andy. Mr. Kessler just wants to have a word with you."

Browning hoped that was true. He wondered how the enterprise had all gone so wrong. The plan had seemed so simple. Buy the women in San Antonio, shackle them in his van, take them to Pinyon, and hand them over to Novak. Novak had assured him there was no risk, that nothing could go wrong. After all, they had an ace in the hole, the chief deputy of the Noble County sheriff's department.

The UTV shook as it slammed into yet another of the unpaved road's cavernous potholes. Where were they going? Browning shuddered as his imagination came up with several possibilities, none of them good. This morning he had arrived at his shop to find three men waiting. When he told them he had a busy day planned and had no time for a road trip, Enrique patted the pistol tucked into his belt and said, "Mr. Kessler insists." One man demanded Browning's van key. Enrique shoved him into a Ford Bronco and followed the van to this place in the middle of nowhere. He then jerked Browning from the Bronco and packed him into the back seat of the UTV. Squeezed between the other two men, Browning trembled at the memory of Kessler's icy warning: "Don't get caught."

But they had been caught. All because of that idiot Noteboom. Clovis Ward was an idiot, too. The guy who was supposed to take the fall for Turner's murder not only slipped through his fingers but figured out who was behind the killing. If only his cousin Griff had agreed to turn a blind eye to their plan, they wouldn't have had to kill him. But he had revealed himself to be a self-righteous jackass, so Novak said he had to go.

Enrique slowed to a stop at a ranch gate. He lowered his window, punched in a code on the keypad, and the gate swung open. Once they were clear, the gate shut behind them.

They rolled through a lengthy cedar brake, decades-old trees lining the dirt road on either side. Browning saw a ranch house off to the left a hundred yards distant. They turned right.

"Where are we going?" Browning asked, trying to keep his voice from shaking. No one replied.

They entered another stand of cedar. Enrique dodged trees for twenty yards before coasting into a clearing. Kessler was waiting for them, hands on his hips. Beside him were two other men. One held a dirty shovel.

The UTV stopped. "Get out," Enrique said.

Browning's knees wobbled as he climbed out of the vehicle. Why was that guy holding a shovel? Then he saw it. Behind the man was a hole. A hole big enough for a body.

"Mr. Kessler, please," Browning said. "I won't tell them anything."

Kessler stared at him with cold eyes. "No, you certainly won't."

"I haven't even been arrested."

"A lucky break for us."

Browning went limp as powerful hands gripped his arms and dragged him to the hole. When the men released him, he collapsed in the dirt.

"Please don't kill me." He was sobbing now.

Kessler flicked a hand and said, "Enrique."

Enrique stepped forward and raised his gun. It looked like a cannon to Browning.

Without warning, six armed men and women burst from cover. One shouted, "FBI. Put your hands in the air." Kessler pulled a pistol and got off two shots before he fell under a hail of bullets. Enrique and his companions dropped their weapons and put up their hands. The FBI agents rounded them up and restrained them with zip ties.

Browning spotted a familiar face. "You!"

"Hello, Andy. I'm Adam Cash."

***

The FBI agents loaded their prisoners into two black SUVs. The agent in charge of the operation, a woman named Yolanda Deaver, came over to him and said, "You got that warrant for the GPS tracker you put on his van, right?"

"I did."

"Because if you didn't, we'll have to let these guys go."

"Like I said, I got it. I can show you a copy."

Deaver smiled. "I'm just yanking your chain. I already saw it."

Cash extended a hand. "Thanks for letting me join the party." They shook.

"What's next for you?" Deaver asked.

"I've got some people to see."

"Is one of them Edie James?"
"She's high on the list."

63

At three in the afternoon, Cash strolled into Bill and Ted's Excellent Pizza, looking for its surviving owner. The young woman at the counter—the same one who had served his drink the night of the murder—pointed toward a back hallway and said, "He's in his office."

Cash made his way to the closed office door and rapped on it. "Come in," a voice called from within. Pushing the door open, Cash found Ted Hubbard seated at a desk. "Do you have a minute?"

"Sure. Have a seat."

He slid into a chair. "It was Noteboom."

Ted dropped his hands and looked away. "How do you know?"

"The bullet that killed Bill came from a gun we found in his house."

"He kept the gun? What a dumb bastard."

Cash told Ted about finding the hammer in Noteboom's truck. "They were cocky. Ward wasn't planning on conducting a real investigation, so they didn't think they needed to be careful."

"What did that son of a bitch have against Bill?"

"From what I can tell, nothing. Bill was just in the wrong place at the wrong time. Noteboom was chasing two women they were holding prisoner. Bill got between them." Cash paused. "He was trying to protect them."

"That sounds like Bill."

"They were running oxycodone too."

"Where'd they get that?"

"San Antonio. Trotter had a friend working at Santa Rosa Hospital who would tip him off about incoming drug shipments. Browning and Noteboom would hijack the truck and steal whatever oxy they could find."

"And now Bill's dead because of those sick bastards."

Cash didn't know what to say. Ted saved him by standing up and extending his hand. "Thank you. It helps to know what happened."

"I'm sorry, Ted. I really am. Bill was a good man."

"He was."

"What will you do with this place now that he's gone?"

A look of surprise replaced Ted's somber expression. "What do you mean? I'm not going anywhere."

"So, I'll still be able to come here for an excellent slice of pizza?"

"Any time. On the house."

***

Fred Uecker drained the last of his coffee and said, "Can you and Cash handle the department by yourselves? It's a big job for just two people."

"Don't forget Deke," Santos said.

"It's my understanding he won't be back for at least a month."

"Even so, I think we're up to it. Besides, Ward was sitting on a pile of resumes, and the budget already called for two deputies over the ones we had. We won't be shorthanded for long."

"Do me a favor and give me a heads-up before you hire anybody. It's your choice, of course, but the other commissioners and I would appreciate an opportunity to voice an opinion."

"Of course."

Uecker turned his gaze on Cash. "Are you okay with the pecking order? Gabe as sheriff, you as chief deputy?"

"No problem."

"Good." Uecker stood up and gathered his briefcase. "I have a feeling that Noble County is in good hands."

***

Cash smoothed his hair and got out of the Fiesta. As much as he had cursed the piece of junk over the past year, he was happy to be driving it again. Anything was better than rotting in prison. And now that he had a better-paying job, he'd be able to afford an upgrade soon. He had his eyes on a Ram 1500 Laramie Sport pickup like Steve's.

Dodging cracks in the sidewalk, Cash made his way to the door of the double-wide trailer. He sighed at the thought of his daughter being raised in such a ramshackle home. What had once been bright white siding was now covered by a layer of grime accumulated through years of neglect. Warped plywood covered a broken window. A sprawling live oak tree so completely shaded the yard that no grass could grow in the packed dirt beneath it. The small wooden porch was missing one of its rails.

Cash pulled the torn screen door open and knocked. He slipped his hat off as the door opened. A middle-aged woman in polyester slacks and a Pinyon Javelinas T-shirt blocked his path. "What do you want?"

"Hello, Mrs. Fenster. I came by to see how Emma and Bernadette are getting along."

"They're just fine." Her voice had a hard edge.

"Are they home?"

After a long, stony silence, she stepped back and said, "Come on in."

He started to sit in the same battered rocker he recalled from his earlier visit, but the old lady said, "That's my chair. You sit on the sofa." The chair squeaked in protest as she wedged her ample bottom into it. Turning her head, she hollered, "Bernie! Somebody's here to see you!"

Cash endured several seconds of awkward silence before Bernadette emerged from the hall. She was holding a bottle to Emma's mouth. "She won't take no more, Momma."

"Then don't give her no more. She'll eat when she's hungry."

Bernadette set the bottle on a wobbly coffee table and sat at the other end of the sofa. The corners of her mouth crept up into an almost imperceptible grin. "I'm glad they didn't catch you, Cash."

"Thanks."

The electric hum of a wall clock provided the only noise breaking the thick silence. Bernadette slid closer to Cash and held Emma out. "Would you like to hold her?"

"I would." He took the infant in his arms. Marveling at her tiny hands and beautiful face, he cuddled her against his chest. She felt warm and soft. Intense longing overcame him. There was nothing he wouldn't do for this child.

"I've been thinking," Bernadette said, "maybe you'd like to come spend the night with her sometime."

"I'd like that."

Mrs. Fenster leaned forward. "Don't you think you ought to run that past me?"

"No, Mama, I don't. She's my baby." She smiled at Cash. "And his."

***

Steve set the full glass of beer on the bar. "Try it."

Cash eyed it without picking it up. "What is it?"

"Beer."

"What kind of beer?"

"The good kind. Just try it."

Cash picked up the glass and brought it to his lips. "No avocados?"

"I promise."

He sipped. A smile creased his face. "Hey, that's actually pretty good."

"It's a wheat beer. With just a touch of Fredericksburg peaches."

"This one's a keeper. Unlike that avocado crap."

Steve poured himself a glass. "Are you kidding? People love that shit."

"There's a sucker born every minute." He sipped the beer again. "So, you never caught any grief for letting me stay in your basement?"

"No. I got lucky."

"I found an arrest warrant for you on Ward's desk. I guess he was too busy with me to enforce it."

"Is it still active?"

"Yeah, but don't worry. I talked to the DA. He said to ignore it."

Steve let out a sigh. "That's a relief."

"By the way, remind me how much Griff was squeezing out of you each month."

"Five hundred. Why?"

"I'll do it for half."

"Do what?"

Cash held up his glass. "Drink your lousy free beer."

Steve laughed. "On one condition."

"What?"

"You drink the rest of that avocado crap first."

***

"Honey, your father and I are so relieved that you were able to prove your innocence."

Cash swigged his bottle of Packsaddle peach wheat beer and spoke into the phone. "Thanks, Mom. It's a big load off my back, that's for sure."

"Now that that's out of the way, you'll have time to fill out law school applications. Remember, we'll still pay half your tuition."

"Mom, I don't want to go to law school. I got a job here with the county. I'm a deputy now."

His father's booming voice came through the phone. "See, Janet, I told you he wouldn't do it."

Cash said, "Are you guys on speakerphone?"

His mother said, "Cash, baby, it wouldn't hurt to fill out an application or two."

"Mom, I said no."

"I'll send you the links."

His father butted in. "Damn it, Janet, is there wax in your ears? He doesn't want to."

There was a long silence. Cash said, "There's something I need to ask you about, Mom."

"What is it?"

"Clovis Ward told me he had an affair with you."

After another long silence, his mother said, "I'm sorry we never told you."

"Do Reid and Emily know?"

"No. I guess it's time they found out."

"Maybe so."

"I want you to know your father and I have a strong marriage now. We've moved past all that. I hope you can too."

"Sure, Mom. One thing, though."

"What?"

"I'm not going to law school."

64

"It takes more than what goes on in bed to keep two people together," Edie said, her eyes glistening in the soft light.

Cash eased her head into his lap so that she lay on her back looking up at him. He stroked her hair. "I know."

She took his hand, kissed it, and held it against her cheek. "I just don't want to make any more mistakes."

"We don't have to do anything if you don't want to. I can go home."

Flipping over onto her stomach, she massaged his crotch and said, "Oh, I want to do it, all right. I'm just saying there's more to it than that."

***

Cash woke early the next morning and rolled over to look at Edie. He smiled at the sight of the drool puddle under her chin. Her breathing was soft and regular. Barely audible snoring noises escaped her mouth. A lipstick smear ran across one cheek. It occurred to Cash that, if he were to take a picture of her like this and show it to her later, she would punch his arm and tell him to delete it from his phone. He wouldn't delete it, though. He thought she looked perfect.

He slid out of bed and padded into the kitchen. Luke, clad in Spiderman pajamas, sat at the table, rolling a toy car back and forth over its smooth surface. "Good morning," Cash said.

"I'm hungry," said the boy, not taking his eyes off the car.

"I'll make breakfast." Cash opened the refrigerator. Rummaging through its contents, he found milk, eggs, cheddar cheese, an onion, and a pack of corn tortillas. He spread everything out on the counter and returned to the refrigerator.

Edie sauntered into the kitchen and rubbed the top of Luke's head. "Hey, buddy." Spotting the items on the counter, she said, "All right. Migas."

Cash's head emerged from the refrigerator. "Dang it."

"What?"

"Still no chocolate syrup."

***

Cash twirled Vicky as the last notes of "Amarillo by Morning" faded away. "That's one of my favorite songs," she said.

"Can't go wrong with George Strait."

She squeezed his hand. "One more? Please?"

The band struck up "Remember When," Alan Jackson's ballad about a married couple's enduring love. "Sorry, I promised the slow ones to Edie."

She made a pouty face but let go of him. "All right. I'll go ask Gabe."

Cash made his way back to their table and extended a hand to Edie. "May I?"

She smiled and followed him to the dance floor. As he slid his arms around her, Edie said, "That poor girl's got a crush on you the size of Texas."

"She's a good kid, but I'm spoken for."

They swayed to the music, relishing their closeness. Edie leaned her head on his shoulder. Cash shut his eyes and imagined the song going on forever. When he opened them again, he put his mouth to her ear and whispered, "I'm lucky to have you back."

"You're damn right you are." She gave him a lingering kiss. "But I'm lucky too." After a few seconds, she added, "Want to stay over tonight? I have to warn you; you won't get much sleep. But I will make you breakfast.

"Migas?"

She grinned. "With chocolate milk."

Thank you ...

... for reading *Blunt Force Trauma*. Want to keep up to date on my upcoming books and giveaways? Sign up for my newsletter and I'll send you a free copy of *Cash*, a collection of three exciting short stories featuring *Blunt Force Trauma* protagonist Adam Cash! Just click on this link:

jeffreykerrauthor.com/newsletter-signup

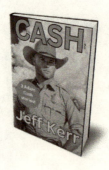

Got a moment?

The best way to help an independent author like me is to post an honest review on Amazon or any other reading platform you use. Reviews are critical to a book's success. And success is what allows any author to continue writing the books you want to read.

To leave an Amazon review, **click here**.

If you're reading this the paperback or pdf version, please visit the book's Amazon page and scroll down to the customer reviews. Then click on "Write a customer review."

Word of mouth and posting on social media also help. I appreciate anything you can do to spread the word!

If you enjoyed Blunt Force Trauma

You'll love **Second Death!** In this second installment of the Adam Cash series, the newly hired Noble County deputy investigates the fatal explosion of a pickup truck that the driver had outfitted for stealing diesel fuel. Cash's discovery of a gold coin in the dead man's pocket leads him to suspect the death was no accident. As Cash digs deeper into the mystery, he encounters a web of deceit and betrayal that threatens a violent end to his short law enforcement career. Here's a sample.

"Which brings me to that deputy. He's not going to stop nosing around. We've got to do something about him."

Bonnie sighed at the thought of an early trip to the Lord for the handsome deputy. "It can't be like Alissa. Jeremiah won't be hungry again for months and we can't keep a body that long. I guess you'll have to shoot him."

"Bullets leave too many clues."

"Strangle him then."

Webb cringed at the recollection of Tammy' pleading eyes just before she went limp. "He's a big guy. That's not a sure thing."

"Hit him with the car?"

"Too big a risk. Somebody might see it."

"Okay, genius, that's three ideas of mine you've shot down. What's your brilliant plan?"

Webb refilled his glass. He liked to drink when he was mulling over a problem. It helped free up his mind so he could think outside the box.

"How many of those shotgun shells do we have left?"

"You just said you weren't gonna shoot him."

"I'm not. And we still have that box of burners, don't we?"

"Yeah. It's in the bedroom closet. Are you planning on blowing him up? He's not stealing diesel like Ralph was."

"If I use enough powder, that won't matter. One spark and, boom!"

"It won't look like an accident."

"There's no way they'd be able to trace anything back to us."

Bonnie finished her drink, rose, and stepped over to Webb. She slid onto his lap and gave him a prolonged, open-mouthed kiss. Fingering the abundant chest hair poking up from beneath his shirt, she said, "Come on, let's go make some sparks of our own."

About Jeff Kerr

Jeff Kerr wasn't born in Texas but says "y'all" like a native. He wrote a poem in the third grade that earned him a school prize, a book about the American flag. You'd think that would have inspired him to become a writer but that came later.

Jeff wrote and published his first book twenty years ago. He hadn't planned on doing so until one night at supper his son interrupted a discourse about local history by saying, "Enough, Dad! Write a book." Choosing to interpret a teenager's flip remark as sage advice, he did. Six books later, he calls himself an author. So there.

When Jeff isn't writing you can find him floating a Texas river or battling cedar on his small slice of Hill Country land. When he *is* writing, he stays busy by creating pulse-pounding crime thrillers that, according to one reader, "move along like a runaway locomotive." Thank you, son.

Learn more about Jeff and his work at **www.jeffreykerrauthor.com**.

Drop him a line at **jeffkerr@jeffreykerrauthor.com**. He'll write back!

Twitter: https://twitter.com/jkerr50
Instagram: https://www.instagram.com/jkerr50
Facebook: https://www.facebook.com/JeffKerrAuthor
Bookbub: https://www.bookbub.com/authors/jeffrey-kerr

Books by Jeff Kerr

FICTION

The Adam Cash Mystery Series

Blunt Force Trauma

Second Death

Murder Creek

Stand-alone novels

Refuge

Lamar's Folly

The Republic of Jack

NONFICTION

Austin, Texas: Then and Now

The Republic of Austin

Seat of Empire: The Embattled Birth of Austin, Texas